THE
MAN OF HER
Dreams

Note on the author

Kate McCabe is married with two children and lives in Howth in County Dublin. She is a former journalist and has published several bestselling novels including *Hotel Las Flores*, *The Beach Bar*, *The Book Club* and *Forever Friends*. Kate's hobbies include reading, music, travelling and walking along the beach in Howth while she thinks up plots for her stories.

Also by Kate McCabe

Hotel Las Flores

Forever Friends

The Beach Bar

The Book Club

Casa Clara

Magnolia Park

THE
MAN OF HER
Dreams

KATE McCABE

HACHETTE
BOOKS
IRELAND

First published in Ireland in 2013 by
HACHETTE BOOKS IRELAND

1

Cataloguing in Publication Data is available from the British Library

ISBN 978 144472 629 9

Typeset in Cambria by redrattledesign.com
Cover design by cabinlondon.co.uk

Printed and bound in Great Britain by
CPI Group (UK) Ltd, Croydon, CR0 4YY

Hachette Books Ireland policy is to use papers that are natural, renewable and
recyclable products and made from wood grown in sustainable forests. The logging
and manufacturing processes are expected to conform to the environmental
regulations of the country of origin.

This novel is for three very important people who have supported me right from the start: Anna Fanning, Siobhan Moore and Ursula Lacy.
Enjoy, ladies.

CHAPTER ONE

When Piper McKenzie heard the captain announce that the plane was starting its descent, she put down her book, glanced out of the window and saw the sea suddenly appear. Then it was gone again and, in its place, a parched brown hillside studded with little whitewashed houses. Immediately, she swung into action. In quick succession, she folded her tray into the upright position and tightened the seatbelt around her waist. Then she shut her eyes and started to pray.

Piper had no fear of flying but she was terrified of landing. She had read somewhere that take-off and landing were when most accidents occurred. And she had taken the information very much to heart.

She gripped her armrests, prayed like mad and didn't stop till she felt a heavy thump and heard a loud cheer go up from the other passengers. When she opened her eyes, the plane was safely taxiing along the runway to the terminal building. She thanked God and felt herself relax.

All at once, people were getting out of their seats and crowding the aisles while they dragged their luggage from the overhead bins. She smiled to herself. Each time she flew into Málaga airport, it was the same. All those pasty-faced travellers who had been shivering all winter just couldn't wait to get off the plane and straight to their loungers beside the pool. She'd probably do the same herself, if she was in their shoes.

She slid her travel bag from under the seat and stood up to wait as the crowd pushed and shoved its way down the aisle. A tall, dark-haired man in a light linen suit stopped at her seat and indicated that she should go before him. 'Please,' he said.

Piper smiled and thanked him. At least there was one gentleman on board today. By the look of him, he was a businessman. The crowd moved towards the exit, like a human tide, and then it was her turn. The stewardess wished her a good day and Piper stepped out into the bright Spanish sunshine.

***

Twenty minutes later she arrived in the vast arrivals hall after collecting her luggage from the carousel. The place was packed but she quickly spotted her driver waiting at the barrier holding up a placard that read 'SEÑORA McKENZIE'.

As she drew closer, she could see that he was a handsome young man, almost dwarfed by his chauffeur's uniform and peaked cap. He welcomed her and gave his name as Pedro. Then he took a case in each hand and strode purposefully towards the exit, Piper following in his wake.

Once she was outside, the heat struck her like a smack in the face. But what impressed her most were the flowers. It was only April but already the place was ablaze with bright yellow, red and purple blooms. They were everywhere in pots, baskets and window boxes. That was when she knew for sure she was back on Spanish soil.

Pedro stowed her luggage in the boot of the car, took off his cap and wiped his forehead, then got into the driver's seat and they set off. Before long, they had left the airport behind and were on the motorway. Down below she could see hotels and villas dotted along the coast and beaches crowded with people.

'Did you have a good flight, *Señora*?'

'Yes, thank you, very pleasant.'

'Will you be here for long?'

'Just a couple of days.'

'I can tell you that the weather will be fine. No rain.'

'That's very good to know.'

The driver kept up a steady stream of conversation. Piper quickly realised that he was practising his English with her. They did it all the time. It was important to be able to speak English here on the Costa del Sol, particularly if you were in the tourist trade.

'Have you been to the Costa before, *Señora*?'

'Many times.'

'Then you know the people like to celebrate. It is *feria* week in Marbella. Everyone will enjoy themselves. There will be eating and drinking and flamenco dancing.'

Piper loved flamenco: the throbbing guitars, the clacking of castanets, the women in their bright dresses with flowers in their hair, the men in their tight-fitting gaucho suits and dark hats, the intoxicating rhythm of the dance.

'I am taking my *novia* to the *feria*. Her name is Carmencita. She is very beautiful. She likes the *feria* very much. Perhaps you will go too.'

Piper would certainly like to go to the *feria* but she doubted she would have time. She was here on her father's behalf to look over a hotel he was interested in buying. 'We'll have to see.'

By now they had reached the outskirts of Marbella and their progress slowed as the streets got narrower and they encountered more traffic. But at last Pedro drove into the grounds of a hotel close to the seafront. He pulled up at the entrance and stopped. 'We have arrived,' he said.

Piper gazed out of the car. She checked the information she had been given. Hotel Azul was described as small and comfortable. It had thirty-two bedrooms on three floors, a lounge, dining room, café/bar with terrace, enclosed gardens with a swimming pool and a gate that led down to the beach. It seemed a fair description of the building she was looking at now.

She got out and tipped the driver. A porter in a red waistcoat came hurrying down the steps to collect her luggage. He was followed by a stout little man in a dark suit, who made an elaborate bow and introduced himself as the manager, *Señor* Hernandez.

'Welcome to Hotel Azul, *Señora* McKenzie. We have been expecting you. I trust you are well. Your journey has gone to plan?'

'My journey was perfect, thank you.'

'Very good. *Señor* Guzman has called to say he will be here at four o'clock. He has instructed me to make you at home.

So, if you would follow me, please?'

They went up the steps and into the lobby, *Señor* Hernandez leading the way and the porter struggling behind with the cases. Piper glanced about her: the lounge seemed neat and comfortable, quite spacious. They got into the lift and the manager pressed the button for the third floor. Then they were walking along a corridor. *Señor* Hernandez stopped when they came to a room at the end, produced a key and, with a flourish, pushed open the door.

Piper stepped into a beautiful room, with a large sliding window leading on to a bright terrace. She could see pots of crimson geraniums flaming in the sun. In the centre of the room was a table with a large bowl of freshly cut flowers. Above was a sparkling crystal chandelier. There was a writing desk, built-in wardrobes, a dressing-table and, to the side, an en-suite bathroom.

The manager beamed. 'Do you like it, *Señora*?'

'Yes, indeed, it's beautiful.'

'It is the bridal suite. You will find drinks in the mini-bar. And there is a menu on the writing desk. If you wish to have something to eat, please call Room Service and they will be happy to oblige.'

'Thank you.'

'Is there anything else I can do for you?'

'I don't think so.'

Hernandez smiled again, made another elaborate bow and was gone.

Piper opened the sliding door and walked out on to the terrace. Down below, she could see trim lawns, trees and flowers, and in the centre the calm blue water of the swimming pool. The beach and the sea seemed almost within touching distance. Yachts scudded on the horizon. What a magnificent view, she thought. I could sit here all afternoon.

But she had things to do. She returned to the room and drew the curtains. Then she undressed and went into the bathroom. As she stepped under the shower and felt the cold water hit her skin, she remembered what the manager had told her. The bridal suite, she thought. That's interesting. She thought of her own honeymoon, just a few years earlier, and the high expectations she had entertained.

They hadn't all been realised.

CHAPTER TWO

Some jealous people muttered that Piper had been born with a silver spoon in her mouth. Usually they said it behind her back, never to her face, for Piper didn't take criticism lightly.

Her father was Henry McKenzie, a self-made man with a personal fortune of at least €50 million earned from his hotel empire, which he had built up from nothing in the space of thirty years. The family lived in a magnificent mansion on Howth Head, with stunning views over Dublin Bay. Henry kept a vintage Mercedes Benz in the garage, a yacht in the marina, and a holiday villa in Nice on the French Riviera. It was meant to be a retreat where he could get away from the pressures of business, but he worked so hard that he rarely found time to use it.

Henry and his wife, Rose, were not aristocrats. They were humble people who had never forgotten the hardship and poverty of the small farms where they had been reared in the west of Ireland. They knew the value of hard work and had tried to instil that understanding in their children, Piper and her older brother Jack. The pair had been sent to private schools because Rose, in particular, placed a high value on the benefits of a good education.

Sadly, Jack had shown little talent for study. He was a lackadaisical student with more interest in sport than books and dropped out of school at the first opportunity. He now worked as a manager in one of the family's hotels and played rugby in his spare time for the local club, Suttonians.

Piper was different. She was the clever child, who had studied hard and passed her Leaving Certificate exams with distinction, gaining enough points to secure a place on almost any university course she wanted. Instead, she had chosen to study hotel management, and now worked closely with her father, helping him to run the business.

But her good fortune didn't stop with wealth and intelligence. She had also been blessed with good looks. By the age of eighteen when she had left adolescence behind, she stood five feet seven inches tall, with a trim figure, long, slender legs, blue eyes, blonde hair and the face of a Botticelli angel.

Of course, she had men beating down the doors to woo her. But Piper had a high opinion of her own self-worth and wasn't about to throw herself away on the first smooth-tongued Romeo who crossed her path. She had dozens of boyfriends, but if they didn't hold her attention after a few weeks, she discarded them, like cast-off handbags.

By the time she was twenty-two, many of her friends were secretly whispering that Piper would never marry. She had set the bar too high. No mortal man could ever match her expectations. Then she ran into Charlie White.

***

They met one evening in Aunt Polly's Boudoir, an exclusive club off Grafton Street where visiting rock stars and celebrities gathered to escape the attention of their fans. Piper being Piper, she had managed to secure a coveted membership card. She was enjoying a night out with some girlfriends when someone introduced her to Charlie. From the get-go, electricity sparked between them.

Charlie was twenty-eight, which might have accounted for some of the attraction, but he was also stunningly handsome. He was six feet tall, well-built, dark-haired and very good-looking. He had a droll sense of humour and a quick line in smart talk. He was in the music business and managed a rock band called Hell's Kitchen, which gave him an edgy street cred. Piper thought at last she had met the man of her dreams. Within weeks they were seeing each other almost every night.

Not everybody was happy about it. Her mother, especially, was nervous about Charlie's intentions.

'What kind of job is band manager?' Rose wanted to know.

'It's exciting, Mum. Charlie meets all these important people in the music industry. He gets invited to glamorous parties. Mick Jagger is one of his friends.'

Rose crinkled her nose. 'I'm not sure that's any recommendation. How do you know he's not after your father's money?'

'Because he doesn't need it. He's got plenty of his own. The music industry is very lucrative.'

'That doesn't mean anything. Some people can never get enough money.'

'Not Charlie. I think he'd still love me if I didn't have a penny.'

'Has he got a roving eye?'

'What do you mean?'

'You know damned well what I mean. Is he interested in other women?'

Piper was shocked. 'Not at all! He only has eyes for me.'

'Well, let me give you some advice. Keep your legs crossed till he puts a ring on your finger. Then you'll know if he's serious or not.'

Before long, Charlie and Piper were the best-known item in Dublin, the acknowledged king and queen of the social scene. The photographers adored them and the gossip columnists were forever writing stories about them. Their pictures were rarely out of the tabloids, coming out of nightclubs or going into parties in fancy hotels. Piper loved every moment. She couldn't get enough of the glamour and the limelight. She knew that thousands of women would have cut off an arm for just a little of what she had.

After just six months, Charlie proved her mother wrong and proposed. There was no question of Piper turning him down. By now she was madly in love. She thought that, with Charlie as her husband, her life would be complete. But she kept him waiting for another two weeks before she accepted, just to let him know that she wasn't desperate.

They were married in her local church, the wedding of the year. The road was blocked for half a mile with reporters jostling for position and celebrities trying to park their Jaguars.

Piper looked radiant as she glided down the aisle on Charlie's arm. The triumphant notes of the organ swelled up to the ancient rafters. The congregation rose as one from their seats and their applause followed her as she passed. In row after row, she saw smiling faces.

As the couple walked from the church into the bright morning sunlight, more people pressed forward eager to catch a glimpse. The official photographer pushed through, weighed down with cameras, and indicated that the groom should kiss the bride. She tilted her head and felt Charlie's soft lips brush her cheek as the moment was recorded for posterity. Then people were showering them with confetti, blithely ignoring the signs that forbade littering the church grounds.

By now, the groomsmen and the bridesmaids had also filed out of the church and the photographer was lining them up for more pictures, fluffing up the folds of Piper's dress and squeezing the group closer together so that he could fit them all in. Right on cue, Piper displayed the famous smile that had lit up the pages of dozens of newspapers.

'Look into each other's eyes,' the photographer said, and Piper turned to her husband and gazed soulfully into his face. 'Now, if you would please hold your bouquet a little higher ...'

She followed his instructions and the photographer went down on one knee and shot yet more pictures.

The congregation was pouring out of the church and the bridal party was in danger of being engulfed. The photographer shook his head in dismay. 'That's all we can do for now,' he said, bowing to the inevitable. 'We'll have to finish the shoot at the reception.'

As Piper and Charlie passed out of the gates of the church, mayhem ensued. A horde of press photographers and reporters burst past the posse of burly security guards and descended on them, like a swarm of magpies. Piper continued to smile as the guards forced a way through to the waiting limousine, she and Charlie following. Piper stepped into the car, drew her dress in behind her and sat down. Charlie got in beside her. The door closed and the driver began to make his way slowly through the throng.

She felt Charlie's arm slip round her shoulders. She gazed into his handsome face as he drew her close and kissed her, not a mere peck for the photographer but a deep kiss, brimming with passion. 'I'm glad that's over,' he murmured. 'Now it's official. We're man and wife.'

'Yes,' Piper whispered.

'You know I love you,' Charlie went on. 'The memory of this day will be engraved on my heart for ever.'

Piper closed her eyes. She had dreamed of her wedding day since she was a little girl. She had prepared for it for months, endured endless sessions with the dressmaker, spent countless hours poring over guest lists and menus, talked to florists and caterers, and prayed that everything would go off just right.

And it had. The weather had been perfect – a bright, sunny May morning without a cloud to dull the sky. She knew she looked gorgeous in her beautiful silk dress. The media had their photographs. Tomorrow her face would be splashed all over the front pages.

Beside her sat one of the most sought-after men in Dublin. Ahead of her was a lavish reception, to be attended by the great and good of Irish society. And then they were off on honeymoon – two weeks in a sun-drenched hideaway with nothing to do but relax and enjoy their good fortune.

Piper thought she would never be happier.

***

That had been four years ago. Now she put all her energy into her marriage and the family business. She had a three-year-old daughter, named Sofía, and a live-in nanny, Margie Cooke, so she could continue to work with her father. People said Piper had finally grown up.

But not everything had turned out as she had hoped. Charlie's work had continued to grow as Hell's Kitchen's career took off. It took up most of his time. He was constantly negotiating contracts with promoters and recording companies so she saw less and less of him. Even when he was at home, his phone was rarely silent until she insisted that he turn it off. Piper resented the way his work intruded into their married life. She wanted him to herself, and didn't like sharing him with strangers. They had argued about it, and Charlie had promised to slow down but he never did.

Sadly, the wonderful future she had hoped for with her husband was colliding with cold reality. There were even times when she began to wonder if her mother had been right and she had made a terrible mistake by rushing into marriage with Charlie White.

CHAPTER THREE

Piper stepped out of the shower, dried herself and put on a light dress. She took a bottle of mineral water from the mini-bar, poured it into a glass, added some ice and went to sit on the terrace. She took out her phone and rang home.

'How is my darling daughter?' she asked, when Margie answered.

'Oh, Piper, it's you! Did you get to Spain all right?'

'Yes, everything went to plan. Is all okay at home?'

'We're fine. Sofía is right here beside me. We're reading a story. Would you like to talk to her?'

'Sure, put her on.'

Her little daughter was on the line at once. 'When are you coming home, Mummy?'

Piper smiled. 'I've just got here, honey. Are you being a good girl?'

'Yes.'

'Are you behaving yourself for Margie?'

'Yes, Mummy. Will you bring me a present?'

'What would you like?'

'A dolly.'

'I'll bring you a Spanish one. You can start thinking of a name for her. But I want you to promise you'll do whatever Margie tells you.'

'I promise.'

'I love you, sweetheart. I'm missing you.' She felt a tug at her heart-strings as she ended the call. She hated being separated from her daughter.

Next, she tapped in her father's number. 'I've arrived.'

'How was the flight?'

'Smooth as silk.'

'Well, I don't need to ask about the weather. I've already checked. Twenty-two degrees Celsius. Not too hot for you?'

'Not at all. I love it.'

'You're at the hotel?'

'Yes.'

'Room okay?'

'It's beautiful. They've given me the bridal suite.'

She heard her father laughing. 'Probably the best room in the house. What's your initial impression of the place?'

'It looks clean. The staff seem smart and efficient. It's close to the beach. There's a stunning view of the sea from my terrace.'

'Have you seen Guzman yet?'

'He's meeting me at four to take me on a tour of inspection.'

'You know what to look for – hygiene, comfort, defects and potential problems. Make sure he shows you the kitchens. That's important.'

'I know, Dad.'

'Don't let him try to negotiate with you. Just find out how keen he is to sell. Keep your cards close to your chest.'

'Okay. I'll have more to report tomorrow. Love to Mum.'

There was a click and the line went dead.

Finally, she rang Charlie but was put through to his message-minder. She wasn't surprised. Getting through to Charlie was like getting an audience with the Pope. She left a message for him to ring her as soon as he was free, then cancelled the call.

She went back out to the terrace, lay down on a lounger and let the sun warm her face. From somewhere near the beach, guitar music was drifting up to her on the breeze. Hotel Azul was small, thirty-two bedrooms in all, what was known in the trade as a boutique establishment. Her father had heard about it on the grapevine from one of his friends and sent Piper to carry out some reconnaissance. Once she had completed the inspection, she would type up a report and that was her work done. He would make the final decision about whether or not to buy.

It was very pleasant here. She felt herself relax. She closed her eyes and was dozing off when her phone rang.

'Miss McKenzie?'

'Yes.'

'Guzman here. I'm on my way to see you. I should be with you in fifteen minutes. Can I take it that the staff are looking after you properly?'

'Yes, indeed.'

'Good. I'll meet you in the foyer. I'm looking forward to talking to you.'

'Me too,' Piper said.

She got up quickly and went back into her room. For this meeting, she would have to dress up a little. She had brought a grey business suit. She went to the wardrobe where she had earlier hung her clothes and pulled it out, then put it on with a plain white blouse and black heels, brushed her hair and applied a little makeup. She selected a plain gold chain for her neck. She was just adding the finishing touches when the concierge rang to say that *Señor* Guzman had arrived.

Piper locked the door and went down in the lift. She found a tall, dark-haired man waiting. As she approached, he turned towards her. *Señor* Guzman had an olive complexion, a tiny moustache and creases around his eyes that told her he was about forty. He grasped her hand warmly and addressed her in perfect English, with only a trace of an accent. 'My dear Miss McKenzie, it's so good to see you. I hope you are rested after your journey?'

'Yes, thank you.'

'How is your dear father?'

'He's very well.'

'Please give him my kind regards when you return. Now, you are here to see the hotel. Would you like a cup of tea before we begin?'

'No, thank you,' she replied. 'I'm anxious to get to work.'

'In that case, where shall we start?'

'With the kitchens,' Piper said.

She had brought a small voice recorder to note her observations. The drawback was that *Señor* Guzman would hear everything she had to say, but that couldn't be helped.

17

The alternative was to write notes, which would take for ever.

Señor Guzman led the way to a large area at the back of the hotel. The staff had obviously been warned that the owner was on the premises and were on their best behaviour.

The head chef and his assistants stood aside in their starched white aprons and watched silently as Piper inspected the polished surfaces, the ovens, the cooking utensils, the freezers and food cupboards. She knew how jealously chefs guarded their territory and resented intruders but she wasn't going to let that deter her. She smiled politely as she continued her inspection and recorded her observations. It took forty-five minutes. Then *Señor* Guzman led her to the bedrooms.

She looked behind furniture and on window ledges for dust, opened wardrobes, inspected baths and showers. Then it was the turn of the games room, the laundry, the reading lounge and the bar. It was seven o'clock when they finally arrived in the dining room, with its large bay windows looking out on the gardens and the pool. Piper switched off her recorder.

'We still have the gardens to see,' *Señor* Guzman said.

'Why don't I leave that till the morning? The sun will be out. It will give me a better impression. There's no need for you to come with me.'

'As you wish.'

'I'd also like your permission to take some photographs for my father.'

'Take as many as you wish. Have you eaten yet?'

Piper had skipped lunch and now she was hungry. 'No.'

'Then you must allow me to buy you dinner. I know a very select little restaurant. You'll like it. Shall I ring now and make a reservation?'

'Let's eat here.'

Señor Guzman looked surprised, but then he grinned. 'Ha, ha, I can read your mind. You want to check the quality of the food and the service?'

'Of course.'

'Very good, Miss McKenzie. I can see you know your business very well.'

***

Señor Guzman had a word with the head waiter, who led them to a discreet table for two in a corner. Piper noted the gleaming cutlery, the starched white tablecloth, the sparkling wine glasses. By now the dining room was beginning to fill, which she took as a positive sign.

The meal that followed was one of the best she had ever eaten. They began with grilled sea bass and king prawns, and followed it with tender roast lamb, baby roast potatoes and peppers. To accompany the food, her host chose a delicious white wine from Galicia called Albariño.

Eventually *Señor* Guzman ordered coffee and leaned across the table to look into her face. 'So, am I allowed to ask if the meal met your rigorous standards?'

'It certainly did.'

'And the service?'

'Perfect.'

He clapped his hands. 'I am so pleased. Hotel Azul really is very good. We run a tight ship here.'

'Why are you selling it?'

He sighed and a melancholy look came over his face. 'I'm afraid I overextended myself in the boom years, like so many people in your own country. I borrowed too much money and now the banks are looking for it back. I will be very sorry to let the hotel go. I built it from nothing and put a lot of work into it.'

Piper had come to like *Señor* Guzman in the few hours she had spent in his company. He had been courteous and charming. Now she felt sorry for him. 'You realise that I'm only here to report? My father will decide whether we buy.'

'I appreciate that.' He seemed to cheer up. 'Now, would you like a little brandy to complete your meal?'

It had been a long day and now it was after ten o'clock. Piper was feeling tired. 'I think I'd rather go to bed.'

'As you wish.'

Señor Guzman accompanied her to the foyer. When they came to the lift, he kissed her cheek. 'I have enjoyed your company, Miss McKenzie. Sleep well.' He turned on his heel and was gone.

Piper made her way up to her room. By now it was dark outside and the moonlight lent the room a yellow glow. She drew the curtains, got undressed, and as she was slipping into bed, she remembered that Charlie still hadn't called. She took out her phone and checked it. Not even a text.

Chapter Four

She woke at seven. The sun was coming up and bathing the landscape in a brilliant orange light. In the distance, the sun-parched mountains sloped down to the sea. Outside her window, she could hear birds singing in the palm trees. She decided to have a dip in the pool.

She had packed a swimsuit, she remembered. She got it out of her case, put it on, slipped into a cotton dressing-gown the maid had left in the bathroom, stuck a towel under her arm and set off. A few guests were having an early breakfast on the bar terrace and waved to her as she went by.

As she walked through the gardens she took in the trim lawns and the profusion of flowers slowly opening their faces to the sun: roses, carnations, bright bougainvillaea. The air was already heavy with their scent. She made a mental note to put this into the report she was writing for her father. When she arrived, she found the pool deserted, gleaming blue in the morning light, and plunged straight in.

She came to the surface, gasping – the water was icy. She swam for fifteen minutes, then climbed out and returned to her room. She felt vibrantly awake. She ordered a pot of coffee and croissants and had breakfast on her terrace. Then she made a series of quick calls to Margie, her father and Charlie. He was still not answering. She cursed under her breath, sat down at her laptop and began to transcribe the notes from her voice recorder.

The bright morning seemed to lend energy to the task and by one o'clock she had finished. She had addressed all the issues her father had mentioned and added a note that the hotel was comfortable, clean and efficiently run. She spent another half-hour taking photographs so that Henry would get an idea of what it looked like. Then she typed a message, attached the photos and the report and emailed the package to him.

Her return flight to Dublin was scheduled for the following morning so now she had almost a whole day to relax. She decided to have a snack lunch at the hotel bar and spend the rest of the afternoon sunbathing by the pool. This evening she would treat herself to a good dinner in a pleasant restaurant near the port.

The bar was doing a lively trade when she arrived. She had a prawn omelette, with some salad, and drank a glass of white wine. Then she walked the short distance to the pool, found a vacant sun lounger, applied sunscreen to her face and arms, opened her novel and began to read.

The sun was now at its height. It was warm but not as warm as it would be later in the summer when the temperatures would climb into the mid-thirties. She was happy to be back in Spain even if it was only for a couple of days. She loved the lifestyle here: the climate, the food, the beautiful scenery, the natural ease and charm of the Spanish people.

But her pleasure was marred by thoughts of Charlie's continuing refusal to return her calls. She had been gone for a whole day and he still hadn't bothered to reply to any of her messages. She had known before they married that her husband was a very busy man, always rushing from one business deal to the next. The music industry was cut-throat, certainly not an occupation for the faint-hearted. But it wasn't so busy that he couldn't spare a few minutes to ring her or simply send a text. Well, she wasn't going to ring him again. He could contact *her*.

The problem had been there from the beginning, she could see that now. Even in the early days of their whirlwind romance, she had lost count of the times when he had turned up late for a dinner date, always with a plausible excuse about being delayed because of some last-minute hitch. She had overlooked it then because she was starry-eyed with love. That had been a mistake. She should have put her foot down and set rules. But Charlie had been so charmingly apologetic that she had always forgiven him.

It would have to change. He was now a married man, the father of a child. He had responsibilities. She made up her mind. When she got back to Dublin, she would sit down and have a really serious talk with him, let him know that she was no longer prepared to put up with his errant ways. She wasn't some punk musician in one of his bands whom he could treat with disdain. She was his wife, the mother of his daughter. The time had come for him to show her more respect.

She put Charlie out of her mind and spent a pleasant few hours beside the pool. She had another swim and, when the sun began to go down, retreated once more to her room and began to prepare for the evening. She had a bath, dried herself and thought about what she should wear. This was a short trip so she hadn't packed much.

In the end she chose a simple white dress, sandals and a little jacket in case it turned cool. She locked her bedroom door and set off through the winding streets towards the port. The evening air was scented with flowers and the sea.

When she reached the promenade, she found it packed with people, and a lively buzz spilled out from the bars and restaurants. There was throbbing guitar music on the night air and dark-haired women in brightly coloured dresses. Suddenly Piper remembered that Pedro the driver had told her it was *feria* week in Marbella. The town was in carnival mood. She quickly found herself entering into the spirit of the night.

The aroma of roasting garlic gave an edge to her appetite, and when she came across a small place set back from the seafront, she went in and was shown to a table in the garden. It was lit with lamps and hung with baskets of red geraniums and bright yellow nasturtiums. A lattice supported a climbing clematis and the lavender flowers cascaded almost to her table. She ordered roast chicken, which came with a half-carafe of wine, a dish of olives and a basket of fresh-baked bread.

It was almost eight o'clock when she paid the bill. She set off again along the promenade, which was ablaze with lights.

There seemed to be even more people about, including parents with children, all decked out in bright costumes. Jugglers and mime artists entertained the crowds, and men did a brisk trade in bootleg CDs or watches.

She was drawn by the sound of music further along the Paseo Maritimo. When she arrived, she found a crowd gathered around a group of dancers. She watched, entranced, as they performed an elaborate flamenco, the women stamping their heels and clacking castanets above their heads as they swirled and twisted to the intoxicating rhythm of the guitar.

When the dance ended, the crowd melted away and Piper found herself looking at a deserted building, the windows boarded up, the paint peeling and the walls plastered with posters for bullfights and concerts. Above the door was a rusting sign: 'Club Xanadu'.

She felt her heart skip a beat as memories flooded into her mind. She had been here before.

***

It was the summer of 2000. Piper was eighteen and had just finished her Leaving Certificate exams. As a special treat, her mother had given her permission to go for a week's holiday to Marbella with her best friend Jo Ferguson. It was the girls' first trip abroad on their own and they were madly excited, chattering about the sun, the beach and the handsome Spanish boys they were sure to meet at the discos.

Their bags had been packed for days with all the things they thought they would need – dresses, shoes, bikinis, sunscreen, cosmetics and their iPods for listening to their favourite music on the beach. Rose McKenzie drove them to the airport and before she let them out of the car she gave them a stern warning: 'Don't stay out in the sun too long. Don't drink too much. Don't talk to strange men.'

Then they were racing for the departure lounge, laughing uproariously. Which men were they supposed to talk to if not strange ones? They didn't know anyone in Spain. That was part of the excitement.

Their hotel was close to the beach. They spent the first afternoon at the pool and then they got ready to go out, putting on their makeup, brushing their hair and deciding what to wear. By the time they set off, it was dark and the moon shimmered on the sea. They stopped at a little bar to get up their courage, and then they were off in search of somewhere to dance.

Music was booming out from Club Xanadu when they approached, and as they walked past the potted palms and stepped into the gloom, Piper knew they had found the right place. The strobe lights cast shadows on the walls and there was a faint whiff of marijuana in the air, mingled with scent and perspiration.

Around them, couples were dancing, the men in open-necked shirts and jeans, the women slender and elegant, with sultry Andalucían good looks. Piper and Jo found a vacant table and sat down. They were just about to order drinks when two Spanish boys approached and asked them to dance.

They got up and joined them on the floor. The boys introduced themselves as Eduardo Garcia and Cesar Alvarez.

'*Chicas ingles*?' Eduardo asked, in a garbled mix of English and Spanish.

'*Irlandesas*,' Piper explained.

'Ah. You know Bono?'

'Not personally,' Piper said, and everyone laughed.

It was difficult to talk because of the din so after fifteen minutes they all retreated to a table in a quiet alcove and the boys insisted on buying a bottle of wine. After further attempts at conversation, the girls discovered that they were students from Málaga and worked as waiters at the Metropole, one of the big tourist hotels, to earn summer money.

'Do you like your work?' Jo asked, and Cesar shrugged. It was a job, he explained, not a career. When the season was over they were hoping to go to university to study medicine. This opened up another line of conversation and the girls explained that they, too, were planning to go to college.

'What will you study?' Eduardo asked Piper.

'Hotel management.'

'You want to work in a hotel?'

'My father's in the business.'

'Maybe I should work for him. Maybe he will pay better than Hotel Metropole.'

They laughed. Piper was enjoying the company of these good-looking boys. 'Medicine is a difficult subject. At least, it is in Ireland,' she said.

'In Spain too,' Eduardo replied. 'Many years of study. I just hope I am successful.'

27

Piper was impressed by the boys' good manners and respectful behaviour. They were about nineteen but seemed far more confident than Irish boys of their age.

They danced again, and when Piper next glanced at her watch, she saw, to her amazement, that it was two o'clock. 'We have to leave now,' she said regretfully.

The boys said they would take them home but the girls refused. They said their hotel was close and they would find a taxi.

'Will you be here again tomorrow evening?'

'Perhaps.'

Before they left, they exchanged telephone numbers. Eduardo and Cesar insisted on kissing them chastely on each cheek. Then Eduardo paused and his dark eyes looked deep into Piper's. He drew her close and kissed her cheek once more.

'That is special,' he said.

'Why?'

'For a friend, two kisses. For a special friend it is three.'

There was a row of taxis waiting outside the club. The girls sank back on the thick upholstered seats and gave their destination.

'What lovely guys!' Jo sighed. 'And they certainly know how to treat a lady, unlike some of the gougers you meet back home.'

'Yes,' Piper said. Her eyes were closed. She was thinking of Eduardo and what he had just said to her.

After that, they saw the boys every evening. They would go for a drink at a bar overlooking the marina and watch the crowds parading along the Paseo Maritimo as the moon reflected off the water. Sometimes they might end up at a club. After the first night, Piper had made it clear that they expected to pay their own way. The boys were horrified at first: they were *caballeros* – it was their responsibility to take care of the bills. It was a matter of honour and etiquette.

But Piper insisted. 'You're just students like us,' she said. 'You should save your money. You work hard at the hotel.'

'It's not so hard,' Eduardo said, with a shrug. 'And we get good tips.'

'You'll need your money when you go to university. Now, we don't want to hear any more about it. If we are going to see you, we expect to pay our share.'

The boys laughed and Eduardo tapped his head. '*Irlandesas loco, no?*'

Piper was growing fond of Eduardo. He was very handsome, with a bright, intelligent face and dark, proud features. Likewise, Jo had taken a shine to Cesar. But in the light of day, Piper had to ask herself where it was leading. Perhaps if she lived here permanently, it might grow into something serious. But she knew it was nothing more than a holiday romance. And, like the holiday, it would come to an end. Before long they would return to Dublin. The boys would eventually go back to Málaga and university. The odds were highly stacked against them ever meeting again.

The days flew past until it was time for their final meeting. The boys had dressed for the occasion in light linen suits, shirts and ties. They presented Jo and Piper with single red roses, then took them to a little bar near the water's edge where they drank wine and listened to the waves lapping softly on the shore.

Despite their best efforts to be cheerful, a sombre mood settled over the group and their final farewell was tearful. When they finally stood up to leave, Cesar insisted that they take some photographs. He recruited the barman and they stood locked together with their arms around each other, smiling for the camera. Then Eduardo drew Piper to him and kissed her passionately on the lips. She felt a warm, tingling thrill run along her spine.

'I will always think of you,' he said. 'And perhaps, some day, you will come back.'

'Yes,' she whispered. 'I will.'

'The world is not so large. The distance that separates us is not great. Perhaps the next time we meet, you will be a successful businesswoman.'

'And you will be a brilliant doctor.'

***

That was nine years ago. She had returned to Dublin and, within a year, she was a frequent visitor at Aunt Polly's Boudoir and men were throwing themselves at her everywhere she went. Then she had met Charlie White. She hadn't seen Eduardo since.

Piper turned away and began walking back along the promenade towards Hotel Azul. But the brief remembrance of that carefree holiday had affected her mood, and by the time she got undressed for bed, melancholy had overtaken her.

CHAPTER FIVE

The following morning at eleven o'clock she arrived back into Dublin airport to find wind and dull skies. She had left her car in the short-term car park. She ran through the rain, which had started to fall, opened the door and threw her luggage onto the back seat. Then she set off for Howth. She had already called Margie to say she would be home around one o'clock.

The morning rush hour was over, and once she was out of the airport it took a mere twenty minutes to reach her destination. She couldn't help contrasting the vivid green fields she passed with the parched landscape she had left behind in Spain.

Elsinore was a splendid mansion on the south side of Howth Head overlooking Dublin Bay. It had extensive gardens, which required the services of two full-time gardeners, and fantastic views right along the coastline from Killiney to Booterstown and as far as the Dublin mountains. It had been built in the nineteenth century by a wealthy brewery magnate, but by the time Henry McKenzie had bought it, it had been a wreck.

He had spent half a million pounds restoring it, and now it was one of the best addresses north of the Liffey.

It was also the headquarters of McKenzie Leisure, the company that ran her father's group of a dozen hotels. The nerve centre was a large room at the top of the house. It was equipped with top-of-the-range communication facilities to enable Henry to run his business without ever having to leave his front door.

Piper pulled up at the gates and used her electronic buzzer to let herself in. She waited till the heavy gates had slid open, with a loud grating sound, then drove in and parked beside the garage.

Her mother opened the front door, hugged her, then held her at arm's length to look her up and down. 'You didn't get much of a tan.'

'What did you expect? I was only there for two days and one of them was taken up with business. Anyway, tanning's very bad for the skin.'

'Well, you're welcome back. When did you last eat?'

'I had a snack on the plane.'

'That wouldn't feed a sparrow. I'll rustle up some bacon and eggs. Go and see your father. He's waiting for you upstairs.'

Piper went straight up to Henry's office. She pushed open the door and found him seated at a huge desk in front of the window where he could look out over the bay. He was on the phone but signalled for her to take a seat.

His voice was raised and he sounded angry. It was several minutes later that he slammed down the phone. 'That boy

32

will be the death of me,' he declared, as he got up from his chair to kiss her.

'Jack?'

'Who else?'

'What's he done now?'

'What's he not done, more like? He never listens. Thinks he knows better than me. He won't take advice, won't even take instructions. If he wasn't my own son, I'd fire him straight away. I wouldn't even give him time to put his coat on.'

Jack was the manager of the Majestic, the largest hotel in the group, but he was a disappointment to their father. He complained that Henry wouldn't give him more authority, while Henry was forever giving out about his son's sloppy attitude and lack of attention to the job.

'It makes me sad, Piper. When he was younger, I was so proud of him. You know the way he was always first at sports events, winning cups and medals, captaining the rugby team? I thought he'd carry that spirit into the business but I was mistaken.'

Piper was fond of her brother. They had always got on well. When she was a teenager, Jack had looked out for her, scaring off any boyfriends he thought were unsuitable. 'You're my little sister,' he used to say. 'It's my job to protect you.'

Once when she was fifteen and developing an adolescent crush on an older boy called Dale Doherty, Jack had drawn him aside and threatened to take him apart if he didn't leave her alone. At the time, Piper had thought he had ruined her life for ever, but when she was older and discovered that Doherty was a drug dealer, she was glad that Jack had got rid of him.

'Why don't you give him a break, Dad? Don't you think you're a bit hard on him?'

Her father stared at her. 'Hard on him? You don't know what you're talking about. When I was his age, I was working eighteen hours a day as a kitchen porter in the Gresham Hotel to scrape together the money to start my own business. Jack expects everything to be handed to him on a plate. He's had life too easy.'

He softened and smiled at her. 'Why am I giving out to you? You never let me down. Tell me about Guzman. I've read your report.'

'You wanted to know how keen he is to sell. I think he's desperate. The banks are chasing him for money.'

'So his back's to the wall?'

'Looks like it.'

'What about the hotel? You think we could make a go of it?'

'I do. It's well-run, comfortable, good location down near the seafront. It doesn't cater for the package trade. The clientele are older, more up-market.'

'Those are the type of guests we want,' Henry said. 'They're prepared to pay extra. And they don't go in for rowdy parties and end up thrashing the place. Did he mention price?'

'No. I told him you would conduct any negotiations.'

'Quite right. I saw the photos you sent. The hotel looks fine. It might need a bit of a makeover but not much.'

'So, are you interested?'

'That depends if the price is right. I need a few more days to think about it and then I'll make up my mind.'

He leaned back in his chair. Henry was a large man with a mat of silver-grey hair. Ever since Piper was a child, he had always looked fit, with a strong chest and arms and a healthy complexion from years of hard, physical work. Today, she thought, he looked tired. His face was bright red and the veins in his neck were pulsing. 'Are you feeling okay, Dad?'

'Fit as a fiddle.'

'You look like you could do with a rest.'

He laughed and waved away her concerns. 'Don't worry about me. Go down and see your mother. She's dying to talk to you. You did good work in Marbella. I'm very pleased. Thank God I have one child I can rely on.'

As she went downstairs, Piper was met with the smell of bacon. She found her mother in the kitchen, cracking eggs into a pan.

'Take a seat. This is almost ready.'

Piper sat at the table and her mother placed a pot of tea in front of her, with a steaming plate of bacon and eggs. She poured two cups, passed one to her daughter and sat down beside her. 'I don't think you eat properly,' she said. 'You're too skinny.'

'Please,' Piper protested. 'Don't start that again.'

'You have to keep your strength up. You have all that work to do for the company, plus you have a young child to care for.'

'Margie does most of that.'

'How is Sofía, anyway?'

'She's fine. I'm going straight home to see her as soon as I've finished this.' She indicated her plate.

'Why don't you bring her to visit next Sunday? You know she enjoys coming out to Howth. We can take her down to the harbour to see the yachts.'

'I might just do that,' Piper said.

'And Charlie? How's he?'

At the mention of her husband's name, Piper felt a coldness grip her. 'He's okay. You know Charlie, always working.'

'That makes two of you. Not a good combination for a marriage, if you ask me. Anyway, it's none of my business.'

Piper decided to change the subject. 'Has Dad been keeping all right?'

'Why do you ask?'

'I thought he looked tired.'

Rose put down her cup. 'He *is* tired. He's worn out. He'll be sixty-eight next birthday and he hasn't the energy he had when he was thirty.'

Piper nodded.

'I've being trying to persuade him to retire. We have that lovely villa in Nice lying empty most of the year. We should use it. I keep telling him the time has come for him to put his feet up. But he won't listen to me.' She lowered her voice. 'There's one big problem. He doesn't trust your brother.'

'I know. They were arguing earlier.'

'They're always arguing. It's a sad thing for me to say this but Jack rubs your dad up the wrong way. He should make more effort to get along with him. And, between us, he should work harder. He hasn't been seen around the Majestic for three days. Took off on a jaunt down the country to some rugby tournament and left the under-manager in charge. Your father is furious.'

So that's what they were arguing about, Piper thought. Jack went AWOL. No wonder Dad's angry.

Her mother's voice dropped to a conspiratorial whisper. 'I blame Corinne. I don't know what he sees in that woman. It's not as if she's a raving beauty. She's pretty ordinary, if you ask me. But he's infatuated with her. She leads him round by the nose. She just has to snap her fingers and Jack comes running like a puppy.'

Corinne Delaney was Jack's girlfriend. She was a junior solicitor in a large practice in town, petite with dark, curly hair and, as Rose McKenzie had remarked, pretty ordinary-looking. Jack had met her nine months earlier at some rugby function and had now moved out of the family home to share a luxury apartment with her in nearby Portmarnock.

Piper usually minded her own business where her brother's girlfriends were concerned but she shared her mother's opinion of Corinne. Jack seemed always to be at her beck and call. She had never seen him behave like that before. 'Who knows? Maybe he'll see sense and the whole affair will blow over.'

'Are you kidding?' Rose exclaimed. 'She won't allow a catch like Jack to slip through her fingers. I wouldn't be surprised if she had him marching up the aisle one of these fine days.'

Piper put down her cup. 'You're not serious?'

'I'm deadly serious. I've seen her sort before. And I've lived a lot longer than you.'

***

37

Piper lived in Sandymount, in a beautiful penthouse apartment on the beach that had been Charlie's before they were married. It was spacious with four large bedrooms, two bathrooms, a vast lounge and modern kitchen. One of the bedrooms had been allocated to Margie. Another had been converted into a nursery for Sofía.

The apartment was bright and comfortable but Piper wanted to move to a house with a garden where Sofía could play, preferably in Howth so she'd be near her parents and the company's headquarters. But Charlie kept putting off the decision. Any time she raised the subject he said they should wait. The apartment was fine. It was close to town and, besides, if they sold now, with the property market depressed, they wouldn't get back the money he had paid for it. So, for the time being, they stayed where they were.

As she drove, she kept thinking of the conversation she'd just had with her mother. She had always believed that one day, when her father retired, Jack and she would inherit the family business. She had never contemplated that an outsider might be involved, particularly someone like Corinne Delaney. Piper was polite to her brother's girlfriend but she considered her scheming, bossy and too obviously ambitious. The thought of her having a say in the affairs of McKenzie Leisure sent shivers down her spine.

But that was not the main thing that bothered her as she battled the city-centre traffic. It was two days since she had spoken to her husband. She had tried calling him but he hadn't replied. Her initial upset was now giving way to concern. Where was he? Had something happened to him?

Could he be in trouble?

She drove into the parking bay outside the block, removed her luggage from the car and locked it, then made her way up to the penthouse. The sound of her key in the door brought Sofía running to greet her. Margie came behind.

'Mummy! Mummy!'

'Hello, honey,' she said, scooping the little girl up in her arms. 'Look what I brought you.'

She put her daughter down and unzipped a bag to take out the doll she had purchased in the duty-free shop at the airport. 'Isn't she beautiful? Look at her long black hair! Have you thought of a name for her?'

'Not yet.' Sofía sat down on the floor and began to examine the doll, murmuring to it.

Piper used the opportunity to draw the nanny aside. 'Margie, do you know where Charlie is?'

'No.'

Piper felt fear hammer in her breast. 'When was the last time you saw him?'

'Two days ago. He came back to the apartment shortly after you left for the airport. He seemed to be in a hurry. He packed a bag and said he had to go away.'

'Did he say where?'

The nanny shook her head.

'Or how long he'd be gone?'

'No.'

'Did he leave any message for me?'

'No. I didn't ask. I assumed you'd be talking to each other. Is something wrong?'

CHAPTER SIX

By now, Piper was afraid that something might indeed be very wrong. She took out her mobile, rang Charlie's number again and got the same response as before. Damn, she thought. If he won't answer his bloody phone, what am I supposed to do? She went into the kitchen and made a cup of tea while she tried to think.

She was becoming seriously worried. What if he'd had an accident? Should she call the police and report him missing? Another thought came to her. This might have something to do with his business. Who would be the best person to know?

She asked Margie to take care of Sofía while she went into her bedroom and rummaged through her contacts book till she found the number of Pete Donohue, the drummer with Charlie's band, Hell's Kitchen. He was pretty close to her husband. Pete answered on the third ring.

'Hi. Pete. It's Piper. I'm trying to locate Charlie. Do you know where he might be?'

'He said he was going to London. Has he not come back yet?'

'No. Do you know what he was supposed to be doing there?'

'Sorting out some problem with contracts.'

'Pete, this is very important. Do you know where he is in London? Do you know his hotel, who he was meeting? Can you give me any information that might help me to contact him?'

By now, Pete had heard the urgency in her voice. 'Try not to worry, Piper. I'll put out some calls straight away. Soon as I've got anything, I'll be right back to you.'

The phone went dead. Piper returned to the kitchen. Her head was spinning. At least she now knew where Charlie was. But was he safe? He could come to harm in London just as easily as he could in Dublin. She paced the floor and waited for Pete Donohue to call back while her mind conjured up all sorts of weird possibilities. Had he been kidnapped? Was he being held prisoner in some grimy basement? Was she about to get a ransom note?

When it came, the call seemed to explode into the kitchen.

She grabbed the phone and clamped it to her ear. 'Well?'

'Hi, it's me.' Charlie's voice.

'Where the hell are you?'

'Dublin airport. I'll be with you in half an hour.'

She emptied the tea down the sink, went to the fridge and poured a glass of wine. Her hand was shaking. But the initial relief was rapidly giving way to anger. The selfish bastard, she thought. He disappears to London for two days and doesn't even bother to send me a text while I worry myself sick.

The phone rang again and this time it was Pete Donohue with information about the people Charlie was meeting.

'It's okay, Pete. He's back. He just called me from the airport.'

'Good. You sounded worried.'

That's an understatement, she thought. 'Thanks for your help, Pete. It was just a mix-up.'

'Glad to know that, Piper. See you around.'

She went into the bedroom and began to unpack her bags to calm herself down. She was just finishing when she heard Charlie's car driving in through the gates. A few minutes later, he bounced through the front door, debonair as ever, looking totally unconcerned, as if he had just nipped out to buy a newspaper.

Sofía ran to greet him and flung her arms round his legs. 'Daddy!'

He put down his bag, lifted her up, planted a kiss on her cheek and swung her around. 'How's my little princess? Have you been good?'

'Yes. Where have you been?'

'Away on business.' He turned to Piper. 'And how are you, sweetheart?'

She stared at him with cold fury. 'You and I have got to talk.'

Charlie shrugged, like an errant schoolboy who had been sent to the headmaster. 'Sure.' He gave Sofía to Margie and sheepishly followed Piper into the bedroom. As soon as he'd closed the door, he began apologising. 'Look, I'm terribly sorry for not contacting you sooner.'

'You didn't contact me at all. I've been terrified that

something bad had happened. You just took off without telling anyone where you were going. You didn't leave any message. You didn't return my calls. I didn't know whether you were alive or dead.'

Charlie put his hands up. 'Calm down.'

'Don't tell me to calm down!'

'Don't shout. Margie will hear.'

'I'll shout if I damned well want to.'

'If you listen, I'll try to explain. Shortly after you left, I got an urgent call to go to London to sort out a problem with the recording company. I've been literally tied up for the last two days, locked in a room with corporate lawyers. It's been a nightmare.'

'And they didn't even let you use the bathroom?'

'Don't be silly.'

'Charlie, it takes a minute to send a text message.'

'Listen, I've said I'm sorry. My mind was just totally focused on getting this problem solved.'

'So you had no time to think about your wife and child?'

'It wasn't like that. There were thousands of pounds of revenue at stake. There were these spivs in fancy suits and there was just me on my own. You don't know what those guys are like. It's like swimming with a shoal of barracudas. Blink and they'd have your wallet, credit card and watch.' He paused. 'Anyway, I got it sorted. It's over now. I'm home.'

She looked at him. He seemed contrite. He had apologised. She even felt a little bit sorry for him. 'Charlie, you and I have got to have a serious talk. And I mean serious. We can't go on like this.'

'Of course. Any time you want.' He put out his hands to draw her closer. 'C'mon, Piper. Tell me you forgive me.'

When Charlie looked at her with his smouldering eyes, it was hard for her to resist. 'On one condition.'

'What?'

'You've got to stop taking me for granted.'

'Of course.'

'You've got to spend more time with Sofía and me and stop gadding around town like a bachelor playboy.'

'Done.'

'And you don't disappear again without telling me, no matter how important your business might be. You reply to my messages. You show me the same respect you would show these lawyers you've just been negotiating with.'

'You have my word, Piper.'

'Because if you don't, I'll be gone and Sofía with me. There'll be no second chance.'

She had forgiven him but she knew she wouldn't forget. Charlie had a way of making promises and breaking them. This time she was determined to keep him to his word and set down a list of boundaries. He would have to behave more like a husband and father and less like a single man.

He went into the bathroom to have a shower and ten minutes later emerged with a towel wrapped around his waist. 'I've just had a bright idea,' he said. 'Why don't I take you out for a nice dinner tonight? It'll be a homecoming, an apology and a celebration all rolled into one.'

She looked at him. It would be lovely to have her husband all to herself for a few hours. And it would be an opportunity to tell him about her trip to Spain. 'Okay,' she said.

'Let's say eight o'clock. I'll go and book right away.'

Piper spent the remainder of the afternoon with her daughter, playing with the Spanish doll and reading stories. At seven o'clock, she put the child to bed and began to get ready for the evening. Charlie had managed to book a table at the Chalet d'Or, a new restaurant in Dawson Street that had garnered a string of rave reviews from the food critics. She was just putting the finishing touches to her makeup when she heard the buzzer sound to announce the arrival of their taxi.

***

The meal was good – but not quite as good as all those critics had suggested. Afterwards, Charlie suggested they drop into Aunt Polly's Boudoir for a nightcap. It was a short walk to the club and, once inside, they found it packed with familiar faces. Piper felt a buzz of excitement. It was as if she had stepped back a few years to when she was still a bachelor girl, before she had known Charlie.

Loud music was pumping out of the sound system. Couples were gyrating on the dance floor. Piper recognised several fashion models, a television chat show host, a rising young novelist and a celebrity chef. Heads turned as they arrived and people waved.

A voice shouted above the din, 'My God, it's Piper and Charlie! Come and join us!'

She turned to see a small middle-aged man, with dyed hair, in a pink shirt, gesticulating frantically from the bar: Serge Dupont, fashion designer to the rich and famous. He was one of the regulars in Aunt Polly's. A sulky-looking boy clung to his arm as if for dear life.

'Where have you been, my darlings?' Dupont exclaimed, standing up and kissing Piper on the cheek. 'We never see you, these days. We were beginning to think you might be dead.' He laughed. 'Here, have some champers.'

He pulled a bottle from an ice-bucket and poured two glasses. Then he turned and introduced his companion. 'This is Alessandro. Isn't he a little charmer?'

Alessandro scowled.

'We're off tomorrow for a little holiday in Puerto Banús,' Dupont announced. 'Alessandro misses the sun.'

'I'm just back from there,' Piper said.

'What was the weather like?'

'Very pleasant, not too hot.'

'Oooh, I can't wait.'

Dupont addressed Charlie. 'I hear great things about that band of yours. What are they called again? Hell's Gates?'

'Hell's Kitchen,' Alessandro corrected him.

'They keep me busy,' Charlie said. 'They have a major concert tour lined up in a few months' time, six European capitals, kicking off in Paris and ending in Dublin.'

'Too busy,' Piper muttered.

'We must go and see them some time,' Dupont said. 'Can you get us tickets?'

'Just give me a call.'

A crowd had quickly gathered at the bar and drinks were flying across the counter. Piper felt a tug at her sleeve and turned to see a pretty, dark-haired woman smiling at her. 'It is you, isn't it? Piper McKenzie?'

It took Piper a moment to recognise her. Alice McDowell was a former classmate from her student days. 'Alice, my God! What are you doing here?'

'My boyfriend brought me. He's off talking to some people. When I saw you, I thought, That's the famous Piper, so I decided to pop over and say hello.'

'Enjoying yourself?'

'Oh, yes. I've never been here before. It's very exciting, isn't it?'

Piper introduced her to Charlie. She saw admiration in Alice's eyes at the sight of his handsome face.

'So, you guys were at college together. What are you doing now, Alice?'

'I work for myself. I've set up a marketing company.'

'Surviving?'

'Just about.'

'Tell you what,' Charlie said. 'I might be able to put some work your way. Any experience of music promotion?'

'No, but I'd love to try.'

He fished a card from his pocket and pressed it into her hand. 'Give me a call some time and we'll see what we can do. I'm always on the lookout for good marketing people.'

The two women kissed and Alice departed back into the crowd.

'Pretty little thing,' Charlie said.

Piper slapped his wrist. 'You're a married man now, Charlie. You're not supposed to notice pretty little things.'

He shrugged and emptied his glass of champagne. 'Is a man not allowed to pass a compliment any more?'

***

They left the club at around one o'clock. As they stepped outside to find their taxi, a figure emerged from the shadows. 'Mr White, sir?'

Charlie spun round. There was a series of flashes. The man ran to a waiting car and it roared away. 'Bloody paparazzi,' he muttered. 'Wouldn't you think they'd find someone else to photograph? There's a whole club full of people in Aunt Polly's.'

'But they're not as glamorous as us.' Piper laughed.

The champagne had left her in a light-hearted mood. She couldn't wait to get Charlie home and into her arms.

***

The moment they were in the bedroom, they were clawing at each other. She felt his hands encircle her waist and his warm mouth close on hers.

He lifted her dress over her head and carried her to the large double bed. In a matter of seconds, he had undressed her and his hot lips were caressing her breasts while his hand stroked her thigh.

Afterwards, they lay exhausted in the tangle of sheets, her head cradled in the crook of his arm.

'You're so beautiful,' Charlie whispered, as they cuddled closer together.

Piper closed her eyes. Charlie White had many faults but he was far and away the most romantic lover she had ever known.

CHAPTER SEVEN

It was her best friend Jo Ferguson who alerted her to the photograph the following morning. Piper was just leaving to drive over to Howth when her phone rang and her friend said, 'I suppose you know you're on the front page again.'

'Which one?'

'The *Tribune*.'

'I didn't, but thanks for alerting me. Charlie and I were in Aunt Polly's last night and there was a guy waiting outside when we were leaving. He snapped us before we could do a thing.'

'It's nothing to worry about. You're not falling around drunk.'

'Well, thank God for that.'

'In fact it's quite a flattering shot. You look quite the attractive young couple.'

'It's the price you pay for being in the public eye.' Privately, Piper was quite happy to see her photo in the papers. She liked the publicity. When she was younger she had actively courted it. She could hardly complain now.

She stopped at a filling station and purchased a copy of the tabloid. Jo was right. Her picture was splashed all over the front page but it showed Charlie and her to very good effect, both so glamorous. She smiled at the headline.

CELEBRITY COUPLE OUT ON THE TOWN

Music supremo Charlie White and his beautiful wife, Piper McKenzie, were in happy mood last night after spending the evening with their celebrity friends at an exclusive Dublin nightclub.

White is the successful manager of the rising young rock band Hell's Kitchen. McKenzie is the daughter of Henry McKenzie, the hotel tycoon, and is widely tipped to take control of the business empire when her father retires. There's no recession for this fortunate young couple.

Piper tossed the paper onto the back seat. Apart from the snide last sentence there was nothing to get upset about.

As she continued along the coast road, the green slopes of Howth Head seemed to rise closer to meet her. At last, she was pulling through Elsinore's gates, then stepping out of her Lexus. Yesterday's rain was gone and now the sun was out.

She went up the stairs to her father's office and found him waiting for her. He looked pleased to see her as she sat down across the desk from him.

'How are you this morning? Everybody okay at home?' he asked.

'Everyone is fine, Dad.'

'And my little angel, Sofía, how is she?'

'Bright as a button. I might bring her over on Sunday.'

'I'll certainly enjoy that. Now, Hotel Azul.'

'Yes?'

'I've been studying your report again. I think we might buy it. It would be a good acquisition for our portfolio. The market in Spain is depressed right now so we'd probably pick it up cheap.'

'Okay.'

'I'm thinking of the future. This recession won't last for ever and people will always want holidays in the sun. Besides, it would be easy to manage. It's small and the overheads will be low.'

Piper thought of the beautiful little hotel, the terrace and the gardens with the flowers in bloom. 'I agree. When are you going down there?'

'I'm not,' Henry said. 'I'm too busy here in Dublin. I want you to go.'

'Me?' she said, surprised.

'Why not?'

'But I've never done anything like that before. You always insist on carrying out the negotiations.'

'That's about to change. You're working with me to learn the business. This is an opportunity for you. Regard it as a learning curve. I want you to go back to Marbella and do this deal with *Señor* Guzman. You'll have to be tough, Piper. I want that hotel as cheap as possible.'

He shuffled some papers on his desk till he found what he was looking for. 'I've made some enquiries. He's looking for three million euro. If you can get him down to two and a half, we'll buy. But that price has to include all the fittings and equipment. Get a list of payroll costs and accounts from him and an inventory of the contents. I also have the name of a reliable lawyer in Marbella who'll assist you with the legal side.'

Piper took a deep breath. Her father had never asked her to do anything as important as this before. She knew he was placing a lot of trust in her. But he was right. It was a major opportunity to get involved at the highest level of the McKenzie business. How could she refuse?

'When do you want me to go?'

'Tomorrow morning. Ring him today and tell him you're coming. Ask him to meet you tomorrow afternoon. And one final thing, don't sign anything. Leave that to me. You can pick up the phone at any time and speak to me if you're in doubt.'

He leaned back in his chair and smiled. 'Are you nervous?'

'A little.'

'I remember the first place I bought back in 1972. It was a bed-and-breakfast establishment in Gardiner Street. The clientele were mainly students and backpackers. I sweated blood over it for months, couldn't sleep I was so worried. I paid ten thousand pounds for it. Three years later, I sold it for seventy grand and bought my first small hotel. It's like a baby learning to walk, Piper. You have to take that first step, and after that, you don't have any fear.'

'I'll start making the arrangements right away.'

She stood up to go but her father signalled for her to stay.

He drew a copy of the *Tribune* from a drawer, the one with Charlie and her on the front page. 'You've seen this, I suppose.'

'Yes.'

'I know you can't stop them taking your photograph. You're a beautiful woman, Piper, and you're married to a glamorous man. It's inevitable the press should be interested in you. But I don't like the firm getting dragged into the papers. That's a different matter.'

'I understand.'

He held his hand up to silence her. 'I don't want Jack upset. He's your brother. You're my only children. I want you to get along together. I don't want him reading in the papers that you're going to inherit the business. Nothing has been decided about that.'

'It didn't come from me.'

'It doesn't matter. What you do with your life is your own affair. Just keep the family out of it. I have enough trouble with Jack as it is, without provoking him even further.'

On her way out, Piper called into the office of her father's secretary, Sally Burrows. Sally was not much older than Piper, dark-haired, attractive and super-efficient. 'I'm off to Spain again. I'll need you to take care of the travel arrangements.'

'When are you going?'

'Tomorrow morning.'

'No problem, Piper. I'll check the flights right away.'

Before leaving the house, she went into the large lounge where she found her mother watching one of her favourite soaps on a giant screen. She switched it off as Piper came in. 'I have to get my daily instalment of *Paradise Square* or I

53

don't feel right,' Rose said apologetically. 'Have you time for a quick cup of tea?'

'Sure.' She followed her mother into the kitchen where Rose set about filling the kettle. 'Dad wants me to go back to Spain and negotiate for Hotel Azul.'

'I thought he might. He was talking about it last night. It's a first for you. How do you feel about it?'

'You know me, Mum. Where the company's concerned, I do as I'm told. But just between us, I don't like leaving Sofía behind.'

'Why don't you take her with you? She'd love it. And bring Margie too. You could leave Sofía with her while you get your work done.'

'I hadn't thought of that.'

'It's the perfect solution. It means everybody gets a break.'

***

On her way home, Piper turned her mother's suggestion over in her mind. She might even add an extra day to the trip and have a little holiday. But before she did anything, she had to clear it with her father. She rang him and he agreed at once.

'Trust your mother to think of that,' he said. 'Go right ahead. You have my blessing.'

When she explained her plan to Sofía and Margie, they were both excited.

'Will I be able to play on the sand?' Sofía wanted to know.

'Of course, darling, and ride on a donkey. And fly on a plane. There'll be lots of wonderful things to do.'

Margie said she would pack while Piper got on the phone

to *Señor* Guzman. She had been entrusted with an important mission by her father. Now that she had solved the problem of her daughter, she would be able to give the negotiations her full attention. Once they were concluded, they would all be able to relax together in the warm Spanish sun. But when she managed to contact the hotel owner she encountered a setback.

'Tomorrow is out of the question, Miss McKenzie. I have to be in Madrid to talk to my bankers.'

'So when would suit you?'

'The following day.'

'Fine. Leave the afternoon free. I'll let you have a precise time once I've arranged flights.'

'Excellent. One other thing, I must insist that you stay with us at Hotel Azul again, my dear Miss McKenzie.'

'I'll be travelling with my young daughter and her nanny.'

'That is not a problem.'

'Are you sure?'

'Of course!'

'How very kind of you.'

'Not at all. We will enjoy your company.'

The situation was getting better by the minute. Hotel Azul would be perfect for Sofía, with its gardens and pool. As soon as Piper had hung up, Sally called with flight times so she asked her to check for a day later, then book the flights for herself and the others.

When Charlie heard about the trip, he pretended to be upset. 'So you're all disappearing to enjoy yourselves in the sun while I'm left behind. I don't call that fair.'

'It'll be no picnic, Charlie. I'm going to be negotiating for the purchase of a hotel. You should know all about negotiations. You certainly spend a lot of time on them.'

Her husband laughed. 'Do I hear a note of sarcasm creeping into your beautiful voice?'

'Let's just put it this way. Now you'll know how I feel when you disappear for days. At least I'll be available to take your phone calls.'

'Ouch.'

***

Piper spent the following day preparing for the challenge that lay ahead. Her father had invested his faith in her and she was determined not to let him down. She contacted the lawyer in Marbella Henry had mentioned and asked him to get hold of the inventory of contents and payroll costs and fax them to her. She also asked him to compile a list of recent sale prices of similar hotels in the Marbella area. The more ammunition she had, the better.

That evening, after Sofía had been put to bed, Charlie and Piper had a quiet dinner together.

'This is a big deal for you, Piper. I assume your father's briefed you thoroughly.'

'Of course.'

'Let me give you one piece of advice about negotiating. Don't dig yourself into a hole you can't get out of. Always leave yourself an escape route. And be prepared to make concessions so long as you achieve your main objective.' He placed his hand over hers and gave it a reassuring squeeze. 'Just hold your nerve and you'll be fine.'

Chapter Eight

It was as if she had never left. The moment they stepped outside the terminal building she felt the heat and saw the flowers in bloom, the sun like a big ripe orange in the clear blue sky. Piper closed her eyes and sniffed.

Pedro was waiting. He took the luggage from them and led the way to the car. They all got in, and he set off for the motorway. 'So you have come back, *Señora*,' he said, with a smile.

Piper remembered the conversation they had had just a few days before. 'Did you take your girlfriend to the *feria*, Pedro?'

'Oh, yes. Carmencita enjoyed it very much. Did I tell you we are going to be married?'

'No. But you have my congratulations. When will it be?'

'When I get a better job. Her father is very tough.'

'You mean strict?'

'Yes, strict. He will not give his permission until I am able to buy a house. He says his daughter deserves only the best.'

'Well, of course she does. What does Carmencita say?'

'She would marry me in the morning but she doesn't want to fight with her father.'

'So you will have to wait.'

'Yes,' he agreed sadly.

'Don't worry, Pedro. You're a good worker. Something will come along.'

'You think so?'

'I know about these things. I can tell.'

The young driver turned to her and grinned. 'You are so kind, *Señora*. You cheer me up.'

He kept up a stream of conversation while Margie and Sofía gazed from the car window at the scenery flashing by and the sea sparkling in the distance. At last, they reached the outskirts of Marbella and began the descent towards the seafront.

When they arrived at the hotel, the stout little manager, *Señor* Hernandez, was waiting once more, with a couple of porters, to greet her. 'Welcome, *Señora*. I hope you had a pleasant flight. Your rooms are ready. *Señor* Guzman has given instructions, if you will kindly follow me, please.'

The porters took hold of the luggage and they set off.

This time, the rooms were on the ground floor at the back of the hotel where it was quiet. *Señor* Guzman had obviously taken safety considerations into account because of Sofía. The rooms were adjoining and led out to the gardens. They were spacious and comfortable and almost as elaborate as the bridal suite Piper had been allocated on her previous visit.

'These are lovely rooms,' she said, as she tipped the porters.

'Thank you, *Señora*. *Señor* Guzman has asked me to say that he will meet you in his office at three o'clock. He has instructed me to offer you lunch.'

Piper checked her watch. It was now a quarter past one. The negotiations might take a long time. It might be wise to eat something but perhaps not a full lunch. 'Thank you. We'll have a snack from the bar.'

'As you wish, *Señora*. If you prefer to eat here, Room Service will be pleased to assist you.' He bowed and was gone.

By now, Sofía was bouncing up and down on the bed, filled with excitement at her strange new surroundings. 'When can I play on the sand, Mummy? When can I see the donkeys?'

Piper turned to the nanny. 'What do you think, Margie? I could be tied up with *Señor* Guzman for some time. I don't know when I'll be free.'

'I'll take her to the beach as soon as we've had lunch.'

'Brilliant.'

***

The bar served a good range of light snacks. Piper ordered ham and salad rolls for Margie and herself while Sofía happily tucked into a plate of spaghetti. They drank chilled sparkling water. At two o'clock, they returned to their rooms to get ready. Margie organised towels and the beach stuff. Sofía was impatient to set off.

'Don't let her get too much sun,' Piper advised. 'Put on plenty of factor fifty and make sure she wears her baseball cap.'

'Don't worry, I'll take good care of her.'

Piper knelt down and looked into the child's eyes. 'I want you to listen to Margie now, do you hear?'

'Yes, Mummy.'

'You must be a good girl or I won't let you go again.'

'Yes, Mummy. Can I go now?'

Piper gave her daughter a kiss and she set off with Margie through the hotel grounds towards the back gate that led down to the beach. It had been agreed that Sofía would sleep in Piper's room so she quickly unpacked the cases and put their clothes in the wardrobe. Then she got undressed and stepped into the shower.

She was still a little nervous about the meeting. *Señor* Guzman was a pleasant man and they had got on well but she had to set aside her feelings and concentrate on getting the best possible deal for the company. She dried herself, brushed out her blonde hair, then put on a skirt, a blouse and a little light jacket. She sat down at the writing desk beside the window and quickly ran over the material she had gathered to familiarise herself with it.

When she was satisfied, she stood up and put the papers in her briefcase. She checked her appearance in the mirror. She looked smart and businesslike. She locked the door and set off for *Señor* Guzman's office. When she arrived, it was two minutes to three. She straightened her jacket, took a deep breath and knocked politely. A voice invited her to enter. Piper turned the door handle and walked into the room.

Señor Guzman was seated behind a shiny mahogany desk with a pile of papers before him and a worried look on his face. A giant ceiling fan gently stirred the air. He rose from his chair as she came in and politely took her hand. 'My dear Miss McKenzie, you look as charming as ever. Please take a seat. Would you like some tea?'

'No, thank you.'

'Some fruit juice, perhaps?'

'That would be nice.'

He opened a mini-bar and produced two bottles. He uncapped one and passed it across the desk with a glass.

Piper sat down, opened her briefcase and placed her documents in a neat pile in front of her.

'So your father has decided to purchase Hotel Azul. You are familiar with the asking price? It is three million euros.'

'I'm afraid that's too much for us.'

He looked disappointed. 'But you will be getting a beautiful hotel. You have inspected it and you know I am telling the truth. You have seen the accounts. You know what the turnover is. You are an intelligent young woman. You know this is a good business.'

'I also know that Hotel Victoria sold last month for much less. And it has more rooms.'

Señor Guzman forced a smile onto his face. 'My dear Miss McKenzie, you surely do not intend to compare Hotel Victoria with us? Hotel Victoria is a mere two-star hotel. We have four stars.'

'Hotel Magenta sold six weeks ago for two million euros. It has four stars.'

'But it is a mile away from the seafront and has no swimming pool.'

61

'*Señor* Guzman, I know the price of every hotel that has been sold in Marbella in the past six months. You're asking too much. If we're to do business, you must lower your price.'

He opened the top button of his shirt and loosened his tie. Piper could see the sweat glistening on his forehead. She, however, remained cool and calm. Now that the negotiations had begun, she felt totally relaxed.

'What do you propose?' *Señor* Guzman asked.

'We have made our calculations. We'll have to undertake renovation work and upgrade the fittings and furniture. It's all extra expenditure. If we're to make Hotel Azul a profitable venture for us, the most we can offer is two million euros.'

At these words, the owner's face collapsed. He raised his hands. 'It is impossible. I cannot sell at that price. It wouldn't even pay off my bank debts.'

Piper gathered her papers together. 'In that case, we cannot do business.'

She stood up but the owner quickly stood up too.

'Please sit down, Miss McKenzie. Let's not be hasty. Perhaps I can come down a little. I would be prepared to accept two million eight hundred thousand euros.'

Piper caught his eye and held it. 'Two million four hundred thousand.'

'No. It cannot be sold at that price.'

'Two and a half million, and that is my final offer,' Piper said.

By now, the sweat was streaming down *Señor* Guzman's forehead. He took out a large white handkerchief and wiped his face. 'Miss McKenzie, I regard you as my friend. But I must be entirely honest with you. Hotel Azul has been my life's work. I have put all my savings and my energy into it. It breaks my heart to have to sell it. The very lowest price I can accept is two million six hundred thousand euros. That is what I require to clear my debts. I would like you to have the hotel. I know you would look after it. But I really cannot go any lower than that.'

Piper stared into his eyes. He was telling the truth. 'Let me take a break of fifteen minutes while I consider the situation.'

She left the room and walked out into the gardens. She found a bench beside a rose-bed, took out her phone and called her father. 'I've pushed him as far as he can go. I also feel sorry for him. I think we should cut him a little slack.'

'Where have you got him?' Henry asked.

'Two six.'

'Take it.'

'You're sure?'

'Yes. It's a very good price. I don't believe in grinding people's faces in the dirt, Piper.'

'Neither do I. That's why I called you.'

She returned to the negotiating room. As she came in, *Señor* Guzman glanced up, a nervous look on his face.

'We'll offer two million six hundred thousand euros. And the price is to include all fittings and equipment.'

A wave of relief passed over *Señor* Guzman's face. His eyes brimmed with tears and, for a worrying moment, she thought he was going to weep. He took her hand and kissed her fingers. 'Miss McKenzie, you are my saviour. You don't know how much this means to me. Now I am content that Hotel Azul will be in good hands.' He opened the mini-bar again and produced two small bottles of champagne and two glasses. 'I invite you to drink a toast with me to seal our agreement.' He removed a cork, poured and passed a foaming glass across the desk. 'To Hotel Azul.'

'To Hotel Azul.'

The cold bubbles tickled Piper's throat. A warm feeling of satisfaction enveloped her. She had achieved the task her father had set for her and now she felt vindicated. 'You are a shrewd businesswoman, Miss McKenzie. Perhaps if you had been working for me, I would never have had to sell my little hotel.'

CHAPTER NINE

They spent another half-hour tying up the fine details of the deal. *Señor* Guzman undertook to have his solicitor draw up a contract detailing the purchase price and an inventory of the fittings and equipment that would be included in the sale. One copy was to be faxed to Piper's lawyer in Marbella and a second to her father in Dublin.

When the work had been completed, he invited her to have dinner with him that evening, but Piper was anxious to be with Sofía and Margie. 'I'm afraid I can't, *Señor*. I was planning to take my daughter out this evening to show her Marbella. This is her first visit to Spain.'

'How long to you intend to stay?'

'One more day.'

'You are welcome to stay longer if you wish.'

'Thank you but I really must return to Dublin.'

'If you require transport to visit some of the countryside, I will put Pedro at your disposal.' He made a little bow and they shook hands.

Piper returned to her room and immediately rang her lawyer to brief him on the outcome. 'The agreed price is two million six hundred thousand euros and that will include the fittings and equipment. *Señor* Guzman has undertaken to send you a copy of the contract as soon as it is completed.'

'I will take care of the legal work, *Señora*. You can relax now.'

'How long do you think it will take?'

'That depends. I would expect a month or six weeks.'

'Please keep in touch with us.'

'Of course, *Señora*.'

Next she rang her father. 'It's a done deal,' she said, when she heard his voice on the line.

'Congratulations, Piper. I'm proud of you. We've got a good bargain. How does Guzman feel?'

'He's happy with the outcome.'

'That's important. A successful negotiation should leave both parties feeling satisfied. So, now you've cut your first deal, are you ready for more?'

A smile came over Piper's face. 'You're a hard taskmaster. Won't you even let me get my breath back?'

She heard her father laugh. 'You've shown you can do it, Piper, and I'm very pleased. Now that you've proved yourself, I'll be relying on you more and more.'

Finally she rang Charlie. He answered on the first ring. 'I'm pleased you're sticking to your promise,' she said jokingly.

'Of course. I'm always available for you, Piper.'

'That's good to know. How's your day?'

'All my days are the same: busy, busy, busy.'

'Well, you'll be happy to learn that you aren't the only

member of the family who can conduct serious negotiations. I've just bought a hotel.'

There was a slight intake of breath and then Charlie was gushing praise.

'That's fantastic. Did you get the price you wanted?'

'More or less. We got a deal Dad's very pleased with. Now we can add Hotel Azul to our portfolio.'

'That's brilliant. Well done, Piper.'

'I took your advice. I held my nerve and I made a small concession.'

'I'm delighted. I really am. When are you coming back?'

'Day after tomorrow.'

'I'm missing you and Sofía. It's lonely here without you.'

'Do you mean that, Charlie?'

'Every word. I can't wait to see you. Do you want me to pick you up at the airport?'

'I'll decide tomorrow. We'll talk again.'

'I love you, Piper.'

'I love you too, Charlie.' She turned off her phone and gazed out across the gardens. The sun was still strong but shadows were creeping across the lawn. Charlie really was the nicest man, the best husband any woman could wish for. How could she ever have doubted him?

She decided to have a swim while she waited for Margie and Sofía to return from the beach. She slipped out of her clothes, put on her swimsuit, then pulled a hotel dressing-gown around her and set off through the gardens.

There were a couple of people sunbathing beside the pool but otherwise it was deserted. She had a shower, then slipped into the water and had an invigorating swim. She was getting out when she heard the excited cries of her daughter coming up the garden with Margie. 'Mummy! We had a lovely time at the beach. I went for a paddle in the sea and then we had ice-cream. And I had a ride on a donkey.'

Piper swept her daughter into her arms. 'Were you a good girl, like I said?'

Margie nodded. 'She was a little angel, Piper. Good as gold.'

'And I made a sandcastle and we saw a clown. Oh, Mummy, can I go again tomorrow?'

'We'll see, sweetheart. Now let's all go back to our rooms so that poor Margie can relax. I'm sure you must be exhausted?'

Margie shrugged. 'Not really, she was very well behaved. Most of the time, I just sat in the sun and watched her.'

They walked back to their rooms and Piper helped Margie put Sofía down for a little nap before they went out for dinner. Once the child was asleep, she opened a bottle of wine and poured two glasses, which they took out onto the terrace.

The sun was sinking fast but the air was balmy and warm. The lights of the town were coming on and twinkled like stars in the distance.

'Isn't this the most relaxing thing you can imagine?' Margie said, lying back in her chair and stretching her feet.

'It's wonderful,' Piper agreed. She felt a sense of contentment steal over her. She had just concluded a successful deal for her father and now she had an evening to look forward to with her daughter and Margie. If only Charlie was here to share her pleasure, the day would be perfect.

'You know something, Piper? If I was ever lucky enough

to win the lottery, I'd buy a little apartment down here and never go home again to the wind and rain.'

Piper listened to the cicadas chattering in the trees. Margie had a point. It would be marvellous to wake every morning to the sun and see the flowers opening. 'It rains here too, Margie. I was here one time and the heavens opened. It poured for two solid days.'

'But I'll bet the sun came out and everything was bright again.'

'Yes,' Piper admitted. 'That's exactly what happened.'

At seven o'clock, she reluctantly got up and dragged herself under the shower. Then she got dressed while Margie woke Sofía and readied her for their evening excursion. It was seven thirty when they set off into the town. The shops were open and the streets were crowded.

They found a pretty little restaurant at the seafront and sat at a table outside where they could watch people strolling up and down the Paseo Maritimo.

'I was thinking of taking a jaunt up into the mountains tomorrow,' Piper said. '*Señor* Guzman has offered us a car and Pedro to drive. It would give us an opportunity to get away from the tourists and see some of the countryside.'

'I want to go to the beach,' Sofía protested.

'There's no reason why we can't do both. We could go to the beach in the morning and take a drive in the afternoon.'

Later, when they had eaten, they set off again through the throngs on the seafront. They stopped several times so Sofía could watch a mime artist and a gypsy girl dancing a wild flamenco, her heels tapping like castanets on the hard pavement and her skirts swirling like flames. By the time they got back to Hotel Azul it was ten o'clock and they were tired.

Piper stopped briefly at the reception desk to leave a message for Pedro, asking him to drive them to Ronda the following afternoon at two o'clock. Then they went to their rooms, where she said goodnight to Margie and put Sofía to bed.

She was just slipping under the sheets herself when it occurred to her to check her phone for messages. There was only one and it was from her mother: *Ring home urgently.*

CHAPTER TEN

Piper's heart jumped into her mouth. Her first thought was that something bad had happened. It wasn't like her mother to be alarmist. She checked the time the message had been sent. Two hours earlier, at eight o'clock, when they were sitting down to eat.

She pressed her mother's number and immediately heard her voice on the line.

'It's Piper. You asked me to ring. Is everything all right there?'

'Yes, everything's fine. When are you coming back?'

'Day after tomorrow.'

'You did excellent work in those negotiations. Your father's been singing your praises all day long. You've certainly impressed him, Piper. But I wanted to warn you.'

'What?'

'Not everybody's happy.'

'How do you mean?'

'Jack was here this afternoon and Corinne was with him. I overheard them talking in the kitchen. She was telling him he should have been sent instead of you. She said he had more experience and it was an insult.'

Piper felt her temper flare. 'The cheek of her. It's none of her damned business.'

'My sentiments exactly.'

'Does Dad know about this?'

'Not unless Jack's complained. Your father was in such good form that I didn't want to upset him. But I thought I'd better warn you so when you come back you'll be prepared.'

'That woman's getting far too big for her boots. McKenzie Leisure means exactly what it says. It's the McKenzie family company. She's an outsider. I think someone will have to take her down a peg or two.'

'Do nothing till you come home. I just wanted you to be aware. Now, in the meantime, just enjoy what's left of your break. How is my favourite granddaughter?'

'Oh, she's loving it, Mum. She spent the day on the beach with Margie while I was with *Señor* Guzman. She's having a ball.'

'And the weather?'

'It's beautiful.'

They talked some more, and finally Piper ended the call. She snuggled down under the cool sheets. The news from home had put a dampener on her day but it had made her more determined. If Corinne Delaney was intent on meddling in the family business, she'd better understand what she was taking on. Piper would resist her every inch of the way.

***

The birds chirping in the trees outside her window woke her at eight o'clock. The sun was up and the gardens were bathed in a luminous light. It was going to be another beautiful day. She put on her swimsuit and walked the short distance to the pool, then swam for twenty minutes. On the way back, she called into the bar and picked up a tray of pastries and croissants.

When she arrived at their rooms, she found that Margie and Sofía were up. They sat on the bright terrace and had breakfast together.

'Now, here's the drill for the day,' Piper said. 'After breakfast, we go off to the beach till one o'clock. Then we have lunch and at two o'clock Pedro is taking us for a drive into the countryside. Everyone agreed?'

'Yes, Mummy,' Sofía said, and disappeared to find her bucket and spade.

Piper finished her coffee and began to pack the bags with towels, sunscreen, water bottles and reading material. Half an hour later, she locked up and they set off through the back gate and down the winding road to the beach. She was looking forward to spending a few hours with her daughter and Margie.

There was only a handful of people on the beach when they arrived and the sea looked cool and inviting. In the distance, they could see a large cruise ship ploughing towards Málaga. They hired two sun loungers and an umbrella from the beach attendant while Sofía sat down and immediately began to dig a hole in the sand. Piper applied some sunscreen to the little girl, then to herself, and lay back to relax.

She recalled what Margie had said yesterday about living permanently in Spain. There was something about the warmth and the bright sunshine that put people in a good mood. The idea of living in Spain was an enticing one but it was totally unrealistic. Her life was busy now but it would be hectic before long.

Some time in the near future, her father would retire and control of the company would transfer to Jack and her. She knew how hard her father worked. The same prospect awaited her: busy days cutting deals, travelling, negotiating, organising staff, sorting out problems. And then, of course, there was Charlie. His music business was based in Dublin. There was no way he could operate from Spain. No, living down here was just a pipe dream. Attractive as it was, Spain would have to remain a place she came to for holidays.

Thinking of Charlie reminded her to call him. He replied at once and she found herself smiling. Perhaps he had taken her lecture to heart and really had turned over a new leaf. No more leaving messages and waiting in frustration for him to return her calls.

'How are things in Dublin?'

'Do you really want to know? I'm struggling to put the Hell's Kitchen European tour together. You can imagine the nightmare that is, booking hotels and venues, talking to promoters, organising publicity. Incidentally, I've hired that friend of yours to give me a hand.'

'Which friend?'

'Alice McDowell. Remember? You introduced us at Aunt Polly's.'

'Is she any good?'

'Time will tell. She's certainly energetic and hungry for

work. That's always a good sign. So you can see, Piper, I'm not exactly sitting here twiddling my thumbs. You, meanwhile, are probably lying on a beach somewhere soaking up the sun.'

Piper laughed. 'That's exactly what I'm doing. But tomorrow I'll be home and I'm not looking forward to it. Jack's miffed that I got sent down here to do the hotel deal instead of him.' She related what she had learned from her conversation with her mother.

'If he gives you trouble, tell him to take a hike. And if he's such a hot-shot, why didn't your father send him? Your dad's a wise old owl, Piper. He sent you because he knew you'd do a better job.'

'Well, it may not be that simple. Dad wants us all to get along together. I want to avoid a blazing row with Jack, if possible. Besides, I'm not sure he's acting alone in this. I suspect Corinne's egging him on. I don't like her, Charlie. I think she's scheming to get her hands on the company.'

'I haven't time to get involved in the McKenzie family problems, Piper. I've got enough of my own. But sometimes you're better off speaking your mind to someone and letting them know exactly how you feel. Now, how's my darling daughter? Is she enjoying herself?'

'You can speak to her. She's here beside me.' She handed the phone to Sofía, who babbled away to her father about the beach and the donkeys. Finally she handed the phone back to Piper.

'About tomorrow,' Piper said to Charlie. 'I think I'll take you up on that offer to pick us up at the airport, unless you're too busy.'

'Piper, how many times do I have to tell you? I'm never too busy for you. What time do you land?'

'Three o'clock.'

'I'll be there. *Adios, amiga.* Don't stay too long in the sun and spoil that wonderful complexion of yours. Remember, blondes burn faster than brunettes.'

They said goodbye and Piper cancelled the call. Yes, she thought, as she lay back and let the sun warm her face. Charlie's got the message. He really does sound like a new man.

***

Before they knew it, it was five to one and time to return to the hotel. They gathered up their belongings, packed them into the bags and started back up the winding road.

By the time they reached the bar, they were thirsty and Piper ordered cold beers for herself and Margie and lemonade for Sofía. No one was really hungry so they had a snack, then went back to their rooms to change for the drive up into the mountains. Piper packed a couple of sweaters in case it got chilly later on.

When they got downstairs Pedro was waiting for them in Reception, wearing his ill-fitting chauffeur's uniform and cap. They settled into the car and headed inland. Before long they could look down and see the tourist resorts spread out along the coast.

The air-conditioning was on in the car but Piper noticed that little rivulets of sweat were running down the driver's neck. 'Are you hot in that uniform?' she asked.

Pedro glanced at her in the rear-view mirror and smiled. '*De nada*, *Señora*. It is nothing. I don't mind.'

'It's making you uncomfortable.'

'I like my uniform. Carmencita says it makes me look smart, like a soldier.'

Maybe, Piper thought, but one of the first things we're going to do when we take over Hotel Azul is get rid of that outfit.

By now they had climbed high into the hills and the road had become narrow and twisting, with huge gorges falling away on either side. She was glad when at last the white houses of Ronda came into view. She had been there before: it was one of the most scenic towns in the region, boasting the oldest bullring in Spain. They parked the car on the outskirts and made the rest of the journey on foot. As she had suspected, it was slightly cooler than it had been on the coast so walking was pleasant. They visited several of the main attractions, then Sofía complained that she was hungry. They found a restaurant with tables set out in a shady courtyard and sat down.

'I will leave you now,' Pedro said, 'and return in one hour.'

'Where are you going?'

'I will take a walk.'

'You'll do nothing of the sort,' Piper said. 'You will eat with us.'

The young driver looked embarrassed. 'You will want to talk in private. I will find a bar and have a *bocadillo*.'

'No,' Piper said firmly. 'I insist. Sit down – please – and tell us what is good to eat.'

Pedro took off his cap, lifted the menu and studied it for a few minutes. 'The food here is excellent. I will recommend a range of tapas. Would you like me to choose?'

'Please do, and in the meantime, I'm going to order some beer.' She signalled to the waiter. When the man returned with the drinks, Pedro ordered in quick Spanish and he hurried away again. Piper turned her attention to their surroundings. There was an ancient fountain bubbling in the centre of the cobbled courtyard and pots of the ubiquitous bright-red geraniums along the window-ledges. 'I'm going to miss Andalucía when we go home.'

'Me too,' Margie agreed. 'Still, we'll have pleasant memories.'

At the mention of memories, Piper rummaged in her bag and produced her camera. 'I almost forgot! We'll have to take some photos to make everyone jealous when we get back.'

They huddled together around the table and Pedro obliged with the camera.

'Make sure to get the fountain,' Piper instructed.

He had just finished taking the photos when the waiter appeared with an array of little dishes. Pedro took great delight in explaining what each contained. 'This is *tortilla de gambas*. It is an omelette made with prawns. These are *albondigas*, meatballs in sauce. Here is *queso con anchoas*, cheese with anchovies.'

Piper selected a piece of garlicky chicken and gave a sigh of delight. 'Yum.'

Soon everyone was tucking in, including Sofía, who had a plate of *patatas bravas*, fried potatoes with herbs.

'You like the food?' Pedro asked.

'It's wonderful,' Margie said.

'And not too heavy,' Piper added.

Since she wasn't driving, she decided to chance some wine, which she shared with the nanny. Once again, Pedro came to their aid. He spoke to the waiter and soon a bottle of deliciously chilled white wine appeared. She examined the label. It appeared to be a local wine from the Ronda region. 'You really know your food and wine, Pedro.'

He blushed. 'I once trained to be a chef.'

'And what happened?'

He shrugged. 'The wages for a trainee chef were small. I was young and in a hurry to earn bigger money so I left.'

'That's a pity,' Piper said.

'What will be will be. Now I am a driver. I enjoy my work very much.'

They sat in the little courtyard until gradually the sun began to sink over the hills and it got chilly. 'Time to go back,' Piper said. She paid the bill and they walked the short distance to the edge of the town where Pedro had parked the car. They strapped themselves in and he began the careful descent down the mountainside to Marbella. Below, they could see the lights of the town twinkling in the gathering gloom.

An hour later, at eight o'clock, they were back at the hotel. They shook hands with Pedro and thanked him for a wonderful trip.

'You are returning to Ireland tomorrow, *Señora*. Will you require me to take you to the airport?'

'Yes, please. Can you be here for nine o'clock?'

'Certainly, *Señora*.' Pedro made a polite bow and left them.

'He's a lovely young man,' Margie said, once he was out of earshot. 'So polite and handsome.'

'He's engaged,' Piper confided, 'but there's a large fly in the ointment. His fiancée's father has said they can't marry until he gets a better job and earns more money.'

'That's sad.'

By the time they reached their rooms, Sofía's eyes were drooping with fatigue. Piper undressed her, gave her a quick wash and put her to bed. 'I feel tired myself,' she said. 'Why don't we just sit on the terrace, drink a glass of wine, then have an early night?'

'My thoughts exactly,' Margie agreed.

The two women sat outside in the balmy night air, listening to the sounds drifting up from the town. In the distance, they could hear someone singing. From closer by, the insects were making a racket in the bushes. Over the sea, a big yellow moon was sailing through wisps of cloud.

'I haven't changed my mind,' Margie said. 'If I had the chance, I'd live here permanently.'

Piper was thinking of her brother's reaction to the trip and the tension that awaited her when she returned to Dublin. 'If only things were so simple for me.'

***

She woke at seven thirty, had a quick swim and picked up the breakfast croissants. Then it was a matter of getting Sofía dressed and the bags packed. At nine o'clock they were outside the front door of Hotel Azul where Pedro was waiting with the car.

The drive to the airport took twenty-five minutes and he insisted on accompanying them with the luggage to check-in. Piper withdrew an envelope from her pocket. Inside were two fifty-euro notes. She pressed it into his hand.

'There is no need, *Señora*.'

'Yes, there is. It's a little thank you for the way you've taken care of us.'

'But it is my job.'

'Enough,' Piper said. 'Take it.'

'*Gracias, Señora. Adios, amigas*,' he said, and kissed each of them on the cheek. 'When will you return?' he asked, as they turned to go.

Piper shrugged. 'God knows, whenever my father decides.'

They waved goodbye and set off for Departures. Piper was a little sad to be going home. It seemed that in Spain she had discovered the knack of leaving her troubles behind.

Chapter Eleven

Charlie was waiting, as promised, when they emerged through the arrivals gate. He took Piper in his arms and kissed her. 'It's so good to see you home again,' he said. Then he lifted Sofía and held her at arm's length while she squealed. 'Now, miss, I want to hear everything you did on your holiday.'

'We went to the beach and had nice things to eat and we had a ride in a car up the big mountains.'

'Can you talk Spanish yet?'

'No, Daddy! You're silly!'

He grabbed the bags and they trooped out to the waiting car. The weather was mild and bright, but not as warm as it had been in Spain.

'So now you're back to hard reality,' he said to Piper. 'No more gallivanting with those dashing *caballeros*.'

'As if!' Piper laughed.

It took half an hour to reach the Sandymount apartment. Charlie unloaded the bags and carried them up to the flat, then took off again for his office in town, explaining that he had some important people to meet. 'Perhaps we might eat out tonight to celebrate your homecoming,' he said, as he kissed Piper.

'Let's see,' she replied.

As soon as she was alone in her bedroom, she took out her phone and rang her father. 'I'm back. I should be with you in forty-five minutes.'

'Excellent,' Henry replied. 'We've a lot to talk about.'

She left Sofía with Margie, got into her Lexus and started the journey to Howth. The traffic in the city was heavy, but once she reached Sutton, it thinned out and she was at the house for half past three. Her mother opened the door and gave her a hug. 'Welcome back. Good trip?'

'Great.'

'Come and have a cup of tea in the kitchen and tell me all about it. Your dad's got Jack in his office. He told me to keep you down here for a few minutes.'

Piper followed her mother into the large kitchen and sat down at the table. 'What are they talking about?'

Her mother rolled her eyes. 'Need you ask? I told you Corinne was complaining that you were sent to Spain and not your brother. Plus your father is very unhappy with the way he's managing the Majestic. He's never there.' She paused. 'Jack's never applied himself, just expected everything to be given to him as of right. That's not the way business works, Piper.'

'I know.'

'He's never been a very good worker but recently he's got much worse. He's behaving very erratically. You don't think he's on drugs, do you? I know they're all at it nowadays.'

'Not all of them, Mum, just the stupid ones.'

'Anyway, your poor father's at his wits' end. I'm sorry to say this but Jack is a real trial for him. And now he's got Corinne winding him up every chance she gets. By the way, she's coming for lunch on Sunday.'

Piper pulled a face.

'You and Charlie are invited too. And don't say you won't come. The thought of being in a room alone with that wagon is too much to contemplate. You have to come to give me support. And bring Sofía. I'm dying to see her.'

'Okay, we'll be there.'

Rose brought the teapot to the table, sat down and poured two cups. 'To tell you the truth, Piper, I'm worried about your dad. He's reached the stage in his life when he should be able to relax and put his feet up. But he can't do it till he has someone he can rely on to take over the company.'

'I don't know what to say, Mum. I'm willing to play my part but I'm still only learning the business.'

'Well, he was delighted with your work in Marbella. That certainly cheered him up. Although, as I told you, it set Jack off.'

Piper sipped her tea. She was thinking of what her mother had said about Jack and drugs. Was it possible? It would explain a lot. There were times when she had seen her brother ranting and raving like someone who wasn't quite sane. 'Listen, Mum, I know you disagree with me but Jack has a history with girlfriends. He must have had at least a dozen in the last five years. None of them's lasted very long. He goes through phases when he's madly in love and then he's dropped the poor girl and got another. I'm betting the same thing will happen with Corinne. And once she's out of the way, he'll get his act together.'

'Corinne isn't like the others. She's cunning and ambitious. And they're the worst. She's encouraging him. She'll not rest till she gets her own hands on the company and then God help the rest of us.'

Piper finished her tea and went up the stairs to her father's office. She knocked at the door and pushed it open. Jack was sitting in a corner with a sullen look on his face. He scowled at her and didn't speak.

'Here she is,' Henry declared. 'The heroine of the hour. You did excellent work down there in Marbella and I'm very pleased. I've been in touch with Rodriguez, our Spanish lawyer, and he tells me he's expecting a contract from *Señor* Guzman's lawyer in the next few days. Once he gets it, he'll scrutinise it. If it's okay, we'll fix a completion date and transfer the first tranche of cash as a deposit. It's all been arranged with the bank. Are you happy with the deal you did?'

'Very. We've got a great little hotel for a very good price. It's basically solid and comfortable. It appears to be well managed. You have my report. I saw nothing to concern me.'

'Good. Well, you and I will sit down later and discuss any alterations that might be required. What about this Hernandez fellow who's managing it? Are you happy with him?'

'He seems on top of the job. The hotel is clean and well maintained. The staff seem happy and efficient. As for the clients, they were mainly middle-aged couples and appeared to be enjoying themselves. I didn't see any families or party animals.'

Henry smiled. 'Perfect. And now that's taken care of, I have another task for you. The accountants are coming tomorrow to go over the books and I'd like you to sit in with us. It'll be good experience for you. You'll get an insight into how the whole enterprise is run.'

'What time?'

'Ten o'clock. Bring a notebook and don't be afraid to ask questions.' He turned to Jack. 'Your brother is being promoted. I'm making him manager of the Excelsior. The Majestic is too big for him, too many demands on his time. The Excelsior is smaller but it has great potential. It will give Jack an opportunity to develop his managerial skills. I've set him the task of doubling the bed nights within twelve months.'

Piper grinned at him. 'Congratulations!'

He glared at her.

'Now I have to make some calls. Jack, I want you to go over to the Excelsior right away and take over. Introduce yourself to the staff. Give them a pep talk. Let them know you're the new boss and that you expect their co-operation in growing the business.'

'Where's the present manager of the Excelsior going?' Piper asked.

Her father gave her a look that said he wished she hadn't asked that question. 'He's been transferred to the Majestic.'

Once they were outside on the landing, Jack turned on her. 'I suppose you're happy with your work?' he said.

86

'What do you mean?'

'Undermining me after everything I did for you. I always regarded you as my best friend. I looked after you when you were a kid and kept you out of harm's way. And this is how you repay me, by stabbing me in the back.'

'What on earth are you talking about?'

'I'm the eldest child. I should be working with Dad, learning the business, instead of running these bloody hotels, organising the stupid staff and doing all those menial jobs. It's boring. I should have been sent to Spain to negotiate for Hotel Azul, not you.'

'I only did what Dad asked.'

'You should have turned him down. You should have suggested me.'

Piper's jaw dropped. 'Jack, I've never turned down any task that Dad asked me to do. He knows this business far better than me. He built it up from nothing and I trust his judgement. If he asks me to do something, I do it. You should do the same.'

'What's that supposed to mean?'

'Isn't it plain? You go out of your way to annoy him. You never listen. You argue with him. You contradict him. That's not the way to earn his trust! Why don't you just knuckle down and do what he asks?'

'You mean I should just jump up and down whenever he says so? I'm fed up with it. He acts like a dictator, ordering me around and giving me all the dirty jobs to do while you get the plums.'

'That's outrageous.'

'Is it? You know what the problem is? He's too old. He's losing his grip. He should retire and let me take over.'

Piper gasped. '*You*, Jack? Aren't you forgetting something?'

'What?'

'I have a role in the company too.'

'But I'm the son and heir. It's natural that I should be the successor. That's what I intend to do. I read what the *Tribune* had to say about you inheriting McKenzie Leisure.'

'I had absolutely nothing to do with that!'

He came closer and stared into her face. 'Well, I'm warning you, little sister. I'm taking over the company when Dad retires. Get in my way and you'll live to regret it.'

Chapter Twelve

Piper left her parents' home unhappy after her confrontation with Jack. Things were far worse than she'd guessed. The atmosphere was upsetting her mother and God only knew what it was doing to her father. It was plain to her that Henry didn't trust Jack. His transfer to the Excelsior wasn't a promotion at all. He was being moved to the smaller hotel because he wasn't capable of running the larger one.

Yet he persisted in his delusion that he was being victimised and overlooked. He seemed blind to his own failings. Instead of studying to enhance his skills, as she had done, he had dropped out of college at the earliest opportunity, preferring sport to study. Her parents were right. Jack expected everything to be handed him on a plate. He had been spoiled.

If he would only do what she suggested and listen to their father's advice, co-operate with him and try to learn the business. It wasn't rocket science. Any sensible person could see that was the way to gain his trust and progress in the company. And now Jack had blamed her for his setbacks. She was horrified to think that the brother she loved now saw her as his enemy.

As she was passing through town, she had a brainwave. She hadn't seen Jo Ferguson for several weeks. Jo had remained her best friend since schooldays. She had gone on to complete a business degree at Trinity College and now held down a senior management position with a leading multinational company. She worked nearby. Piper pulled over, took out her phone and rang her number. 'Hi, I'm in the neighbourhood. Any chance of a quick cup of coffee and a natter?'

'Of course! Where are you now?'

Piper told her.

'Okay, there's a little coffee shop at the corner of Townsend Street. Can you get parking?'

'Sure.'

'See you there in ten minutes.'

Piper found an off-street car park and walked the short distance to the coffee shop, which was almost empty. Jo was one of the very few people she could talk to honestly and she badly needed to talk right now. She had barely sat down at a corner table when the door opened and her friend swung in, dressed in a smart navy business suit. She was an attractive young woman, slim, with shoulder-length brown hair. Unlike Piper, she was still single although she had been dating a young management consultant called Carl for almost a year.

She gave Piper a friendly hug and sat down beside her. 'Cappuccino?' she asked.

'Yes, please.'

'Want a muffin with that?'

'Just the coffee.'

Jo caught the waitress's attention and ordered two cappuccinos. 'Well, what have you been up to? You look smashing. How's Sofía?'

'She's fine. I'll have to give serious consideration to getting her into a school soon.'

'You've got some time yet. She's happy with Margie, isn't she?'

'Thank God for Margie. I wouldn't be able to function without her.'

Jo laughed.

'What are you laughing about? You're going to face the same problem, one of these days. How is Carl? No sound of wedding bells yet?'

Jo's eyes twinkled. 'He's keen but I'm not. I want to wait, gain more experience in my job. I've been watching you. It's not easy trying to manage two careers, is it?'

'Tell me about it,' Piper said. 'I've just had a row with my brother. I'm afraid he's turning into a major problem.'

Her friend frowned. 'I'm sorry to hear that. I always thought he was a nice guy and very hunky. In fact, I sort of fancied him when we were younger.'

'Well, he's become a right pain in the arse. He's driving my poor dad round the bend. Dad's almost sixty-eight. Mum wants him to retire but he won't go till he's confident he's got someone to take his place. Naturally he wants to be sure it's in safe hands before he goes.'

Jo took a sip of coffee. 'There's always you.'

91

'Are you kidding? I'm not ready to take on a big job like that single-handed.'

'Don't underestimate yourself, hon. You're bright, you're already learning how the business operates. Why not you?'

'I've got a young child, and it would cause a civil war with my brother.'

'So what are you going to do? Wait till your father drops dead from exhaustion? If I was in your shoes, I'd go for that job. I'd have a word with your father and tell him I was willing to shoulder the burden. He'd know he had someone who could replace him and could plan accordingly.'

'Then the civil war would begin in earnest. And Dad wants us all to live in peace with each other. I think he's hoping we could share the company between us. But Jack seems to think he's entitled to it. He actually threatened me today. He said if I got in his way, I'd live to regret it.'

Jo looked shocked. 'That's serious. He sounds deranged!'

'I haven't told you the whole story. He's got a girlfriend called Corinne Delaney. She's a solicitor, very ambitious. And Jack is like putty in her hands. I'm certain she's prompting him.'

Jo shook her head. 'I don't like the sound of that. Something will have to be done to stop her.'

'But what? Short of murdering her, there's nothing I can do. Jack's mad about her. I've never seen him behave like this with any other woman. It's like she's cast a spell on him.'

'Listen, Piper, you have no option. Unless you want McKenzie Leisure to go to an outsider, you've got to fight this. You'll have to stand up to your brother and that woman. You're entitled to inherit half the company. You're a woman and the second child, but that doesn't mean you should let yourself be pushed aside. Don't roll over. Stand up and fight your ground.'

Much as she dreaded the thought of a battle with her brother, Piper knew her friend was right. And she knew it was what her mother would want too.

'Changing the subject, you've got some colour in your face. Been somewhere sunny?'

'Marbella. Dad sent me to negotiate the purchase of a hotel.'

'And how did it go?'

'We got it for the right price.'

'That just proves what I've been saying. You are capable of taking big decisions about the company. Your dad probably knows that too. That's why he sent you.'

'You'll never guess what I came across down there.'

'What?'

'Remember Club Xanadu?'

'Sounds like a nightclub.'

'It used to be a nightclub. It's derelict now. Have you really forgotten?'

Jo screwed up her face. 'Remind me.'

'It's where we met those Spanish students. Remember our first holiday abroad? We'd just finished our Leaving Cert.'

Jo clapped her hands. 'Eduardo and Cesar? I remember them, all right. The red roses, the kisses on the cheeks, the moonlight on the sea ... It was my first romance. I have the photographs somewhere.'

'Well, the building's still there but it's boarded up now.'

'I wonder what happened to them? They were such lovely boys.'

'Probably married with loads of kids.'

Jo was rummaging in her bag. She pulled out her purse, opened it and left some money on the table for the coffee. 'I've got to get back to work. Remember what I said. Fight your corner, Piper. And keep in touch. If you ever want someone to talk to, give me a call.'

They kissed.

'Say hello to Charlie for me,' Jo said. 'How is he?'

'Far too busy for my liking. Managing Hell's Kitchen takes up all his time. But we had a little tête-à-tête recently. I laid down some markers and he seems to have turned over a new leaf.'

'Keep your eye on him. He's a fine-looking specimen and I wouldn't be surprised if he still has women throwing themselves at him.'

'I don't think that's a problem. Charlie knows my limits. If he ever strayed, I'd be gone like a puff of smoke.'

***

Piper drove home feeling much better. Jo had simply reinforced the conviction that was already growing in her heart. McKenzie Leisure was her inheritance. She could not stand by and see it fall into the hands of an outsider. She would take her friend's advice and talk with her father. God knew how she would juggle the demands of being a mother and a full-time businesswoman but she'd manage it somehow. If that was what was required to keep the company in the family's hands, she'd do it.

By the time she got home it was half past six but her mood had lifted. She rang Charlie at work. 'I've been thinking. We haven't seen much of each other in the last few days. Instead of going out tonight, why don't I cook dinner at home? I'll light the fire and we can watch a DVD.'

'Sounds perfect. I can't think of a better way to spend an evening.'

'So what time can I expect you?'

'Eight o'clock.'

'Okay, I'll have everything ready.'

She went into the lounge to find Margie and Sofía watching television. 'Charlie and I are eating at home tonight. Eight o'clock, when he gets back. I'm just nipping down to the supermarket to pick up some shopping.'

'Do you want me to help you? Margie offered.'

'No, you've got your hands full with Miss Chatterbox. I shouldn't be long.'

***

At the supermarket, she went straight to the Fine Foods section, chose a duckling and asked the assistant to chop it into pieces for her. Next she went looking for fresh peaches, then some broccoli, carrots and potatoes. She picked up a lettuce, tomatoes and some yellow peppers, then a raisin tart from the bakery.

When she got home, she went straight into the kitchen and put on her apron. Then she got out her cookery book, propped it open at the appropriate page and set to work. Duck with peaches was a meal she had been served once at a dinner party. It had been ambrosial. She had never cooked it before but she was sure she could follow the simple instructions in the book.

But first she had to make the salad. That was the work of minutes. She washed the lettuce, sliced in some tomatoes, then scattered it with olives and Parmesan. She put the bowl into the fridge. She'd toss in the dressing later.

She poured herself a glass of white wine and began working on the main dish. First she washed the pieces of duckling, put them into a roasting pan with a little oil, some spices and garlic, and stuck it in the oven. Then she sliced the peaches and poached them in a little water. She peeled the potatoes, dropped them into a pot of boiling water, chopped the carrots and broccoli and put them to steam above it.

Margie put her head into the kitchen. 'Anything I can do?'

'Yes, please, Margie. Would you mind setting the table and putting out the candles?'

Everything was almost ready when she heard Charlie's car. Five minutes later he was coming through the front door.

'Mmm!' he said, coming into the kitchen and clasping her to him. 'Something smells good.'

Piper kissed him. 'Dinner's almost ready. You've got ten minutes to get changed, if you want to.'

***

The duck was a great success. 'That was much better than the meal we had in the Chalet D'Or last week,' Charlie said.

'Thank you, darling. It was also a hell of a lot cheaper.'

Charlie topped up the wine glasses. 'Let's drink a toast to

my wonderful wife, Piper McKenzie, superb mother, fabulous wife, successful businesswoman and now celebrity chef.'

'I'll second that,' Margie said, and sipped.

They sat around the table chatting and catching up on Charlie's progress with the forthcoming European tour of Hell's Kitchen. Then Margie helped Piper clear the table and put Sofía to bed. Finally she said good night, leaving Piper and Charlie alone.

The lights were dim and the fire from the grate cast shadows around the room. Charlie drew her close and kissed her passionately. She felt her pulse quicken. In the four years that they'd been married, she had never lost her passion for Charlie. He kissed her again, and this time, his hand dropped to her knee and began to move slowly up her thigh.

'Wait,' she said. She stood up, took his hand and led him into the bedroom. Once the door was closed, they fell on each other. Within seconds they were on the bed, their lips and hands exploring each other eagerly. Piper closed her eyes and was carried away on a tide of pleasure.

Chapter Thirteen

The following morning at ten o'clock, Piper was in her father's office for the accountants' visit. She had never been much good at maths so she was expecting a dull few hours, full of figures and statistics, but she knew it was at the heart of the company's business and that her father had bestowed an honour on her by inviting her to attend. She was wearing a plain grey suit with a blouse and dark shoes and in her sleek black briefcase she had a notebook and pen, as Henry had advised.

She heard footsteps on the stairs, then the door opened and her father came in, followed by two men, both in dark suits. One was middle-aged, introduced to her as Mr Campbell, but the other was younger, about Piper's age. His name was Tim O'Brien. They all shook hands. Henry poured coffee from a pot and then the work began.

The accountants went over each of the company's twelve hotels in turn, presenting figures to show how much profit each was making. They showed the areas where revenue was being generated: bed nights, dining, bar sales and so on. Then they produced statistics of payroll costs, taxes and overheads. It was anything but boring, Piper discovered. She was getting a fascinating insight into what made McKenzie Leisure tick.

Mr Campbell did most of the talking. At one stage, he drew attention to the situation at the Majestic Hotel. 'It's the biggest in the group but, as you can see from the figures, it's generating the least profit. It needs a shake-up. There's no reason why it shouldn't be contributing twice as much to the company.'

Piper glanced at her father. He looked slightly embarrassed. 'That situation is already in hand. I've appointed a new manager. He's taken up his duties today.'

'Good. And the hotel you've purchased in Marbella. When's it coming on stream?'

'We're waiting for the contracts to be drawn up. It's in the hands of the lawyers.'

'Great,' Mr Campbell said. 'Diversification is a clever move. There's always a demand for holiday accommodation, even in a recession. And it should generate revenue all year round.'

'That's my thinking too,' Henry said.

The meeting concluded at twelve thirty, and the accountants left. By now, Piper's notebook was filled with observations. Her father smiled at her. 'Did you learn anything this morning?'

'Oh, yes, indeed!'

'I rely heavily on that pair. I've been using Peter Campbell for twenty years and I'd trust him with my life. He's sharp as a knife, doesn't miss a thing. And young O'Brien's cut from the same cloth. Now, I have another job for you.'

'Yes?'

'You heard what Campbell said about the Majestic. I'd like you to spend a few days there with the new manager. Don't interfere, just observe. Campbell is quite right. The hotel has been underperforming with Jack at the helm. I'll ring the manager and tell him to expect you. When you've finished, write me a short report. Outline your ideas about how things can be improved.'

'Right.'

'And when you've finished with the Majestic, I'd like you to do the same with each of the hotels in the group. When I was younger, I used to make an annual inspection but it's been allowed to slip in recent years. It's time to revive it. Apart from anything else, it keeps the managers on their toes.'

This was the moment she'd been waiting for. She cleared her throat. 'There's something I want to say to you.'

'Yes?'

'Have you given any thought to retiring?'

He looked at her for a moment and then he was laughing. 'Don't tell me you're worried about my health?' he managed, when he had calmed down.

'You work very hard and you're not getting younger. I just wanted you to know that I'm always available to help you. I'll do anything to get some of the load off you, anything at all, including taking over the reins, if necessary. This is your company. You built it up from nothing. I'd hate to see strangers reaping the benefit of your hard work.'

Henry's face softened. He drew her close and kissed her cheek. 'I appreciate that, Piper. And I want McKenzie Leisure to stay in the family. I hope that when I retire, you and your brother will run it between you.'

'And if that isn't possible?'

'We'll cross that bridge when we come to it.'

Piper left him, feeling she had sent her father a clear message. She had let him know that he could rely on her in the days ahead if things went wrong. In the meantime, she would enjoy the task he had set her. She would throw herself into the inspection and gain a close knowledge of each hotel in the group.

The following morning, at ten o'clock, she presented herself at the Majestic. It was a 120-bed hotel in the centre of town near the Financial Services Centre. She was met by the new manager, an eager young man in his early thirties called Ed Brannigan. He appeared a little nervous to have the boss's daughter on the premises but Piper soon put him at ease. 'I'm not here to spy on you, Ed. My father's asked me to report on how we can grow the hotel. I'll keep out of your way, but if you have anything to contribute, I'll be glad to hear it.'

She spent three days at the Majestic and looked at every area, from catering to bedrooms. She found very little to criticise with Ed Brannigan's management. On the final day, she sat down with him in his office and had a frank talk.

'The hotel seems to be functioning very well, Ed, yet there are nights when we have only forty per cent occupancy. Why do you think that is?'

101

'Perhaps our pricing is wrong. Some of our competitors are undercutting us.'

'No,' Piper said. 'It's not that. I think we're in the wrong market. The Majestic isn't a budget hotel. If we can attract the right kind of guests, price won't be a factor. I've noticed we have a conference centre here. When was the last time it was used?'

'I'd need to check that.' The young manager went onto his computer. 'Six weeks ago.'

'Do we promote the conference centre in our marketing?'

'It's included in the list of facilities.'

'But do we actively promote it? We're situated in one of the best areas in town, right in the centre of the city with all these financial institutions around us. I think there's an opportunity here for growth. Let me have a talk with my father and I'll get back to you.'

She went home, wrote up her report and, the next morning, went to see Henry.

'How did you get on?' he wanted to know. 'You didn't scare the daylights out of Brannigan, I hope?'

'No, Ed's fine. He manages the hotel efficiently and he's keen to make a success of it. However, one thing strikes me. We have a fine conference centre with very modern facilities yet it's underused. How about we forget the tourist trade and pitch the Majestic at the conference market? We're so close to the Financial Services Centre. We could do special packages. It's my guess we could have one hundred per cent room occupancy all the year round.' She pushed her report across the table. 'It's all detailed in here.'

Henry's face lit up. 'My God,' he said. 'You might be on to something there.'

***

Piper saw nothing of her brother who was concentrating on his new job as manager of the Excelsior, a thirty-bed hotel in the fashionable Ballsbridge area of town. As she had learned from the figures presented by the accountants, it had excellent potential for growth. Even Jack, with his lackadaisical approach to work, would find it difficult not to make a success of it.

But she was happy to avoid him. His angry threats were still fresh in her mind. There was one situation, though, that she couldn't avoid. The weekend was approaching and with it Sunday lunch at Elsinore. She had promised her mother to come and bring Sofía. She wasn't looking forward to it but at least she would have Charlie for support.

Sunday was Margie's day off and she usually spent it with her mother in Monkstown, so at eleven o'clock Piper, Charlie and Sofía set off for Howth with Charlie driving. Piper had thoughtfully bought a box of expensive chocolates and given it to Sofía to present to her grandmother. When they arrived, the house was shining in the sunlight, the lawns immaculately trimmed, the sea gleaming like a pane of glass and the daffodils tossing their yellow heads in the gentle breeze.

Henry was sitting outside on a bench, leafing through the papers when they came up the drive. He put the papers down and went to meet them, lifting Sofía in his arms. 'How's my girl? You're growing up very fast. You're going to be a heart-breaker, just like your mother.'

'Hello, Henry,' Charlie said. The two men shook hands and began chatting about sport. Piper led Sofía inside in search of her grandmother. She found her in the kitchen, checking the leg of lamb she was roasting for lunch. Piper kissed her and Sofía gave her the chocolates.

'That's very kind of you, sweetheart. I love chocolates. Now, in return would you like some juice?'

'Yes, please.'

'Sit down,' Rose said to Piper. 'I'll put the kettle on and we'll have a nice cup of tea. Your father hasn't stopped talking about your report on the Majestic.'

'The others haven't arrived yet?' Piper asked.

'No, but they're on their way. I had a phone call from her ladyship five minutes ago. Thank God you're here, Piper. A couple of hours in that woman's company and I'd be ready for the lunatic asylum.'

It wasn't long before they heard the car approaching, and Jack and Corinne arrived. Piper and her mother moved into the lounge with Sofía, and a few minutes later, the door opened. Charlie and Henry came in, followed by Jack and Corinne, carrying a bouquet of flowers for Rose and a bottle of wine.

She began by kissing everyone and dispensing bonhomie like confetti at a wedding. Piper glanced dismissively at the purple party dress she was wearing, which revealed a wide extent of thigh and lots of cleavage. Corinne tossed her head, her black curls cascading in ringlets around her ears. Her dark eyes flashed beneath her long lashes as she accepted a glass of wine. She sat on a sofa beside Jack and stretched out her shapely legs.

'Well, Dad,' she said, to Henry, 'I'm surprised you're not down in Nice enjoying the warmth.' She had started to address him as 'Dad' as if she was already a member of the family. Henry disliked it intensely, but he didn't allow his annoyance to show.

'Why is that, Corinne?'

'I checked the weather forecast on the computer. It's eighteen degrees down there and the sun's shining. If I had a villa in Nice, I'd spend as much time in it as possible.'

'But you don't have a business to run,' Henry replied tartly.

'You have Jack to rely on. He's quite capable. He'd be happy to deputise for you so you could have a break.' She turned to Piper. 'Don't you agree? Dad should be down on the Riviera instead of slogging away at his desk every day.'

Piper exchanged a glance with her father. 'I think my father knows his own mind, Corinne.'

'I'm only thinking of his welfare. Running McKenzie Leisure must be very stressful. Why buy a villa in France if you don't use it?'

'We do use it. I was there last summer.'

'Well, I know what I'd do if I was in Dad's shoes,' Corinne said.

Thank God, you're not, Piper thought. You'd drive us all to distraction and run the company into the ground. She glanced at Jack. He hadn't spoken. He sat beside his girlfriend and avoided her glance. The tension was only broken when Rose appeared in the doorway to announce that lunch was ready.

The unease followed them into the dining room. Piper attempted to lift the mood. 'There's definitely a touch of spring in the air,' she said.

'I might take the boat out one of these days,' Henry said. 'She hasn't been out all winter. Remind me to give the yacht club a call next week.'

'Do you sail too? Corinne asked Rose.

'Get away,' Rose replied. 'I've got more sense. I can't see the attraction of being tossed around in a boat and getting my head blown off by the wind only to finish up being seasick.'

This riposte brought the first laughter of the afternoon, but a minute later, Corinne was back. 'I wouldn't mind going out in it some day,' she said. 'I think I'd enjoy it. You're always looking for crew, aren't you?' she said to Henry.

'Have you any experience?'

'No, but I'm a quick learner. You could give me lessons.'

'Let's wait till the weather improves some more,' he said.

Corinne seemed to think it was her duty to keep up a constant stream of chatter which grated on Piper's nerves. Piper stole a look at her. She had obviously spent some time prettifying herself but she still looked plain and ordinary. Yet she had managed to bewitch Jack and now she had him eating out of her hand. Instead of enjoying this meal with her family, Piper waited impatiently for it to end so she could get back to Sandymount with Charlie and her little daughter.

However, Corinne had one more contribution to make. She waited till the coffee was served. 'Jack and I have something to say.' She simpered.

The table fell silent. Piper glanced nervously from one face to the next.

'You'd better tell them, Jack,' Corinne prompted, giving his arm a little squeeze.

Jack coughed and looked at his mother and father. 'We're getting married,' he said.

Chapter Fourteen

Piper's heart plummeted. It was exactly as her mother had predicted. Corinne had sunk her claws into Jack and now she had persuaded the idiot to marry her. Her worst nightmare was coming true. Corinne would become a member of the family and have a claim on McKenzie Leisure.

She glanced at her parents. Her mother's expression betrayed her horror. Henry sat with a stony face as if he was too shocked to register any reaction. Meanwhile Corinne was grinning in triumph.

Charlie glanced across the table at her, bewilderment on his face. For a moment, there was a stunned silence. Finally Rose spoke. 'Have you fixed a date yet?'

'Yes. It's going to be June.'

'You're not giving yourselves much time.'

'But it's all organised. We've been planning it for months. We wanted to surprise you. We're just finalising the guest list.'

'Are you having a church wedding?'

'Oh, yes. I just adore all the ceremony. But not in my parish church. The father of one of Jack's rugby friends is letting us hold the reception in his country estate. It will make the security arrangements easier.'

'Security arrangements?' Rose was clearly amazed.

'We'll need security guards to keep the crowds of spectators away.'

'How many guests are you expecting?'

'Several hundred at least.'

Rose collapsed back in her chair. Her face said that Corinne had lost all contact with reality.

'Of course, it's a terrible nuisance,' Corinne continued, 'but all the big society weddings attract crowds, these days. It's just a fact of life.'

It was Henry who restored a sense of order. He stood up and raised his glass. 'I would like to propose a toast to the young couple on the occasion of their engagement. Long life and happiness.'

Piper took a sip of wine. It tasted like poison.

***

The lunch limped to an end, and Corinne and Jack departed. The rest of the party retired to the lounge. Piper was still reeling from Jack's announcement. 'I never thought I'd see the day ...'

'I did,' her mother chimed in. 'I predicted it.'

'Do you think she's entirely sane?' Charlie wondered.

'All this talk of security, who does she think she is? Kate Middleton? Does she believe someone will try to kidnap her?'

'Oh, she's sane, all right,' Rose replied grimly. 'Believe me, she knows exactly what she's doing. She's planned this campaign right down to the smallest detail.'

'And what is its purpose?' Henry asked.

Rose turned to her husband. He was usually so immersed in business matters that he never had time for gossip. He was obviously unaware of Corinne's scheming. 'To get her hands on the company.'

'She planned this so she could get involved in McKenzie Leisure?'

'Yes,' Rose said.

'Aren't you jumping to conclusions? Why shouldn't we accept the simple explanation that Jack and Corinne are in love and, like any young couple in that situation, they want to get married?'

'They hardly know each other,' Rose retorted. 'They've only been going out together for nine months.'

'I seem to recall that you and I were married within six months of meeting,' Henry replied, with a twinkle in his eye.

'That was different. Now the business is worth millions of pounds. I'll be blunt with you, Henry. I don't like Corinne. I suspect her motives. And she has Jack completely under her control. She's far smarter than he is, and she's able to lead him around by the nose.'

'I agree with Mum,' Piper put in. 'If Corinne marries Jack, she'll manipulate him. You heard her earlier suggesting that you should go down to Nice and let Jack deputise for you.

And don't be fooled by her "concern" about your health. She wants to get Jack installed as MD and she's not even married to him yet.'

'That's not going to happen,' Henry told her. 'But there's one thing you're all forgetting. If they want to get married, there's absolutely nothing we can do to stop them.'

***

Henry was right. The family had to stand by and watch, helpless, as the wedding preparations went ahead. Corinne was clearly determined not to waste any time. At her insistence, the engagement announcement was placed in the social column of *The Irish Times* to make sure that everyone would see it.

> *Patrick and Mary Delaney of Glasnevin, Dublin are pleased to announce the engagement of their daughter, Corinne, to Jack, son of Henry and Rosemary McKenzie of Howth, Co. Dublin.*

But no one was prepared for the scale of what Corinne was planning. She turned up one afternoon at the mansion sporting a large diamond engagement ring and talking excitedly of a bridal dress with Italian lace and French embroidery, imported from Paris. There would be six bridesmaids and six groomsmen, plus flower girls and page boys. There was even mention of helicopters and armoured cars to ferry the guests, whose number was increasing daily. Before long, the list had reached four hundred.

Then there was the wedding banquet, with an orchestra to entertain the guests while they ate a sumptuous meal that would include roast duckling, lobster, salmon, roast beef and sushi for those who were watching their weight. This was to be followed by the honeymoon – a cruise ship to New York followed by a month-long tour of the United States by train. It was going to cost a small fortune.

'What does her father do for a living?' Rose asked Piper one morning.

'I think Jack said he was a dentist.'

'He'd better start extracting more teeth to pay for this pantomime.'

Since she was the groom's sister, Piper expected Corinne to invite her to be a bridesmaid. She was not looking forward to it. She knew it would require a supreme act of willpower to stand beside Corinne and pretend she was enjoying herself while she hated every minute. However, her fears came to nothing.

One day as they were leaving a meeting in Henry's study, Jack drew her aside. Since his outburst a couple of weeks earlier, relations between them had remained cool. It was clear that he still regarded her as a threat. 'The wedding invitations will be going out soon. I have to tell you that you're not invited.'

Piper gasped. She was the groom's only sister. This was a deliberate insult. 'May I ask why?'

'Corinne doesn't want you. The truth is she doesn't like you very much.'

Piper said nothing to her parents. Personally she didn't care about the wedding but she knew that Rose and Henry would be outraged. She hoped that when the time came, she would be able to find some convenient-looking excuse for not attending.

A few weeks later, Corinne and Jack arrived at Elsinore unexpectedly. Corinne sat down with a sigh and began to complain about how busy she was: the yards of silk required for the bridesmaids' dresses, the innumerable visits to the dressmaker, the flowers, the order of the service, the wedding cake, the choir and the limousines. It was wearing her out, she declared.

Then she got down to the real purpose of the visit. She was anxious to co-ordinate the outfits that the two mothers would wear. Mrs Delaney had decided that pink was her colour and Corinne wanted Rose to wear something complimentary.

'It would be terrible if the outfits were to clash, don't you agree?' Corinne asked sweetly, as she sipped her coffee and beamed across the table at her future mother-in-law. 'It would look dreadful in the photographs. We hope you'll bear this in mind when you make your decision, Rose.'

'I hadn't given it much thought,' Rose replied.

'You should,' Corinne pressed on. 'It has to be decided soon.'

Rose put down her coffee cup with a firmness that made it rattle. 'Are you telling me I've got no choice in the matter?' She had flushed, which was a bad sign.

Corinne chose to ignore it. 'Of course you do. All I'm saying is that we should co-ordinate the colour schemes. And everyone agrees on pink. Besides, it would be a good colour for you. It would make you appear more ...' She trailed off, perhaps realising that she was wandering into very dangerous territory. 'Did I say something wrong?'

'Have you finalised the guest list?' Rose asked.

'Four hundred and fifty,' Corinne said proudly. 'Dad wants to invite his friends from the golf club and the tennis club. He knows an awful lot of people. Then there are all Mum's friends. She's involved in so many groups. And, of course, there are the relatives. It's a nightmare, believe me. If you leave someone out, they can get terribly offended.' She smirked at Piper.

'I know it's none of my business but this is going to cost an awful lot of money,' Rose continued.

Jack, who had been quiet so far, suddenly spoke. 'It won't cost too much.'

'What does that mean? You're running up an awful lot of expense here. The reception alone is going to cost a fortune, not to mention the honeymoon. Have you discussed this with Corinne's parents?'

Jack glanced at his bride-to-be. 'Not really.'

'Are you serious? Don't you think you should talk to the people who are going to foot the bill?'

Jack looked very uneasy. Meanwhile, Corinne had suddenly discovered a spot on the table and was staring at it intently.

Jack sniffed and cleared his throat. 'We were hoping Dad would pick up the tab.'

There was a deathly silence. For a moment no one spoke, and then everyone was talking at once.

'We thought he might be willing to pay for it as a sort of wedding present,' Corinne said.

'He can easily afford it,' Jack added. 'That sort of money is chicken-feed to him.'

'But you're missing the point,' Rose said. 'It's not his job. It's the bride's father who pays for the wedding.'

'You can't expect my father to pay for it,' Corinne replied defensively. 'He hasn't got that sort of cash.'

'And we mustn't forget we're the McKenzies,' Jack said. 'People expect a good show from us.'

By now Rose looked like she was about to explode. 'This is outrageous, Jack. I'm astounded at your arrogance and presumption. You plan to spend several hundred thousand euros of your father's money and you haven't even the courtesy to ask him if it's all right?'

'Calm down. I was getting round to it. I just didn't have a chance yet. Everything's been so hectic.'

'I would have thought that funding the wedding would have been the very first item on your agenda.'

'I'll do it now.'

'I suggest you do,' Rose growled. 'And I sincerely hope you haven't made any commitments you can't get out of.'

Jack got up and left the room.

Corinne suddenly stood up too. 'I have to go,' she announced. 'I've an appointment with the caterer.'

'Don't forget what I said,' Rose warned. 'Don't commit yourself to anything you can't pay for.'

As soon as she had gone Rose went to the fridge and took out a bottle of chilled white wine. 'I need a drink,' she said.

'I've never heard anything like this in my entire life. She's busy spending your father's money like there's no tomorrow and, the ultimate insult, neither of them has discussed it with him!'

Piper shook her head. 'It's much worse than that. If this is how she behaves now, what will she be like when they're married and she's part of the family?'

CHAPTER FIFTEEN

Jack's face was ashen when he came down from talking to his father. He didn't say anything and left in a hurry. Half an hour later Henry appeared. He sat down with a sigh. 'That boy will be the death of me. I suppose you know what they were planning?'

'Of course,' Rose replied. 'We've been hearing about it for long enough, but it was only today that we realised they expected you to pay.'

'He suggested we put the expenditure through the company and write it off against tax. He wanted me to commit a fraud. I could go to prison for that.' He shook his head. 'I'm amazed that he would even suggest such a thing. Either he hasn't grasped the fundamentals of business practice or he just doesn't care.'

'I don't think it was Jack,' Piper said. 'He's not interested in a showbiz wedding. It was Corinne.'

'Then he should have told her it wasn't possible. He should never have allowed things to get so far.'

'He's infatuated with her.'

Piper could see the pain in her father's face.

'Who he decides to marry is his business. But when it interferes with the company it becomes everybody's business. I can only hope that Jack has learned a lesson from this episode.'

'What did you tell him?' Rose asked.

'That there was no way I would pay for the wedding. But as a compromise I agreed to pay for the honeymoon. That will be our wedding present to them.'

'And how did he respond?'

Henry groaned. 'How do you think?'

'He should be damned grateful,' Rose said.

'I know, but I gave up expecting gratitude long ago. Somewhere along the way, something happened to Jack. And before you blame Corinne again, it happened well before he met her. I blame myself. I should have been stricter with him. I should have made him work harder. But because he was my only son, I spoiled him. If anyone is to blame, I am.'

***

The wedding plans proceeded on a much smaller scale. Gone was the Paris dress with Italian lace and French embroidery. The six bridesmaids were reduced to two. There were no flower girls, page boys, helicopters or armoured cars. The guest list was cut to eighty and the reception was booked at a local hotel. Corinne's father obviously couldn't afford the extravaganza his daughter had hoped for on his dentist's income.

The triumphant grin had been removed from Corinne's face but Piper suspected it would be just a matter of time before she began to meddle again. Her only comfort was that Henry was now fully alert to the danger the woman posed and the extent of her control over Jack.

Meanwhile, her father had enthusiastically taken up her suggestion that they utilise the Majestic's conference centre. He asked her to liaise with the firm that handled the company's marketing and she had several productive meetings with a smart young executive called Brian Stanley. The result was a series of adverts in the financial press and a special section devoted to conference facilities on the McKenzie Leisure website. Already, Ed Brannigan was reporting interest from several organisations.

She continued to be busy as she carried out the other task her father had set her: to visit each of the hotels in the group and carry out a short inspection. Henry had already sent a memo to the managers, advising them to expect her. It wasn't a difficult job and she enjoyed it. Apart from anything else, it gave her an opportunity to get to know each manager and gain an overview of the group.

Mostly it was a matter of spending a couple of days looking over a hotel, then writing up a report for her father. She found little to alarm her. All the hotels appeared to be functioning efficiently. In a few instances she found minor problems, which she drew to the manager's attention.

She worked hard but she made sure to balance her work with her home and social life. She left each morning at about eight thirty after having breakfast with Sofía and Margie and tried to be back at her apartment in Sandymount by four o'clock to spend time with her daughter and put her to bed.

Meanwhile, Charlie was still extremely busy with putting the finishing touches to the Hell's Kitchen European tour. As he kept reminding her, this was an important milestone in the band's development, offering them the opportunity to expand their fan base and their earning capacity. But he never failed to return her calls and made a point of getting home by eight o'clock.

After the success of her homecoming dinner, they had taken to eating at home more often instead of going out to a restaurant. Piper found cooking therapeutic and enjoyed sitting in her apartment with the fire lit and Charlie beside her, watching a movie or listening to music.

But they did make a few expeditions to enjoy the Dublin nightlife. On one such occasion, Piper invited Jo Ferguson and her boyfriend, Carl, to join them at Aunt Polly's Boudoir. By the time they arrived, around ten o'clock, the place was packed. A band was letting rip on the stage and strobe lights sent eerie shadows flashing across the ceiling and the walls. Jo and Carl had never been there before and were impressed to see so many famous faces.

'Is that Ricky Stark over there, the fashion photographer?' Jo asked. She nodded in the direction of a thin, rakish figure in a velvet suit.

'Yes – he's a regular,' Piper told her.

'And who's the woman with him? Her face is familiar.'

Piper saw an emaciated girl clinging to his arm. 'That's Chloë Devine.'

'The model?'

'Yes.'

'She looks like she's out of her head on something.'

Piper lowered her voice. 'She might well be. Rumour has it she's got a bad cocaine habit.'

A small middle-aged man in a dark polo-necked shirt and white dinner jacket suddenly pushed through the crowd towards her. 'My dear Piper, how good to see you again,' Serge Dupont exclaimed. 'You look absolutely divine. And who is this gorgeous creature?'

Piper introduced Jo and Carl to him, and they found a table beside the bar where Serge insisted on ordering a bottle of champagne. Meanwhile, Charlie had wandered off to talk to some musicians.

'Where is Alessandro tonight?' Piper asked.

Serge's thin lips turned upwards in a sneer. 'That's over. I've dumped the little bitch.'

'Oh! I thought you and Alessandro were an established item. How long were you together?'

'Too bloody long. Two years of my life wasted on that snivelling little shit.'

'What happened?'

'Haven't you heard?' He was clearly astonished that there were still some people in Dublin who weren't aware of the gory details surrounding the break-up.

'We've been out of circulation,' Piper explained.

'Well a couple of weeks ago, I was dancing with this lovely Brazilian boy when that little prick Alessandro started a fight right there on the dance floor. Oh, the horror of it all. There they were, scratching each other's eyes out and screaming blue murder while everyone stared in utter amazement. In the end, the security staff had to eject him.' He took out a handkerchief and waved it in front of his face. 'I still haven't got over the trauma. Can you imagine? They were fighting like fishwives!'

'How embarrassing.'

'I was mortified, my dear. Mind you, I wasn't entirely surprised at his behaviour. He was insanely jealous, completely eaten up by the green-eyed monster. I just had to talk to someone, male or female, it didn't matter, and Alessandro would be flashing daggers in their direction. He was so possessive, he thought he owned me. He used to quiz me about my phone calls and text messages like he was the FBI.' He sniffed and tossed his head. 'I'm better off without him, believe me. I still don't know what I ever saw in him.' He sipped his champagne. 'Anyway, you don't want to hear about my misfortunes.' He turned his attention to Jo and Carl. 'How are you young people enjoying yourselves?'

'We're loving it,' Jo said.

'First time at Aunt Polly's?'

'Yes, Piper got us in.'

'Well, you're a welcome addition to the clientele. We need young blood. Too many old fogeys like me.'

'You're not so old,' Jo said.

Dupont's face lit up and he preened himself, like a peacock fluffing out its tail feathers. 'What a delightful thing to say, my dear.'

At that moment, someone pushed through the crowd and Piper recognised the pretty, dark-haired figure of her former college friend, Alice McDowell. 'Hi, Piper! Having a good time?'

'Alice! How are you?'

'Fine. You know I'm doing some marketing for Charlie. I suppose he told you?

'Yes, indeed. How's it going?'

'Really well. The music industry is a good area to break into. I'm making lots of contacts.'

'And Charlie isn't behaving like a slave-driver?'

'Not at all. He's very easy to work with. He commissions me to do a job and then he leaves me alone and lets me get on with it. And he always pays on time, unlike some clients. I never have to chase him for money, thank God.'

'So you must be doing a good job.'

Alice smiled. 'There haven't been any complaints.'

***

It was after midnight when they left, Jo and Carl to get a taxi home and Charlie to drive to Sandymount. This time, there were no photographers lurking in the shadows.

Once they were in bed, Charlie took Piper in his arms and she cuddled close to him.

'That was a brilliant night. We shouldn't stay away from Aunt Polly's too long. I picked up a load of gossip,' he murmured.

'I did too. Did you know that Serge Dupont and Alessandro have split?'

'Doesn't surprise me.' He drew her closer and she felt his warm hand enclose her breast. They kissed. When he released her, he looked into her eyes. 'You're the only woman I've ever loved, Piper. I don't know how I'd exist without you.'

His words sent a shiver of excitement through her. She closed her eyes and once again felt his lips warm on hers. When he released her, she ran her fingers through his hair. 'I love you too, Charlie. You've always been the man of my dreams.'

***

Piper had left her inspection of the Excelsior to the last because she knew it would be the most difficult one. She had seen very little of Jack in the days that had followed his quarrel with their father over the wedding expenses, and any time their paths had crossed, Jack had been surly and blunt with her to the point of rudeness.

The prospect of turning up at the Excelsior with her notebook to check on her brother's stewardship filled her with dread. She knew that Jack would regard it as further proof that she was being favoured over him. He was certain to protest and make things difficult. Before she picked up the phone to say she was coming, she decided to have a talk with her father.

She found Henry in his usual spot, behind the large polished desk in his study, going through a bundle of invoices.

'Piper! How are you today?'

'I'm fine. Have you read my reports?'

'Of course. You've done good work but that's only to be expected. Everything seems to be coming along nicely. It's no harm to drop in on the managers from time to time. Lets them know we haven't taken our eye off the ball. It keeps them up to the mark.'

'Well, there's one hotel I haven't inspected. You've probably noticed that I haven't been to the Excelsior.'

'You've left it to the last.'

'I thought I'd talk to you first.'

'You're expecting trouble?'

'I think Jack will take it badly. He'll resent me inspecting his hotel. I'm afraid he'll kick up a fuss. It'll just fuel his paranoia. But if you want me to do it, then I will.'

'No, you're right, Piper. We don't want to set him off again. He's still fuming over my refusal to pay for the wedding. Leave it with me. I'll go out there myself and have a look over the place.'

'Okay. How's it performing anyway?'

'It's ticking over. It has great potential – good location, modern hotel, not too big. And Jack has a very efficient under-manager. It would take a supreme act of stupidity for him not to make a success of it.'

She stood up. 'In that case, I'll strike it off my list. Anything else you want me to do?'

'Why don't you take a few days off and spend them with my little granddaughter? You've put in a solid performance, Piper, you deserve a break.'

She went downstairs and had a cup of tea with her mother.

CHAPTER SIXTEEN

Piper gave Margie two days off, and devoted herself to her daughter. She took Sofía to the zoo, the beach and for picnics in the park, where they also went to the swings.

When she returned to Elsinore, Henry was grinning. 'Sit down,' he said. 'I've got some news. I've just come off the phone with Rodriguez, our Spanish lawyer. The sale of Hotel Azul has been completed. It took less time than I expected and now it's all ours, Piper.'

'That's fantastic!'

'Yes, it is. Now, I have something to ask you. I know this is going to be inconvenient.'

'Go on.'

'I need you to go down there again and oversee the transfer. I would go myself but I'm just too damned busy. And there's no one else I can trust. It has to be you, Piper.'

'How long will it take?'

'That depends on how quickly you get the work finished. It could be several weeks. You'll have to check the stock and the equipment to make sure we get everything we agreed in the contract. Once that's done, we'll release the balance of the funds to Guzman. Then you'll have to get an up-to-date statement of accounts from Hernandez, the manager, and I want you to carry out a thorough inspection of the premises and write me a report about what improvements we might need to carry out.'

'When do you want me to go?'

'As soon as possible. You can bring Sofía and Margie like the last time.'

'I'll have to talk to Charlie.'

'Of course. I'm sorry to spring this on you, Piper.'

'It's not a total surprise, Dad. I knew someone would have to do it. And you can't be spared from the day-to-day running of the company. I'm quite happy to go.'

'Then go home right now and start getting ready. Once everything's in order give Sally a ring and she'll organise your travel.' He stood up and kissed his daughter's cheek. 'I knew you wouldn't let me down. But I'll make it up to you.'

She looked into his face. It was pale and lined, and there was a weary dullness in his eyes. 'You're worn out, Dad.'

He waved his hand. 'Don't fuss.'

'Maybe you should take a break.'

'Are you crazy? There's far too much going on.'

'Listen to me. When I come back from Spain, I want you and Mum to go to the villa in Nice. Promise you'll do it.'

'But who'll look after the company?'

'I will. I can keep things ticking over while you're away.'

He nodded reluctantly. 'Okay. I promise. Now go off to Marbella and sort out Hotel Azul.'

***

She started the car and began the drive back to Sandymount, but her father's pallor had scared her. When was the last time he'd had a holiday? Nine or ten months ago. He was always working – even on Saturdays and Sundays, when most people were off, he would be in his study, poring over accounts. When she came back, she would insist that he take a break. She knew she could rely on her mother as an ally.

As she drove, she silently cursed Jack. If he pulled his weight in the company, it would take the strain off their father. But instead of helping, Jack was just adding more stress and worry. One thing was certain. Matters were coming to a head. Her father could not continue working at the frantic pace he had set himself without inflicting serious harm to his health.

But there was one thing that cheered her. This trip to Marbella gave her the excuse she needed to avoid Corinne's wedding. Now her parents need never know of the snub she had received by not being invited. She felt her spirits rise further when she thought of what awaited her down in Marbella: the sun waking her in the mornings, the scent of the flowers drifting up from the garden and the sea sparkling in the distance. It would be a pleasant challenge to take over the little hotel and make sure everything was in order. And she was glad to do it because it was one less problem for her father to worry about.

It wouldn't all be work. There would be time to take Sofía to the beach, to go for walks along the Paseo Maritimo and have dinner in cosy little restaurants. In fact, it would be like a working holiday. And it would make a welcome change from the unpleasant atmosphere that had developed between Jack and her.

By the time she got back to the apartment she was completely sold on the idea. The only downside she could see was her separation from Charlie for several weeks.

'You're home early,' Margie said, when Piper came through the front door.

'How would you like to go back to Spain?'

'Really?' Margie said. 'I'd love it.'

'Me too, Mummy!' Sofía said, climbing onto her lap. 'I want to go on the beach with my bucket and spade.'

'And so you shall. We're going back to Marbella. And this time we'll be staying longer.'

'How long?' Margie asked, her eyes shining.

'A couple of weeks or more, even.'

'When?'

'Just as soon as I can make the arrangements.'

She went into the bedroom, sat down beside the window and rang Charlie. 'Dad wants me to go back to Spain. The sale of Hotel Azul has come through and he wants me there to oversee the transfer.'

'Why do you get all the holidays?' Charlie laughed.

'It's not a holiday and it could take a few weeks. You don't mind?'

'Of course I mind. I wish I could come with you.'

'So why don't you?'

'Just a little matter of finalising the most important tour in my band's career.'

'Oh Charlie, it would be brilliant if you could come. You'd love it there. It would be a nice break before the band goes on tour.'

'You sound like you're working for the Marbella Tourist Board. Hang on while I consult my diary.'

There was a pause and he was back.

'You know what, Piper? I might just take you up on that offer. I just have one or two details to iron out. I might be able to squeeze in three or four days before the tour begins.'

'That would be perfect.'

'I'll make a few phone calls.'

When she hung up, Piper's spirits were soaring. The family would be together in Marbella, if only for a few days. Already she was thinking of the excursions they could take along the coast, the days on the beach soaking up the sun, the pleasant strolls along the seafront in the evening, the moon reflecting off the water.

She rang *Señor* Rodriguez, the Spanish lawyer, and told him of her plans. Then she called the Hotel Azul and spoke to *Señor* Hernandez.

'When are you coming, *Señora*?'

'Tomorrow, if I can get flights.'

'Will you be bringing your daughter this time?'

'Yes, and her nanny. We'll be staying for a few weeks.'

'Then you must have my apartment.'

'But I can't do that.'

'Oh, yes, I insist. It has two bedrooms and a kitchen and a nice little sitting room. There will be plenty of space for you.'

'And what will you do?'

'I am a single man. It is not a problem. I will move to one of the guest rooms.'

'Are you sure?'

'Just ring when you are ready and I will have Pedro meet you at the airport.'

Finally, she rang her father's secretary, Sally, and asked her to find flights. Sally was back within half an hour to tell her she had booked them on the nine o'clock plane to Málaga the following morning.

Piper let out a whoop, put down the phone and went back to the lounge. Margie and Sofía looked at her with anticipation in their eyes.

'It's all arranged. We can start packing!'

***

It was a much bigger job than it had been for her previous trips to Spain. Those had lasted a couple of days and this time she would be there for weeks. When they had finished, six suitcases were sitting in the hall, and Piper was overcome with excitement. It was heightened when Charlie rang to say he had cleared his diary and would join them for four days before flying to Paris for the first concert of the Hell's Kitchen tour. All the pieces were falling into place.

Finally she rang her father. 'We leave in the morning.'

'That's excellent, Piper. I'm going to send you over a list of things for you to check when you get there. You should receive it shortly. Keep in touch with me every day, and if you're in doubt about anything, just pick up the phone.'

'Will do.'

'Good luck, Piper. And before you go, your mother wants to talk to you.'

There was a click and she heard Rose's voice on the line. 'You're one lucky sucker getting down to the Spanish sun and avoiding this bloody wedding. Any chance I could come with you?'

'You'd be very welcome.' Piper laughed.

'Have you heard the latest? You know your dad offered to pay for the honeymoon. Well, you'll never guess where Corinne's chosen.'

'Tell me.'

'Just about the most expensive place she could find. Two weeks in some luxury resort in Bali. That girl is the most grasping bitch I've ever come across and I've met a few in my time.'

'It's still cheaper than that ridiculous wedding she'd planned. At least Dad won't have to pay for helicopters and security guards.'

She heard her mother laughing. 'When your father and I got married, I was driven to the church in a hackney cab. And our honeymoon was a weekend in Ballybunion. But I'll tell you one thing, Piper, it taught us the value of money and how hard it is to earn. It's a lesson Jack and Corinne could do with.'

'She's soon to become your daughter-in-law. You'll have to learn to live with it.'

'Well, one thing's for sure. You know she keeps calling your father "Dad"? If she ever calls me "Mum", I'll clobber her.'

Piper was still laughing when she put the phone down. But behind the laughter was the grim reality that soon Corinne would become Mrs McKenzie, and it wouldn't be long before she was hatching plans for Jack to become managing director of the company. When Piper returned from Spain she'd have a battle on her hands for control of McKenzie Leisure. And it was a battle she couldn't afford to lose.

But she didn't have time to brood on it. Charlie rang to say he was coming home early to spend the last night with them before they left for Marbella. He suggested that they all go out for dinner to the American Diner, an upmarket hamburger restaurant that Sofía would enjoy.

As soon as she finished talking to him, the buzzer rang and she found a courier on the doorstep with her father's instructions and the boarding passes for tomorrow's flight, which Sally had printed out. She'd barely had time to shower and get dressed when she heard Charlie's car. Next minute his key was in the lock and he was coming through the hall door.

He kissed Piper and swooped Sofía into his arms. 'How's my girl? Are you looking forward to your holiday, getting on a big plane and flying to Spain?'

'Mummy says you're coming too.'

'Not straight away, darling.'

'Why not?'

'Because I've still got work to do. But soon I'll come and join you. Now, is everybody hungry? I'm taking you out for hamburgers.'

'Can I have ice-cream as well, Daddy?'

'If you've still got room.'

They got into Charlie's car and drove the short distance to the restaurant. One of the attractions was that the waiters were dressed as clowns; they gave the children hats to wear, with stars and stripes, and paper and crayons so that they could draw. Once Sofía got over her excitement, she settled into her seat and picked up a crayon. A few minutes later, she squeaked, 'Look, Daddy! It's a picture of you.' She pushed it across the table.

'You've made me look sad.'

'That's because we're leaving you behind.'

'I will be sad. I'm going to miss you, guys. Who's going to cook my breakfast in the morning?'

'You'll have to do it yourself, Daddy.'

'Boo-hoo,' Charlie said, and everyone laughed.

Sofía had burger and chips but only managed about half of it. However, she made short work of the ice-cream that followed. It was after nine o'clock when they left the restaurant.

Once Sofía and Margie had gone to bed, Charlie poured two glasses of wine and they sat in front of the fire while outside the window they could hear the surf pounding on the shore. He took her hand. 'I wasn't joking back there. I really am going to miss you.'

'We'll be in touch every day.'

'It's not the same. I've been thinking ... We don't take

enough holidays together. Sofía is growing up fast. We should make use of the time.'

'What's stopping us?'

'We both lead busy lives, Piper.'

'You need to slow down, Charlie. I don't want to be left a grieving widow.'

'Look who's talking. This is the third time you've been to Spain recently. And if your father ever retires and you succeed him you'll have the whole company to run. What are you going to do then?'

Piper gazed into the fire as the flames danced and flickered. 'I'll decide about that when it happens.'

CHAPTER SEVENTEEN

It was the end of May, and the thermometer at Málaga airport told Piper that it was twenty-six degrees when they walked into Arrivals just after half past twelve. The first thing Pedro did when they got to the car was to switch on the air-conditioning.

'*Mucho calor*,' he said, when the luggage was stowed in the boot and they were all safely strapped into their seats. He waved his hand in front of his face to indicate how hot it was. But, of course, nobody minded: they were in Spain and heat was what they expected. Besides, they had come prepared. Piper had packed plenty of sunscreen and light clothing, and now she slipped on her Ray-Bans as she settled into the front seat beside Pedro.

He turned to her and smiled. 'So you have come back to Spain, *Señora* McKenzie, and this time you will stay longer. I hear you are the new owner of Hotel Azul. I am very glad.'

'Thank you, Pedro. How is Carmencita?'

He shrugged. 'She is happy. Carmencita never worries.'

'You didn't tell me what she does for a living.'

'She is a – how you say? – *una peluquera*.'

'A hairdresser?'

'*Sí*. That is correct. She dresses the ladies' hair.'

'Does she like her job?'

'Very much. And she is excellent. She spent four years training for it.'

'Then she must be good. Perhaps she will cut my hair for me some time?'

'For her, it would be an honour, *Señora*.'

They continued chatting as the car sped along the motorway towards their destination. Piper could feel the excitement mounting. She knew that the coming days would be busy as she took possession of Hotel Azul, met the staff and checked that everything was in order, but she would enjoy it.

As she gazed from the window, she could see the sun glittering on the ocean and the yachts drifting in the breeze. They had now entered the summer tourist season, the busiest time of the year, and the beaches were packed with bodies. Tonight when it got cooler, the bars and restaurants would be bustling.

At last they entered the town. A few minutes later, Pedro pulled the car into the forecourt of Hotel Azul and stopped outside the front door.

Señor Hernandez was waiting to greet Piper, with what appeared to be the entire hotel staff, including the head chef in his starched white apron. As she stepped from the car, they burst into applause and one of the chambermaids came forward, made a curtsy and presented her with a bouquet of roses.

Piper's eyes misted. This was a regal reception and it was totally unexpected. *Señor* Hernandez stepped out and grasped her hand. 'Welcome once more to Hotel Azul, *Señora*. Please allow me to present the staff.'

He led her along the line and introduced her to each member in turn and Piper shook their hands. In quick succession, she met the under-managers, the bar and kitchen staff, the receptionists, the head waiter, the gardeners, the chambermaids, the porters and the cleaners. It would be a while, she knew, before she had their names by heart.

Señor Hernandez whispered in her ear, 'Perhaps, you might like to say a few words, *Señora*.'

This was another surprise, but when she looked at the row of staff, she could see they were expecting her to speak. She took a deep breath and scrambled together some words. 'Thank you all for your very gracious welcome. It is my honour to become the new proprietor of Hotel Azul. My father chose it because it is the best hotel in Marbella. And I know, with your support, it will continue to hold that proud position. I'm very much looking forward to working with you.'

When she had finished, the manager translated what she had said and the staff broke into spontaneous applause, then dispersed to their jobs. By now, two porters were piling the luggage onto a trolley and *Señor* Hernandez was leading the way into the hotel. Immediately Piper felt at home. Everything was exactly as she remembered it.

The manager was whispering in her ear again: 'That was a very gracious speech you gave, *Señora*. I know the staff appreciated it. It will have meant a lot to them.'

'Thank you.'

'When do you wish to commence your work?'

She checked her watch. It was two o'clock. 'Shall we say three?'

'That is fine. I will accompany you.'

By now they had walked along a corridor on the ground floor and arrived at a door. The manager produced a key and opened it with a flourish. He invited Piper, Margie and Sofía to enter. 'These are your quarters, *Señora*. I hope you will be comfortable.'

She was in a neat little flat. There was a cosy sitting room with sofas, television and a desk, Internet connection and a printer. A drinks cabinet stood in a corner. The floor was of marble and there was tasteful art on the walls. Like the previous rooms she had occupied, the flat had a sliding door leading out to a terrace and the gardens. 'This is very nice.'

'And the bedrooms.' He pushed open the door to a large room with a double bed and an en-suite bathroom. The next room held a single bed. There was also a small kitchen, with a cooker, a table and cooking utensils, and another bathroom.

Piper turned to *Señor* Hernandez. 'This will suit us perfectly.'

He gave a little smile. 'And being on the ground floor, it will be safe for the little one. I will leave you now, *Señora*. I will see you at three o'clock. And, once again, welcome to Hotel Azul.'

He bowed politely and was gone. The porters remained with the luggage. They looked at Piper for directions. '*Ponlo ahí*,' she said, pointing to the main bedroom. The men duly pushed the trolley into it and unloaded the cases. On the way out, she slipped each of them a tip, then realised she was still holding the roses she had been given earlier. She went into the kitchen, found a vase, filled it with water, put in the bouquet and placed it on a table in the sitting room.

She looked around the flat once more. She would be quite at home here.

'I want to go to the beach,' Sofía said.

'Not just yet, honey. We have to get organised first.'

'When?'

'As soon as we're ready.'

'Would you like me to unpack the cases?' Margie asked.

'Would you mind? That would be a big help.'

'No problem.'

Margie went off to the bedroom and set to work, with Sofía who began rummaging through her case for her bucket and spade. Piper went into the kitchen and checked the cupboards and the fridge. The manager had left some provisions but they would need more. She didn't have time to shop now. She had to start on the inspection soon but first she had a couple of calls to make. It was going to be a busy afternoon.

She went out to the terrace and sat down in the bright sunshine. She took out her phone and rang her father. 'We've arrived safely.'

'Good. What's your accommodation like?'

'It's perfect. Did I tell you Hernandez has given us his flat? It's nice and comfortable. And one other thing, we got an amazing reception when we arrived.' She told Henry about the staff lined up to greet her and the presentation of the flowers.

'It sounds like they were expecting royalty.'

'That's exactly how it felt. I'd like to ask your permission to do something, Dad.'

'Yes?'

'I'd like to give them all an extra week's pay as a bonus to mark our takeover.'

'That's very generous, Piper.'

'Look on it as a goodwill investment, Dad. We never know when we might need them to go the extra mile for us. Besides, they deserve it. They really were wonderful.'

'You're right. Talk to Hernandez and tell him to organise it.'

'Okay. I'm under a bit of pressure here. Tell Mum I'll ring her tomorrow.'

'Will do.'

'And, Dad?'

'Yes?'

'Try to slow down, I'm worried about you.'

She heard him laughing. 'There's nothing to worry about, Piper. Don't you know me by now? If I slowed down, I'd die of boredom.'

Next she rang Charlie and was pleased to hear him pick up at once. 'It's me, reporting from Marbella.'

'Lying on a beach again?'

'I wish. We've just arrived at the hotel and I have a very busy schedule ahead of me.'

'How's Sofía?'

'She can't wait to get to the beach. Would you like a word?'

'Of course.'

She called her daughter and Sofía babbled excitedly into the phone. 'Daddy! I'm too busy to talk to you. I'm going to the beach.'

Piper smiled as she took the phone back. 'There you are! Like father, like daughter.'

'What's she going to be like when she's a teenager?' Charlie laughed.

When Piper hung up, Sofía was in her swimsuit. 'Margie, will you take her to the beach for a couple of hours while I see to business?'

'I'd love to!' Margie changed into beachwear, then packed a bag with towels, sunscreen and bottles of water. 'What time do you want us back?'

'Say six o'clock? Then we'll go out and have a nice dinner somewhere.' She knelt down and looked into Sofía's eyes. 'You know the drill. You must do everything that Margie says, okay?'

'Yes, Mummy.'

She kissed her cheek. 'Off you go and enjoy yourselves.'

When they had gone, Piper took out her phone again and this time she rang the lawyer, Rodriguez.

'*Hola, Señor*. This is Piper McKenzie. I've arrived at Hotel Azul to begin my inspection. My father has given me instructions that you are to release the balance of funds to *Señor* Guzman once I'm satisfied.'

'That is correct, *Señora*.'

'This might take a few days.'

'Just call me when you are ready and I will look after the rest.'

Piper just had time to get undressed, slip into the shower and put on some lighter clothes before she locked up and went to the desk to find the manager waiting for her.

'Where would you like to begin, *Señora*?'

'Let's start with the bedrooms.'

She had brought the list her father had given her and attached it to a clipboard. As they began their tour, she ticked off the items one by one: the furniture, the ornaments, the bathroom fixtures, the pictures on the walls. It was a tedious job and progress was slow. By five thirty they had checked only half of the rooms.

'We'll have to stop now, *Señor*. My daughter and her nanny will be returning from the beach shortly.'

Señor Hernandez looked as if he was glad of the break.

'What time do you start in the morning?'

'Eight o'clock, *Señora*.'

'I'll see you then and we'll resume our inspection.'

'As you wish, *Señora*.'

***

Piper went back to the flat, kicked off her shoes and lay down on the bed. She was tired. The heat, the travelling, the walking up and down corridors to check the bedrooms – all had taken their toll. She was dozing off when she heard excited voices coming up the garden. She got up, went to the window and saw Margie and Sofía walking across the lawn. She stepped onto the terrace to greet them. 'Have you had a good time?'

'Can I go again tomorrow?'

143

Piper glanced at Margie, who nodded. 'All right, honey. Now come and have a bath and then we'll get dressed and go out for dinner.'

It was seven o'clock when they set off into the town. The siesta was over, the shops were opening again and the crowds were coming out to stroll through the streets. She was amazed at Sofía's energy. She seemed just as excited now as she had when they'd left Dublin that morning. There was little doubt that she would sleep well tonight.

At last they came to a restaurant on a side street with tables outside so that they could sit and watch people strolling by. Piper was ravenous and decided to treat herself. She ordered a plate of pork chops, chips and a green salad. Margie had fish and Sofía was happy to tuck into an omelette. To wash it all down, Piper ordered a carafe of wine.

She sat back and felt the tiredness seep out of her. Tomorrow she hoped to work until lunchtime, then take the afternoon off to be with Sofía. She planned to have the bulk of the work done before Charlie came down so that they could have a little family holiday. But that depended on how quickly she could complete the inspection. It had been slow today but, hopefully, it would speed up once she got the hang of it.

They finished their meal and decided to walk back to the hotel along the Paseo Maritimo. Like the rest of the town, it was packed with people taking the evening air. The enticing smell of cooking food floated on the night air. Sofía goggled at the mime artists, clowns and musicians who were entertaining the crowds for tips.

It was after ten when they got back. By now, Sofía was dropping with tiredness so Piper undressed her, brushed her teeth and put her to sleep beside her in her bedroom. Then she poured a glass of wine and went to sit on the terrace. Below, the seafront sparkled with lights and she could hear singing and guitar music from the Paseo. She closed her eyes. It was great to be back. And it would be even better when Charlie joined them. She couldn't wait for his arrival.

Chapter Eighteen

The morning sun seeping through a chink in the curtains stirred her awake. When she checked the time, she saw it was ten past seven. She got carefully out of bed so as not to wake Sofía. She slipped on a bathrobe and went out into the garden.

No one else was about and the lawns shone with dew. From some of the trees she could hear birds greeting the morning. She made her way to the pool, climbed in and swam steadily for a while. Then she dried herself, returned to the flat, showered and got dressed.

In the fridge she found milk and butter, jam and a packet of croissants, then switched on the coffee percolator. When everything was ready, she sat on the terrace and had breakfast. At ten to eight she went inside and found that Margie was up. 'Good morning,' she said. 'Sleep well?'

'Like a baby.'

Piper smiled. 'The other baby's still snoozing. I have to go now and meet *Señor* Hernandez, but you'll find everything you need for breakfast in the kitchen. Later we'll do some shopping.'

'I could do it this morning, if you like. There's a supermarket at the top of the road. What do we need?'

Piper made out a short list and gave it to her. 'I'll be back at one o'clock and we can go to the beach.' She set off for the lobby and found the manager waiting for her at the desk, ready to accompany her on her rounds.

'Did you have a good night, *Señora*? Not too hot?'

'Not at all! I had a very good night, thank you. Now, before we begin, *Señor*, my father would like the staff to be paid an extra week's wages in honour of our new ownership. Would you arrange it, please?'

'Of course, *Señora*. That is most kind.'

'And please would you prepare an up-to-date statement of accounts for me. If you send it to me as an email attachment, I'll forward it to my father.' She gave him her email address.

Piper was hoping to finish the bedrooms quickly, then move on to other parts of the hotel. She soon settled into a rhythm and by midday they had completed their task. In a handful of rooms the occupants were still asleep so she made a note to return to them later.

As it was approaching lunchtime, and she knew the kitchen would be busy, she decided to check the linen cupboards. By five to one, she was satisfied with her morning's work. 'That's enough for today, *Señor* Hernandez. You have your normal duties to attend to. We'll start again at eight tomorrow morning.'

The manager smiled and set off for his office. Piper was growing fond of him. He was efficient and polite but there was warmth beneath his formal demeanour. When she returned to the flat, Margie and Sofía were waiting impatiently to get down to the beach.

'We went shopping, Mummy,' Sofía told her importantly. 'I helped Margie at the supermarket.'

'Did you get everything?' Piper asked the nanny.

'We're now stocked up. And the prices were an awful lot cheaper than at home.'

'That doesn't surprise me. Just give me a minute to get changed and we'll head off.'

She went into the bedroom, changed into a bikini, slung a sarong round her waist and packed the beach bag. Moments later they were setting off across the garden.

'Will you be working every morning, Mummy?'

'Only till Daddy arrives.'

'When is that?'

'Next week.'

'And then you'll spend all day with me?'

'Of course, sweetheart.'

The beach was rapidly filling when they arrived, but they were able to secure a couple of loungers and a large umbrella close to the water's edge. It was a good spot because it allowed Piper to keep an eye on Sofía, who immediately decided she wanted to paddle in the sea so Margie went with her.

Piper stretched out on the lounger and took out her mobile. First, she rang her father. 'I've started work.'

'Anything to report?'

'Everything seems to be in order.'

'That's good. Pay special attention to the bar and the kitchen. In my experience, they're where most pilfering takes place.'

'I'll remember that.'

'How is Hernandez working out?'

'He's fine, very helpful. He runs the place well. I like him.'

'Anything else?'

'I told him you wanted the staff to have an extra week's pay and he was very impressed.'

'That was your idea.'

'It sounds better coming from the man at the top. Anyway, it was well received.'

'Weather still hot?'

'It's perfect, Dad. You should try it some time. It'd do you good.'

'Don't start that again. I couldn't lie on a beach all day long. It would drive me crazy. Listen, your mother wants a word.'

There was a click and she heard Rose on the line. 'How's everything working out down there?'

'Fine, so far.'

'You're lucky. It's hectic here. The wedding's on Saturday and Corinne's running around like a headless chicken. She's called me three times already this morning to make sure I've got a pink outfit so I don't clash with her mother. If this keeps up, I'm going to end up on Valium.'

Piper couldn't help laughing. 'I suppose I'll have to send the happy couple a card and a present?'

'That's entirely up to you.'

'I'd better do it or Jack'll have another reason to hate me. Mum, could you buy them something from me and Charlie?'

'What do you suggest?'

'I'll leave it to your discretion. Corinne will understand

149

that I can't be at the wedding because of family business. Tell her we send our best wishes.'

'Okay, Rose said. 'I'll do it but if I get the wrong thing, don't blame me.'

'There's something else. I spoke to Dad before I came away and got him to promise to go down to the villa in Nice when I get back. You should keep reminding him. I think he's in serious need of a rest and it sounds like you are too.'

'Don't worry, I'll keep badgering him.'

'Good. I don't want him trying to wriggle out of it. I'll call again tomorrow.'

She rang off and called Charlie. 'Just checking in. Is the tour on schedule?'

'Yes. Just adding the finishing touches.'

'When are you coming down?'

'Monday morning. I've got one or two details to finalise and then I'll book the flight.'

'That'll be great. I'm really missing you, Charlie. I can't wait to see you.'

'How's Sofía?'

She glanced down the beach. 'Paddling in the sea with Margie. Do you want me to call her over?'

'Let her be. Tell her I was asking for her. We'll talk again tomorrow. Love you, Piper.'

'Me too.' She switched off her phone and lay back. She was glad she was away from Dublin, the wedding and the unpredictable weather. In Marbella she could be sure of sunshine every day. Already she was settling into the pleasant life at Hotel Azul. All she needed was her husband to join her and everything would be perfect. Just a few more days and they would be reunited.

She picked up a novel and started to read but, after a while, her eyelids were heavy and soon she was dozing. She was awakened by Sofía tugging her arm.

'I'm hungry, Mummy.'

She sat up. 'Okay, honey, we'll get you something to eat. What about you Margie? Would you like a bite of lunch?'

The nanny nodded.

There was a little bar further up the beach with tables and seats on the sand. They gathered their belongings and made their way there. It offered simple dishes, like fried fish, squid rings and burgers. Piper ordered various plates, a large salad and a basket of bread. She asked for two beers, and milk for Sofía. Sofía quickly polished off her meal. Soon she was insisting that they get back onto the beach, where she began to build a sandcastle.

***

The following days continued in the same pattern. Piper was out of bed at seven each morning, had a quick swim to wake herself up, ate a light breakfast and was at the reception desk at eight to meet *Señor* Hernandez and continue her rounds. It was a tedious job but she gradually worked her way through the schedule her father had given her. By Friday at lunchtime, she had finished.

Most of the stock and equipment on the inventory was intact. She found some small items missing, such as ornaments and kitchen utensils, but she put that down to breakage or loss. There was no evidence that Guzman was attempting to defraud them. She rang her father to tell him.

'I've completed the inventory and everything seems to be in order.'

'Good, did you check the bar and kitchens carefully?'

'As far as I can see, we're getting everything we've paid for.'

'If you're happy, I'll contact the lawyer and tell him to release the balance of the funds. Did you get an up-to-date statement of accounts from Hernandez?'

'He'll have it ready today and I'll email it to you.'

'Well done, Piper. Now, there's one final thing. I appreciate that you've been very busy but did you get a chance to consider what improvements we need to carry out?'

'Yes. I've been thinking it over and I've decided that Hotel Azul is perfect as it is. It's cosy and comfortable. All it needs is a bit of a face-lift. It could do with some paint, new carpets and curtains, and perhaps some new furniture. But I wouldn't recommend any major renovations.'

'That's a relief.'

'I suggest we leave redecorating till the winter when the season's over. We could close the hotel, get the decorators in and have the job done in a week. That way we cause the least disruption.'

'Good thinking, Piper.'

'Everything okay at home?'

'I wouldn't quite say that. We have your brother's wedding tomorrow. Your mother is going around like a bear with a sore head. I don't think she'll return to normal till the knot's tied and they've been despatched on their honeymoon.'

'That's when the trouble will start.'

'Now, Piper, don't be like that. You know I want you and Jack to get along together.'

'I think you need to say that to Jack. I'm perfectly happy to get along with him, but he seems to think I'm the Wicked Witch of the West out to grab his rightful inheritance and do him down. I happen to see it the other way round. Anyway, enjoy the occasion.'

'Is that meant to be a joke, Piper?'

She smiled. 'I'll leave you to figure it out. *Adios, amigo.* I'll be in touch.' On her way back to the flat she ran into Pedro polishing the car. '*Hola, Pedro.* Busy today?'

'No, today is quiet, *Señora* McKenzie.'

'How's Carmencita?'

At the mention of his fiancée's name, his face broke into a warm smile. 'She is busy cutting the *señoras'* hairs.'

'I haven't forgotten my plan to ask her to do mine. When would be the best time?'

'Whenever suits. She will always be available for you.'

Piper wrinkled her brow. Charlie was coming on Monday. It would be a good idea to have her hair washed and styled so that she looked her best when he arrived. That left today or Saturday to get it done, and Saturday was sure to be busy.

'Could she do it today?'

'I will ring and find out.' He took out his phone and spoke into it. Then he clamped it shut. 'It's arranged. At three o'clock she will be expecting you.'

'You'd better give me the address.' He wrote it on a piece of paper and drew a map. 'Carmencita will give you the special treatment. You will see what a good hairdresser she is. The best in Marbella – no, the best in all of Andalucía.'

An idea occurred to her. Tomorrow, being Saturday, the beach was sure to be packed with local Spanish families as well as tourists. There wouldn't be enough space to swing a cat. 'Are you busy tomorrow afternoon?'

'Tomorrow I am free.'

'I was thinking of taking a drive along the coast as far as Fuengirola. Can you do that?'

'Of course, *Señora*. It would be my pleasure. I know Fuengirola very well. It is a pleasant town. There is much to see.'

'Good. We'll meet you on the forecourt tomorrow at two o'clock. And one other thing, Pedro, don't wear your uniform. Put on something light and comfortable.'

'You mean it?'

'Yes.'

His face brightened. 'Certainly, *Señora*. If you say so, I will do that.'

When she got back to the flat, she found Margie reading to Sofía on the terrace.

'Slight change of plan,' she said. 'I'm getting my hair done at three. You guys will have to go to the beach on your own, unless you want to spend the afternoon at the pool.'

'I want to go to the beach,' Sofía said.

Piper glanced at Margie. 'It's all the same to me,' she said.

'Okay, the beach it is. Now why don't I make some sandwiches for lunch? And tomorrow I've got a surprise.'

'What?'

'Pedro's taking us to Fuengirola. It's got a zoo, Sofía!'

'With monkeys, Mummy?'

'Everything, honey. You'll love it.'

***

Piper made a plate of ham and cheese sandwiches and they ate them on the terrace. Within minutes, a flock of sparrows and blue tits had arrived and Sofía had great fun feeding them crumbs from her plate. At two thirty, Piper got ready for her trip to the hairdresser. She had already studied the map Pedro had given her. The hairdressing salon was nearby and Piper reckoned she could make the journey on foot in twenty minutes. She put on her sunglasses and baseball cap and set off.

This was the hottest time of the day and she began to regret that she hadn't taken a cab. She kept to the shady side of the streets till at last she came upon a large sign reading '*Peluqueria Marbella*'. She had arrived.

She pushed open the door and found a row of women sitting in front of a large mirror. A dark-haired young woman came forward as soon as she entered.

'*Señora* McKenzie?'

'*Sí.*'

'I am Carmencita. Sit here, if you please.'

Piper stole a glance at her. She was very attractive, just as Pedro had said. She led Piper to a vacant chair and placed a large cape around her shoulders.

'Your hair is beautiful, *Señora*, so soft and silky. And natural blonde.'

155

'Thank you, Carmencita. You speak very good English.'

The young hairdresser's face broke into a warm smile of appreciation.

'You are very kind, *Señora*. I worked in London after I finished training. That's where I learned to speak English. Now, tell me what you would like me to do.'

Piper explained what she wanted and Carmencita set to work. First she washed Piper's hair and then she began with her scissors. Forty-five minutes later, when her hair had been dried, Piper was delighted. 'You've transformed me!'

'You are happy?'

'It's the best cut I've had anywhere. And I've been in some of the top salons in Ireland. How much do I owe you?'

Carmencita lowered her voice. 'There is no charge.'

'But I must pay you!'

'Please, *Señora*. Once a week I am allowed to do a friend's hair for free. It is a small perk of the job. And Pedro has told me you have been very kind to him.'

'Well, in that case, you must accept this.' She withdrew a fifty-euro note from her purse and pressed it into the young woman's hand. 'I'll come again. And I'll send my friends. Thank you so much.'

'*De nada, Señora.*'

Piper set off again into the blinding sun. What a lovely young woman, she thought. No wonder Pedro adores her.

Chapter Nineteen

By the time she got back to the flat, Margie and Sofía had returned from the beach.

'Your hair's stunning!' Margie exclaimed.

'I'm really pleased! Carmencita, Pedro's fiancée, did it. How did you guys get on at the beach?'

'We had a great time, didn't we, Sofía?'

'I made another sandcastle, Mummy.'

As they'd be going out for dinner that evening, Piper put Sofía to bed for a nap, then went out to the terrace. 'You look like you could do with a nap yourself,' she told Margie. 'She must have worn you out.'

'Compared with some children I've worked with, she's an angel. I once had a five-year-old boy who set the kitchen stove on fire.'

Piper's hand flew to her mouth. 'Was he hurt?'

'Thankfully not. But the stove was destroyed. When we asked him afterwards what had happened, he said he wanted to cook dinner for the family.'

'Don't ever let Sofía near the stove!'

'Don't worry, Piper. I watch her like a hawk.'

Piper took out her phone and rang Charlie. 'Just checking in.'

'I've bought my tickets and printed out the boarding passes. I arrive at Málaga on Monday afternoon at one o'clock.'

Her spirits soared. 'That's great – oh, Charlie, I can't wait to see you. I'll get Pedro to drive us to the airport and we can pick you up.'

'Who's Pedro?'

'The hotel chauffeur.'

'Hunky, dark-haired, smooth-talking *caballero*?'

'He is, actually.'

'I don't like the sound of that.'

Piper laughed. 'He's engaged to a beautiful girl. She cut my hair today.'

'That wouldn't stop him.'

'Charlie, you should know I only have eyes for you.'

'Damn right!'

'You know what's happening tomorrow, I suppose?'

'Remind me.'

'My loving brother is getting married to his adorable girlfriend.'

'I'd forgotten all about that.'

'I hadn't. That woman's going to cause me no end of trouble. I know it in my bones.'

'Forget it, Piper. You'll be well able for her.'

'You don't know her like I do.'

'And remember something else.'

'What?'

'You'll always have me in your corner, standing right beside you.'

***

At seven o'clock, they were ready to go out. Piper ordered a taxi to take them to Puerto Banús just along the coast. This was a fashionable resort with designer shops, expensive bars and a beautiful marina crowded with magnificent yachts.

It was a lovely evening, the air balmy and filled with the scent of mimosa. As they walked along, Piper stopped occasionally to admire a dress or a pair of shoes in a shop window, till at last, they found a restaurant that appealed to Sofía.

Once seated, they ordered a round of drinks and studied the menu. It had a wide selection of food. Sofía opted for chicken and the adults had the chilli burgers with a side salad.

'It must be expensive to live out here,' Margie said, glancing around the restaurant. 'Everything seems very pricey.'

'It was one of the dearest places in Europe before the recession. But property prices have taken a hammering. I'm afraid a lot of people got burned, Margie, just like back in Ireland. I heard of one man who had to sell a villa worth one and a half million euros for five hundred thousand.'

'I bet that hurt.'

'There are lots of similar stories. Still, it means someone picks up a bargain.'

When they had finished eating, they headed back along the seafront past the buskers and mime artists. There were many strollers like themselves, window shopping or admiring the spectacular yachts berthed in the marina. The discos were opening and the loud sound of dance music reverberated along the street.

When they arrived at the end of the Paseo, Sofía was getting tired. They came to a taxi rank.

'Seen enough?' Piper asked.

Margie nodded. 'One magnificent yacht looks much the same as another.'

By the time they got home, it was almost ten and Piper felt tired too. 'I'll grab an early night,' she said. 'It's been a busy day.'

'I'll sit on the terrace and read for a while.'

'Make sure to lock up.'

Piper put Sofía to bed, then climbed in beside her.

'Tell me a story, Mummy.'

Piper began, 'Once upon a time, there was a little girl who lived at the edge of a big dark forest ...' but before she could get any further they were both asleep.

***

The following morning, Piper was up early but today she didn't swim. She didn't want to get her hair wet after yesterday's trip to the *peluqueria*. Instead, she went down to the bar, ordered some croissants and brought them back to the flat. Then she made a pot of coffee. When the others woke up, they had breakfast together on the terrace.

They spent the remainder of the morning beside the hotel pool, had a light lunch, and at two o'clock, they were out on the forecourt where they found Pedro waiting for them. He had left off his uniform, as Piper had suggested, and was wearing a pair of khaki shorts with a golf shirt.

'That's better, Pedro,' Piper said, as she installed Sofía on the back seat with Margie. Then she got in beside him.

'Your hair is so ...' He kissed his fingers in a gesture of appreciation.

'The work of your own Carmencita.'

'I told you she is the best, did I not?'

'You did. And she is also very beautiful and quite charming. I can understand why you want to marry her, Pedro.'

He blushed. To cover his confusion, he started the engine. 'If everyone has put on the seatbelts, we will now start for Fuengirola.'

Fuengirola was another tourist town about twenty minutes' drive towards Málaga. The road would take them along the coast past some of the smaller resorts. They had barely started before Pedro said, 'When is your husband coming, *Señora*?'

'How did you know we're expecting him? He's arriving on Monday.'

'I heard *Señor* Hernandez talking to the deputy manager, *Señor* Cortes. You will be glad to see him, *Señora*,' Pedro said, eyeing her in the mirror.

She thought of the fun they would have when Charlie arrived.

'If Carmencita was away, I would be very lonely,' he added.

By now they were skimming along the main road towards Fuengirola. On their right, they could see the wide expanse of the sea, like a blue mirror, and the beaches crowded with holiday-makers. Eventually, they saw the outline of the town in the distance. It was smaller than Marbella but much more Spanish.

Pedro knew the town well and soon found a parking spot in a supermarket complex and they continued the remainder of the journey on foot. By now, Sofía was clamouring to get to the zoo. When they got there, they discovered there were no cages and the animals roamed freely in their enclosures. They watched, fascinated, as tigers, chimpanzees, crocodiles and a leopard cub wandered about in what was almost their natural habitat. When they left, the afternoon siesta was over and the shops were opening again.

Pedro suggested they walk towards the old part of town near the beach, an area of small streets and whitewashed houses packed with bars and restaurants. Piper stopped along the way to buy gifts in some of the shops. By now, it was seven o'clock and they were hungry.

'Pedro, you know Fuengirola well and you trained to be a chef. Why don't you take us to somewhere nice to eat?'

He thought for a moment. 'Have you tried paella, *Señora*?'

'Many times.'

'I will take you to one of the best places on the Costa for paella.'

They followed him through the maze of streets till at last they arrived at a small restaurant with a courtyard where he spoke to a waiter wearing a black apron.

'Yes, they will cook paella. What about the *niña*? Will she eat paella too?'

'Yes.'

They were shown to a table in the courtyard, which was lit by lanterns. It lent a cosy romantic atmosphere to the occasion. By now, Piper was ravenous. They ordered some wine. She took a sip and leaned back with a sigh. 'This is beautiful, Pedro. So far, it gets five stars for location.'

'Wait till you taste the food, *Señora*, and then you will give it ten stars.'

It took a while but at last two waiters arrived carrying a large pan of paella, plates and cutlery. They carefully placed the pan in the middle of the table, laid out the plates, stood back and made a polite bow. '*Buen apetito.*'

The aroma rising from the pan smelt delicious. It was a coulorful mixture of rice, prawns, chicken and peppers. Piper was the first to try it. 'Mmm! This is fantastic!'

Pedro smiled. 'I know about food, *Señora*.'

She ladled paella onto each plate and soon everyone was eating.

CHAPTER TWENTY

The insistent ringing of a phone jolted Piper from her deep sleep. For a moment she was confused but when she glanced at her watch she saw it was half past eight. She clamped the phone to her ear and heard her mother's voice. 'Did I wake you?'

'You did, actually.'

Rose laughed. 'Out on the ran-tan last night?'

'Not at all. We took Sofía to the zoo in Fuengirola and afterwards we went for something to eat. I took loads of photos. I'll post them on my Facebook page and you can see them for yourself.'

'I rang to tell you about the wedding.'

Now Piper was wide awake. 'Give me a mo.' She jumped out of bed, slipped on a dressing-gown and went out to the terrace. 'Shoot. I'm all ears.'

'Sit down.'

She lowered herself onto a chair. 'Okay.'

'I'd never witnessed such a performance in my entire life.

I won't go into the bridal outfits, except to say that they were like something out of *My Big Fat Gypsy Wedding*.'

'What about the food?'

'Nothing to write home about. But the airs and graces of your woman were something else. I swear to God, you'd think she was the King of Spain's daughter, not some jumped-up solicitor from Glasnevin. There she was, snapping her fingers and ordering the staff around. I don't know how one of the waiters didn't pour a bowl of soup over her head.

'Then we came to the speeches. Her father made a decent one, but then each of the brothers spoke, and then the uncles and aunts and every other member of the family. I thought I was going to fall asleep from boredom.'

'What about Dad and Jack?'

'Jack rambled on and on, big galoot that he is. Your father was short and to the point. Then your woman started. That was when I thought I was going to explode.'

'Go on!'

'She started by thanking everybody from the priest to the dressmaker. All the time, she was making these remarks that were meant to be funny but nobody laughed. You could see she was enjoying every minute of it, star of the show.'

'I'm glad I wasn't there. I'd've thrown up.'

'You haven't heard the best bit. She finally got on to us, said what a wonderful family we had and how she was so proud and delighted to become part of it. She kept referring to your father as "Dad" and you know how he hates that. I could see him squirming in his seat.'

By now, Piper was listening intently.

'She said Dad was one of the foremost businessmen in the country and he had built up the McKenzie business empire single-handed. But he had been working too hard and now everyone agreed it was time for him to slow down and enjoy the rewards of his hard work.

'She said she intended to give him a hand with the business and was looking forward to the occasion in the near future when Dad would be able to retire and hand over the reins of McKenzie Leisure to Jack and her.'

Piper gasped. 'She did not!'

'She did. I glanced at your father and it was all he could do not to get up and walk out there and then.'

'She said she intended to take over, her and Jack?'

'Exactly. She made him sound like a geriatric imbecile and she was doing him a favour, turning him out to pasture like an old workhorse. Meanwhile your brother was grinning all over his stupid face. I needn't tell you your father was livid.'

'How did the speech go down?'

'They loved it. Everyone was clapping.'

'I don't believe this,' Piper said.

'It's true, every single word.'

'I'm coming home. I can't sit here and let this happen.'

'Calm down, Piper. There's nothing you can do. They've gone to Bali.'

'Did Dad say anything?'

'No, but the first chance he got, he left and came straight home. He looked shocked, Piper, and I've never seen him so angry.'

'We've got to stop her. If she ever gets her hands on the company, we're finished. The first thing she'll do is get rid of me.'

'It's not going to happen. If anything, she's dug a hole for herself. Your father will make sure she gets nowhere near the company.'

'She'll work through Jack.'

'Your father's got Jack's number. They're always arguing. He knows Jack isn't capable of running the company. The only problem is, it'll make him stay longer and he's already working too hard. He really does need to let go. But he won't do it now he knows that Corinne is waiting to pounce.'

'Damn her!' Piper exclaimed. 'Why does she have to meddle in things that don't concern her?'

'Because she's ambitious, and now she's got your stupid brother dancing a jig to please her.'

'I don't know what to say. This has come as a terrible shock. I'll have to think about it. Let me ring you later.'

She went into the kitchen and made some coffee. Her head was spinning. She'd always known that Corinne would cause trouble but she hadn't thought she would move quite so fast. While she was sipping her coffee, she heard movement from the bedrooms. Margie and Sofía were getting up. She'd have to put on a brave face and not alarm them.

Sofía came into the kitchen first, followed by Margie.

'Are you up long, Piper?' Margie asked.

'I slept in.'

'We must all have been tired after yesterday.'

'Today we'll take it easy but first we'll have breakfast. Scrambled eggs for everyone? What about you, Sofía?'

'Cereal.'

'Cereal what?'

Sofía looked sheepish.

'Cereal, please.'

'Get yourself washed and then go and sit on the terrace. This will only take a few minutes.'

She set about preparing breakfast. She was glad of the distraction. At least it gave her something to do while her mind raged over what her mother had just told her. First chance she got she'd ring Charlie and get his advice. He'd know what to do.

She carried the food outside to the terrace, eggs scrambled with chopped tomatoes and parsley, then went back to fetch the coffee pot.

The sun was climbing high in the heavens and there wasn't a cloud in the sky. Already the thermometer was hovering around twenty-five degrees. It was going to be another warm, sultry day. Normally she enjoyed breakfast on the terrace but this morning there was a bitter taste in her mouth.

She tried to disguise her feelings for the sake of the others. 'You're a real sleepy-head, Sofía. It's after nine. Usually you're up before this.'

'I was dreaming, Mummy.'

'What about?'

'Daddy. When's he coming?'

'Tomorrow.'

As soon as breakfast was finished she helped Margie carry the bags and towels down to the pool area. She spread a blanket on the grass and put out Sofía's playthings. Then she excused herself and returned to the flat, saying she had a couple of calls to make. First she rang Charlie. She was put through to his message-minder. She was surprised. It was the first time in weeks that that had happened.

Damn, she thought. Please don't let him go back to his bad old ways. She left a message for him to call her urgently, then rang her father. 'Mum told me about the wedding.'

'The less said about that event the better,' Henry replied wearily.

'Corinne had a damned cheek talking like that in front of all those strangers. McKenzie Leisure is our private business, no one else's.'

'Don't let it upset you. She might have had too much to drink.'

'But it shows what's going on in her mind. You know my feelings about her. She's going to cause trouble unless she's put firmly in her place.'

'I know that, Piper, and I also know the influence she has over your brother. It's just one more headache for me to deal with. But you can rest assured I have no intention of allowing Corinne anywhere near the business and no plans to take early retirement.'

'I'm always ready to do my part, Dad.'

'I know I can rely on you.'

'And you're still going to take that holiday when I get back?'

'Let's talk about that again. Right now, I have a lot on my plate. Is everything okay down there?'

'Yes. Charlie's coming tomorrow to spend a few days with us and then I'll be home. If it's any comfort, I'll take on anything you want to offload.'

'That *is* a comfort. Enjoy your break. When you get back, I'll find plenty for you to do.'

She finished the call, feeling slightly relieved. But Corinne's outburst had prompted her father to have second thoughts about going to Nice. And, by the sound of things, he needed that holiday more than ever.

She went back to the garden and tried to relax while she waited for Charlie to ring her. Margie had taken Sofía into the pool and their laughter echoed around the quiet garden. But it didn't brighten her mood. She was still worried about her father, and growing increasingly uneasy that Charlie hadn't called back.

She tried to concentrate on the novel she had brought but her mind kept wandering. The time ticked away and now she was concerned. She took out her phone once more and rang her husband but got the same response. She heard his voice saying he was unable to take her call and inviting her to leave a message. On this occasion she was more emphatic. *This is Piper. Please ring. It's urgent.*

She hated being put in this situation. It made her feel powerless. It made her feel she was at Charlie's mercy. Yet she had no option but to wait for him to respond. She tried to console herself with the thought that he might be tied up in a meeting. He was busy putting the finishing touches to the Hell's Kitchen tour and she was well aware of all that such a big undertaking entailed.

By lunchtime, when he still hadn't called, she was seriously worried. Perhaps something had happened to him. Her mind filled with Doomsday scenarios. Charlie had been taken ill. He'd had an accident. *Something is wrong.*

By now, Sofía was clamouring to be fed. Piper put her book away and stood up. 'We'll eat at the bar.'

When they got there it was filling up but they managed to get a table on the terrace. They had just given their order when her phone rang.

'Yes?' she said, clamping it to her ear.

It was Charlie. 'Before I begin, let me apologise for not calling you sooner.'

'Charlie, you promised this wouldn't happen again—'

He cut her short. 'I have an emergency on my hands, Piper. I can't come to Spain.'

CHAPTER TWENTY-ONE

She was shocked into silence. Charlie's visit was to have been the highlight of this trip. She had been looking forward to it for days and now he was saying he couldn't come.

'Pete Donohue's had an accident,' he went on.

'Oh, no – what happened?'

'He crashed his car.'

'Oh, my God, is it serious?'

'He'll survive. But he won't be playing the drums for a while. He's broken his leg and his arm. He's in hospital. So now I'm left with five concerts organised, tickets sold, venues booked. And no drummer. It's the nightmare from Hell.'

'What are you going to do?'

'I'm trying to find a replacement. But if I don't get someone in the next twenty-four hours, I'll have to cancel. It's going to cost me a bundle.'

'Don't you have insurance for this sort of thing?'

'The short answer is no. So you can see, Piper, much as I'd love to be with you in Marbella, I've got to stay here and try to sort out this mess.'

'Oh, Charlie.'

'The problem is, all the good drummers are already signed up with other bands. Plus any replacement will have to learn Hell's Kitchen's routines. This is just about the worst thing that could happen.'

'Give him my best wishes.' She had wanted to talk to her husband about Corinne's behaviour at the wedding but this wasn't the time. It would have to wait till the crisis had passed. 'I'm sorry you aren't coming, Charlie. I miss you – we all do.'

'What are you going to do?'

'We'll come home, I suppose.'

'It can't be helped, sweetheart. I'll ring you again as soon as I have any news.'

There was a click and the call ended.

She stared at the silent phone. She could forget about the excursions she had planned, the delicious meals in cosy restaurants. Now she had to break the news to Sofía that her daddy would not be coming. She would be disappointed. But there was nothing to be done. She had better get the bad news over now. She reached out and took Sofía's hand. 'That phone call was from Dad. He can't come.'

Sofía's eyes filled with tears. 'Why?'

'He's got a problem at work.'

'What are we going to do?'

'We have to go home.'

Now Sofía started to cry in earnest. 'I don't want to go home, Mummy. I want to stay here. Daddy said he'd come.'

'One of the boys in the band crashed his car and now he has to find someone to take his place.'

'I want to stay. I like it here.'

'Finish your lunch, honey.'

Piper poked at her own food but she had lost her appetite. First there had been her mother's report of the wedding, now this devastating news.

***

After the meal was finished, she left Sofía with Margie and went out in an effort to clear her head. As she walked along the narrow, whitewashed streets she thought of what lay ahead. Soon she would have to return to chilly, rain-swept Dublin. Then Jack would come back from his honeymoon and civil war would break out in the family.

Eventually she came across a quiet little restaurant and decided to go in for a drink and a rest. She was shown to a table in the garden. Normally it would have cheered her but not today. The gloom that had descended on her with Charlie's phone call hung over her like a shroud.

She ordered a glass of wine and thought of the things she would have to do. Tomorrow morning she would go online in search of flights to Dublin, and talk to *Señor* Hernandez about the future running of the hotel.

As she sipped her wine, her eyes strayed to the other occupants of the restaurant. There was a family eating noisily at a corner table, a father and mother and several boisterous children. A young couple near the entrance were holding hands and gazing soulfully into each other's eyes. They made her feel lonely and added to the gloom.

Her attention was drawn to a young Spanish man sitting alone at a table nearby. He appeared to be staring at her intently. He wore a white suit and was thin and handsome with a bright, intelligent face. There was something familiar about him. She glanced away, but when she looked again he was still staring at her. Then he got up and came towards her. Suddenly she recognised him and her heart skipped a beat. He stopped when he reached her table.

'Hello, Piper. Do you remember me?'

She felt a lump rise in her throat. 'Of course, I do. It's you, Eduardo, isn't it?'

His face broke into a warm smile, and Piper was transported right back to the sultry nights when as young students they had flirted all those years before. How amazing that they should meet again after all this time.

'You look very well,' he said.

'Thank you. So do you.'

'May I sit down?' he asked politely.

'Please do.'

She was all a-flutter. He had caught her off-guard and now she wished she had worn something more fetching than her light summer dress. He continued to look her over till she felt herself blush. Thankfully, the waiter arrived at that moment and saved further embarrassment. 'Will you join me in a glass of wine?' she asked.

'I'd be delighted to.'

He spoke to the waiter in rapid Spanish and the man hurried away.

'So, here you are again,' he said. 'You have changed since we last met.'

175

'Do you think so?'

'Yes. You are more mature, more ... beautiful now. You are no longer a girl. Now you are a woman.'

She smiled. 'You've changed too, Eduardo. Your English is much better for one thing. You're quite fluent.'

He laughed. 'I practise it with every opportunity. But where is your friend, Jo? Isn't she with you?'

'No, she's at home in Dublin.'

'Ah,' he said. 'Are you here with your mother or your husband, perhaps?'

'No, I'm alone.'

This seemed to surprise him.

'What are you doing here?' she asked.

'I'm taking a short holiday.'

'Did you complete your studies?'

'Yes, I am now a fully qualified doctor. I work at a hospital in Málaga.'

'And Cesar?'

He sighed. 'Alas, he failed his second-year exams. He is now working in a medical laboratory.'

Piper thought of Eduardo's friend, the cheerful student who had flirted with Jo. 'I'm sorry to hear that.'

'It is not so bad. He will soon be married. His wife-to-be is a beautiful young woman and they love each other very much. He will be happy. And what about you?' he asked. 'You were hoping to study hotel management. Did you succeed?'

'Yes. I'm working in my father's company.'

'You are a clever woman, Piper. I said you would have a brilliant career in business.'

Piper smiled. Now that the initial shock was wearing off,

she was beginning to relax and enjoy her conversation with this fascinating man.

The waiter was back with a glass of wine for Eduardo. He thanked him and the waiter went away again. He still has those beautiful manners, she thought, the way he talks, the respect he shows to people. She let her eyes travel over his face. If anything, he had grown even more handsome in the intervening years.

They talked for an hour. When it was time to pay the bill, he took a twenty-euro note from his pocket and pressed it into the waiter's hand before Piper could object.

They sat looking into each other's eyes, each of them loath to break up their meeting. At last, he said, 'What are you going to do now?'

'I'm walking back to my hotel.'

'May I accompany you part of the way?'

She stood up and took her bag from the back of the chair. 'I'd be glad of your company.'

By now, the sun was going down. Music drifted to them, the exciting rhythm of guitar spilling from the doorways of dim little bars as they passed.

'It's an amazing coincidence, us meeting again like this,' Piper remarked.

A playful look came into Eduardo's eyes. 'Not really,' he said. 'It wasn't an accident.'

She stopped. 'What do you mean?'

'I have a confession to make, Piper. Every summer since we first met, I have come back here, looking for you. You see, I never gave up hope that I would meet you again. I never stopped believing in you. All this time, I have been thinking of you.'

Her eyes moistened. 'What a beautiful thing to say.'

Eduardo shrugged. 'Well, it happens to be true.'

They continued walking till at last they reached the hotel. 'This is where I'm staying,' she said. 'Thank you for bringing me home.'

He put his hands on her shoulders and gazed into her face. Then he kissed her three times on the cheeks. She felt a delicious tremor pass through her. Three kisses for a special friend.

He didn't move. 'I have a request to make of you,' he said. 'Will you allow me to take you to dinner tonight?'

Piper thought of what lay ahead for her – an empty evening coming to terms with the fact that Charlie would not be joining them. At least the short time she had spent with Eduardo had cheered her up. 'I'd like that.'

His face shone with pleasure. 'So, I will meet you here at eight o'clock. Does that suit you?'

'Eight o'clock will be perfect.'

'Okay,' he said. 'I will be here. Till then, *adios.*'

He turned and walked back the way they had come. She watched him till at last he was out of sight.

Chapter Twenty-two

The despondency that had haunted her since Charlie's phone call was gone. Now she felt light-hearted and carefree as she made her way through the hotel to the flat, where she found Margie and Sofía on the terrace.

'How are you, guys?' she asked.

'Sad,' Sofía said. 'I don't want to go home. Why can't Daddy come?'

'I've already explained, and we'll discuss it tomorrow.' She took Margie aside. 'How has she been?'

'A bit down in the dumps.'

'Hopefully she'll come out of it. I'll think of something to distract her. Now I have a favour to ask. I met a friend when I was out walking and we've arranged to have dinner tonight. Can you look after Sofía for me?'

'Of course. That's no big deal.'

'Thanks a million. Now I'm going to lie down for a bit. Please would you make sure I'm up again by seven?'

'Consider it done.'

Piper went into the bedroom, drew the curtains and turned on the air-conditioning. Then she stretched out on the bed and closed her eyes. She could still feel the tingling pleasure of Eduardo's strong arms holding her and his soft lips kissing her cheeks. She pictured him again in her mind, his tall, manly bearing, his dark hair, firm chin and brown eyes, his impeccable manners. And he had come back again to find her. It must be Fate. They had been brought together again for a purpose.

She listened to the drowsy sounds of early evening as they drifted into the room. What could be more romantic than the story Eduardo had just told her – how he had kept coming back, hoping to find her. It was like something from a fairytale, the very essence of romance ...

A sharp rap at the door woke her. It was seven o'clock.

Tonight she would dress up. She would make a special effort to look her best for him. He had come back for her and she mustn't disappoint him. She went into the bathroom, ran a bath and tipped in some scented foam. She luxuriated in the water till she had finally made up her mind what to wear. She had an elegant cocktail dress in the wardrobe. It fitted her perfectly, showing off her figure. She would wear that with some jewellery and a little jacket in case the evening turned cold.

At seven thirty she sat down at the dressing-table and carefully brushed out her hair. She spent a further ten minutes applying her makeup and finished with a spray of perfume to her wrists and neck. When she stood up and examined herself in the mirror, she saw a beautiful young woman reflected in the glass.

She checked her watch. It was five to eight. Time to leave. She found Sofía, fed, washed and ready for bed. She kissed the little girl. 'Mummy has to go out again. Margie will put you to bed but I'll see you in the morning. Be a good girl now.' She kissed the child again and set out.

***

Eduardo was waiting for her in a smart navy suit and blue tie. 'You look so beautiful,' he said, coming forward and kissing her cheek.

The restaurant he had chosen was called El Cisne, which meant The Swan. It was about fifteen minutes away, near the Don Pepe hotel. He suggested they take a cab but it was a beautiful evening, warm with a cooling breeze, and Piper said she would prefer to walk. She took his arm and they began to stroll down the hill towards the sea.

'Did you have nothing planned for tonight?' she asked.

'I was supposed to see an old university friend but I postponed our arrangement.'

'Just so you could see me?'

'Of course – how could I pass up the chance to have dinner with a beautiful woman like you? I have waited so long for this, Piper. I have dreamed of it.'

He spoke in a simple, honest way and it wasn't flattery. He was saying what he felt in his heart.

'Well, I'm glad you did because I want you to tell me everything that's happened to you since we last met.'

Eduardo had booked a table and they were shown to it right away. The waiter bowed and made a fuss. When she opened the menu she realised that this was an expensive restaurant. The starters began at twenty euros. She looked across at Eduardo in consternation. 'This is far too much. You don't have to spend your hard-earned money like this.'

But he brushed her objections aside. '*De nada.*'

'But I'd be quite happy to eat somewhere cheaper.'

He reached out and touched her hand while he gazed into her eyes. 'This is a very special occasion for me, Piper. I told you how I waited patiently for you, and now that you are here I want it to be perfect.' He smiled. 'Anyway, it is only money. I can earn more.'

His words touched her. But she was still determined not to run up a big bill at his expense. She ordered only simple dishes and refused his offer of champagne.

'So,' she said. 'What's been happening to you?'

'You are aware that medicine is a very long course. I spent a lot of my time with my head buried in books. Two years ago I graduated and I was fortunate enough to find a place in a local hospital. I enjoy my work. It was what I was destined to do.'

'But you must have found some time to relax, Eduardo. What about *señoritas*?' she asked, with a teasing smile. 'You're a good-looking man. Women must find you attractive.'

He looked a little embarrassed. 'There is no one serious.'

'You're too modest, Eduardo. I'm sure you must have plenty of girlfriends.'

'No, Piper. Do you want to know the truth? You have spoiled everything for me. Every woman I meet, I measure her against you and every time they fail.'

She felt her heart flutter as he lowered his eyes.

182

'But you, I see, are married,' he added. He glanced at her wedding ring.

'Yes. He's a wonderful man.'

'You are too beautiful to remain single.'

She blushed. Eduardo had lost none of his charm. But she had detected a note of sadness in his voice.

'What work does he do?' he asked.

'He manages a rock band.'

'An exciting job.'

'Yes, but it takes up a lot of his time. I would like him to spend more time with me but it isn't always possible because he is so busy.'

'But you love him, Piper?'

'Yes, of course.'

'Do you have any children?'

'A little girl called Sofía. She's with me here in Marbella.'

The waiter arrived with the first course. They began to eat and the conversation moved on. Piper told him about the work she did with her father in the family company.

'What about your brother? You told me he is older than you. Will he succeed your father when he retires?'

She paused. How did she explain about Jack and the rivalry between them? This was very personal stuff that should stay within the family. 'Nothing has been decided.'

'But someone must be in charge. Someone must make the decisions. Someone will have to take the responsibility.'

'You're right, Eduardo. What do you think should happen?'

'It should be the person who is best qualified, the one who will be most successful. It is the only way for the business to prosper.'

He had hit the nail squarely on the head. A faint smile passed Piper's lips. 'And that is hopefully what will happen.'

The second course arrived and Piper began to understand why the prices were so steep. The food was superb. Eduardo had obviously chosen one of the best little restaurants in Marbella.

The conversation returned to Piper.

'Do you ever wish you could turn back the clock to those days when we first met, when we were students and the whole world lay before us?' Eduardo asked.

A misty look came into her eyes. 'Sometimes. I couldn't wait to grow up. I should have enjoyed my youth when I was young. It's gone now and will never come back.'

'Don't be sad. Every age brings its own pleasures.'

She wished they could have had this conversation when they'd first met. They had been innocent then ... 'Eduardo, do you believe in love?'

'Certainly,' he said immediately.

'Do you believe that for each person there is another person who is specially meant for them?'

This time there was a slight hesitation. 'Yes. But sometimes you don't realise it till it is too late.'

'And then what happens?'

'Don't you know, Piper? Surely it is obvious. How can you be happy when you are not with the one who is destined for you?'

The dinner continued at a leisurely pace till it was time for coffee. Eduardo asked if she would like a *digestivo* but she refused. She had drunk several glasses of wine and, besides, she was already intoxicated on the conversation. She wished it could go on all evening. Eduardo seemed to think exactly like her.

Inevitably the meal came to an end and the last of the guests were departing into the balmy night. When the bill arrived, Piper took out her purse and offered to pay half but Eduardo looked offended at the very suggestion.

'I invited you,' he said. 'And, besides, it is a man's responsibility to pay for a lady's meal.'

Again he asked if they should take a taxi but she was enjoying the evening and wanted it to last as long as possible. 'Let's walk,' she said, and clung to his arm.

All the way back to the hotel, they talked. Piper was gently probing, attempting to find out more about him. He seemed so certain about everything and he answered all her questions without evasion.

By now they had reached the hotel. They both stood awkwardly for a moment. Then he said, 'May I kiss you goodnight?'

'Yes,' she breathed.

He took her in his arms and their lips met. Piper clung to him. She didn't want him to leave, didn't want this moment to end. But something told her to stop now before it was too late. Gently she pushed Eduardo away.

'What's wrong, Piper?'

She shook her head. 'We have to stop.'

'Have I offended you?'

'Oh, no!' she cried. 'Nothing like that.'

'May I meet you again?'

She felt like weeping with frustration. She wanted nothing more than to spend the night with him, but it was impossible. 'No,' she said, her voice shaking. 'We must never meet again.'

She couldn't have hurt him more if she had whipped him. He turned and began to walk quickly down the street. She watched him go while, inside her head, a small voice told her that she had just made a terrible mistake.

CHAPTER TWENTY-THREE

When she woke the following morning, regret weighed heavily on her mind. She had thoroughly enjoyed the dinner with Eduardo, but had she been guilty of leading him on? Had she allowed him to expect more than a goodnight kiss? The image that remained in her mind was of the young doctor walking away from the hotel, like a faithful dog that had been kicked by its mistress. Why had she been so cruel? Why had she not found a gentler way to let him go?

Because she was a married woman. She had never been unfaithful to her husband but her body had been about to betray her. She could still feel the desire that had overtaken her. It had shaken her to her core. One more minute in his arms and she would have hailed a taxi back to his hotel and climbed straight into his bed. And that would have left her with a legacy of guilt that she could never have erased.

She got up, had a shower and set about preparing breakfast on the terrace. The sun was up. It was going to be another glorious day, possibly the last they would spend here for some time. She set the coffee to brew in the kitchen and was on her way to the café for croissants and pastries when her mobile rang.

'Hello?'

It was Charlie and he sounded excited. 'Have you booked flights to come home?' he asked.

'Not yet. I'm hoping to do it this morning.'

'Good. I don't want you to do anything till I ring again. All may not be lost.'

'How do you mean?'

'I think I've found a replacement drummer.'

Her heart lifted. 'Really?'

'He's a young guy called Sharkie Bolger.'

'What sort of name is that?'

'It's short for Sharktooth. I know it sounds crazy but the fans love him. I found him playing in a little jazz cellar off Camden Street. He's very hot. And he's anxious to take this gig. The other band members are acting like prima donnas and going around with their noses in the air but that'll change when I tell them if they don't accept Sharkie the tour's off. So I might be able to join you after all.'

'When?'

'In about ten days' time when the tour's finished.'

She did a quick calculation. Sofía and Margie would be delighted to stay longer, but could her father afford to let her remain here when there was so much work to be done at home? She'd better ring him and find out. 'That's such good news, Charlie. I'll do nothing till I hear from you again.'

'What's the weather like?'

'Need you ask? It's to die for.'

'Well, if everything goes to plan, I hope to enjoy some of it with the woman I love as soon as the tour's over.'

'You're a flatterer, Charlie, and not a very good one.'

'But you like it. Bye, darling. Give my love to Sofía and regards to Margie.'

She went to the café and collected the croissants and pastries. When she got back to the flat she found Sofía and Margie waiting expectantly. 'I might have good news,' she said, as she set the table with jam and marmalade and poured cups of coffee. 'I had a phone call from Charlie this morning. He might be able to come after all.'

'Can we stay?' Sofía squealed, jumping up and down.

'Provided it all works out. He'll ring me back later. But it's only a perhaps. What do you want to do today?'

'Go to the beach,' Sofía chirruped.

'Okay, but first I have some more calls to make.'

After breakfast, Piper went to her bedroom and rang her father. 'Hi, Dad – how's business?'

'Booming. That idea of yours to promote the Majestic as a conference hotel has really taken off. Ed Brannigan tells me he's booked out right through the autumn. And the clients are happy to pay top dollar. That really was a brainwave, Piper. If things continue like this, we're going to have a bumper year.'

'And how are you?'

'Well, I'm missing you and my little granddaughter and I still haven't found the time to take the yacht out but I'm enjoying myself. I'm never happier than when the business is going well.'

'I've a request to make.'

'Go ahead.'

'Charlie's had a setback. One of his musicians was involved in a car smash.'

'My God! He's not dead, I hope?'

'Thankfully not, but he's out of action and Charlie has the band's tour organised. The point is this. Is it possible we could stay here for another couple of weeks till Charlie's free to join us? It would do Sofía good to spend some time with her father.'

'That's not a problem at all, Piper. In fact, it might be a positive development.'

'How do you mean?'

'I've been wondering what to do when Jack gets back from his honeymoon. I don't want you pair fighting like Kilkenny cats so it might be no harm if you're out of the way for a while.'

'But I was hoping to help you when I came back.'

'That can wait.'

'What about the holiday you promised to take at the villa in Nice? When's that going to happen?'

'We'll get round to it eventually.'

'No, Dad, that's not good enough. You've got to have a break. You've been working far too hard. Mum agrees with me and she's anxious to get a holiday too. You're not Superman. You've got to slow down.'

'Let's see. Stay there till Charlie joins you. Why don't you spend some more time with Hernandez, getting to know how Hotel Azul functions? Use that brain of yours – maybe there are ways of making the place even more profitable.'

She ended the conversation feeling a little uneasy. If she was away for too long, Jack would have a free hand with McKenzie Enterprises. With Corinne at his shoulder encouraging him, what damage might they do?

Then there was the issue of her parents' holiday. At sixty-eight Henry couldn't expect to work twelve- and fourteen-hour days indefinitely without some effect on his health.

Meanwhile, she had two more weeks to enjoy the Spanish sun and she was determined to make the most of it. On the way past the reception desk, she found *Señor* Hernandez going over some accounts. She stopped to have a word with him. '*Señor*, I'd like to spend some time with you learning how the hotel works. When would be most convenient for you?'

He looked up with a smile. 'Whenever suits you, *Señora*. As you know, I am here each day from eight o'clock.'

Piper came to a quick decision. A few hours in the morning would be best: then she could spend the rest of the day with Sofía and Margie. 'Let's say I join you from eight thirty till ten thirty. That should be enough. I won't interfere in your work, simply observe.'

'That is entirely acceptable, *Señora*. I will expect you at half past eight tomorrow morning.' He made a little bow and Piper left.

When she got back to the flat, she found Sofía and Margie ready for their trip to the beach. They set off through the gardens and down the little path. When they arrived, the sand was sparsely populated and they hired some loungers near the water's edge. Sofía was already raring to paddle.

'Make sure you wear your armbands,' Piper warned, but her thoughts were already drifting back to her conversation with her father. He had sounded just a little too keen to keep her in Marbella and away from Dublin. Had he already decided that Jack would assume responsibility for the company when he got back from his honeymoon? Would she return home to find her brother installed as managing director?

No, she thought. Her father would never be so devious. He had always played fair with her and treated her as an equal. He had expressed his dissatisfaction and disappointment with Jack many times. He would never allow him to take the reins of the company that he had so painstakingly built up for the simple reason that he knew he would destroy it.

She was mulling over these thoughts when her phone rang and she heard Charlie's voice.

'It's fixed. Sharkie Bolger's joining the band on a short-term contract. He's an excellent drummer, not as good as Pete Donohue but good enough to carry off this tour.'

'And how are the others behaving?'

'I've whipped them into line. If this tour has to be cancelled, they'll lose a lot of money too. Mind you, we have a lot of hard work ahead of us integrating him into the band's routine. But Sharkie's a fast learner. I think it's going to work, Piper.'

'So when can we expect you?'

'We finish the tour in Dublin, and the following morning I'm on a flight to Spain.'

'I've spoken to Dad and he's given me the go-ahead to stay here for another fortnight.'

'Great! What's that old Irish saying? "God never closes one door but He opens another"?'

'Sometimes God closes a door and it stays closed.'

'Not this time,' Charlie said, with a laugh.

They stayed on the beach till three o'clock, had lunch at the beach bar and returned to the hotel to spend the rest of the afternoon on the terrace. Sofía was thrilled that Charlie was coming after all and that she had two more weeks in Spain, and ran around, giddy with joy.

That evening they went to a pizza restaurant on the Paseo Maritimo. The place was a favourite with young people and was packed with children of all nationalities. Piper sipped her wine and gazed at the lights of the ships out at sea. She felt happier than she had for several days ... but a small doubt niggled at the back of her mind, something she couldn't put her finger on. She knew she wouldn't be completely happy till Charlie was with her once more.

***

The following morning, she was up early, had her swim, then breakfast. Afterwards she put on her grey business suit and presented herself at the manager's office behind the reception desk.

He was waiting for her. 'Some coffee, *Señora*, before we begin?'

'Lovely.'

He lifted the phone and gave the order. Five minutes later, there was a polite knock at the door and a maid entered with a tray. *Señor* Hernandez poured two cups.

'Now, *Señora*, I always begin each morning by checking the previous day's receipts and lodging them in the bank. We don't keep too much cash on the premises, for obvious reasons. There are some bad people in Marbella who would be very happy to relieve us of it. I have it here.' He pointed to a bulging canvas bag on the floor. 'Pedro and two of the security staff are entrusted with this task. I expect them at any moment.'

Just then, there was a knock at the door. Pedro and a couple of burly security staff entered. '*Buenos días, Señora, Señor,*' Pedro said, with a smile. 'Everything is ready?'

Hernandez pointed to the bag. Pedro picked it up and left.

'Next I check the roster to make sure that everyone has arrived for work. Today one maid and one chef are sick so I have to make arrangements to cover for them. The maid is easy to replace. It is very simple work. I will arrange for one of her colleagues to work extra and pay her overtime.'

'Is there much illness?' Piper asked.

'Not so much. The staff are quite dedicated. Sometimes people go sick because of a family problem, a child is not well or something of that kind. The chef, however, is more difficult. He has been sick for three weeks. I have had to hire a temporary chef to take his place.'

'What is the matter with him?'

Hernandez sighed. 'He is suffering from depression. I think he is unsuited for the job. Working in a kitchen is very demanding, as you probably know. Not everyone has the temperament for it. It is always busy and the atmosphere is hot and people shout a lot. But the pay is very good. However, it can get on some people's nerves.'

He sipped his coffee. 'Am I going too fast?'

'Not at all.'

'When I have finished these tasks, I next check the overnight log. This contains notes from the evening staff regarding problems that have arisen, guest complaints and so on. For instance, we have a blocked toilet in Room Twenty-Six. We have a complaint from the guests of Room Fifteen that the air-conditioning unit is not functioning properly. I will ask the technicians to look at them. We also have a request from the guests in Room Six to be moved to a room with a better view.'

'You're certainly kept busy, *Señor*.'

He smiled. 'These are my duties, *Señora*. Later I will make an inspection of the bar and the dining room to ensure everything is in order. Then I will deal with correspondence. We have a booking for a wedding in three weeks' time and we must attend to that immediately. And I also have a gentlemen's golf party requiring accommodation.'

'Aren't golf parties supposed to be rowdy?'

'Not ours. They are mainly retired gentlemen. They are gone by nine o'clock in the morning and don't return till six o'clock for dinner. Then they have a few drinks on the terrace and are in bed by ten o'clock to get ready for the following day. I can assure you they are perfect guests, *Señora.'*

Piper stayed with him till half past ten, then left to let him get on with his work. He had impressed her. She made a note to check what he was being paid and to recommend that her father increase his salary.

CHAPTER TWENTY-FOUR

Piper spent the remainder of the week with *Señor* Hernandez, watching him and making observations that she would later transcribe into a notebook. She quickly came to the conclusion that Hotel Azul was even more efficient than she had previously thought. A quick examination of the computer revealed that it was almost completely full right through the autumn and winter. They were clearly giving their clients what they wanted.

One day as she was having coffee on the bar terrace she glimpsed Pedro, whose demeanour told her he was upset about something. She called him over. 'What's the matter? You look like a bear with a sore head.'

'What does that mean, *Señora*?'

She reminded herself that many of the expressions which slipped effortlessly from her tongue were incomprehensible to foreigners. 'It means you look angry.'

'Well, it is true. I am angry.'

'Let me guess. Has this something to do with Carmencita?'

'You can read my mind, *Señora*.'

'It's not so difficult, Pedro. Please sit down. Let me buy you a coffee.'

He lowered himself into the chair beside her and wiped his brow. When the waiter arrived he asked for a strong black *cortado*.

'Now, why don't you tell me all about it?' she suggested.

He heaved a heavy sigh. 'Carmencita's father, he is a most difficult man. Always he argues with me. Always he makes me small. "You are only a driver," he says. "What kind of job is that? How can you expect my daughter marry a man with such a low profession?" I swear some day he will push me too far and I will murder him with my bare hands.'

'I'm sorry, Pedro.'

'Carmencita and me, we are thinking of running away together to Málaga and getting married without his permission. That would teach him a lesson.'

'But then you would have to give up your jobs.'

Pedro shrugged. 'We will find new ones. Carmencita is an excellent hairdresser, as you know. She has certificates of her qualifications. As for me, I can easily get another job. I could become a taxi driver.'

'But you like it here in Marbella. You would have to leave all your friends behind.'

Pedro sipped his coffee. 'We will make new friends.'

'Don't do anything rash, Pedro. You have a good, secure job here.'

'But what am I to do, *Señora*? Her father is a crazy man. He stops me marrying the woman I love.'

Suddenly Piper remembered the conversation she had

had with *Señor* Hernandez: one of the chefs had been off sick for the past three weeks. 'Tell me about when you trained to be a chef.'

'It was when I left school.'

'How long did you train for?'

'Three years.'

'But you didn't finish your training. Why?'

The pay was too low and I was in a hurry to earn better wages. It was a big mistake. If I had stayed for one more year, I would have qualified and now I would be earning very good money.'

'Did you actually do any cooking?'

'Most of my time was spent cooking. That is how you learn.'

'And did you like it?'

'I loved it.'

'You didn't find the heat and the pressure too much to bear?'

'I enjoyed all that excitement. When you are a true chef it is in your blood. The pressure is part of the experience. Why do you ask, *Señora*?'

'No particular reason.'

Over the next few days, an idea began to form in Piper's mind. But first, she had to check certain details. She went to see *Señor* Hernandez. He was effusively polite, as always.

'*Señora* McKenzie, what can I do for you?'

'Is the chef still sick?'

'Alas, it is so, *Señora*.'

'And you still have the temporary chef to replace him?'

'That is correct. It is not a very satisfactory situation

because the chef I hire has another job in the evening at a restaurant. Sometimes he is too tired to work and sometimes he doesn't come at all.'

'Now,' Piper said, 'how do a chef's wages compare with those of a driver?'

'You mean Pedro?'

'Exactly.'

The manager spread his hands. 'It is a lot more, maybe twice as much.'

'Did you know that Pedro trained for three years to become a chef but foolishly gave it up and now he regrets it?'

'No, *Señora*, I did not know that.'

'Would you do me a favour? It might work out to our benefit.'

'But of course.'

'Would you hire Pedro as a temporary chef?'

Hernandez looked surprised. 'It is a very busy kitchen, *Señora*.'

'I realise that. And if it doesn't work out, it can't be helped. Just give him an opportunity to show what he can do. You can explain that it is a temporary situation. If he proves up to the job, we might consider making it permanent. But we can leave that till later.'

'If you wish, I will do it immediately.'

'There is one other thing. You will need to find another driver.'

'That is not a difficulty. There is a porter called José who stands in for Pedro on his days off. He can do it.'

'So,' Piper said, with smile, 'it's all arranged. I'd be grateful if you'd let me know how Pedro works out, and we can discuss the situation again.'

'Very well, *Señora*.'

She didn't tell Pedro what she had done and pretended to be surprised when she met him a few days later. His frown was gone and he was like a man who had just been given the keys to a bank vault.

'You will never guess what has happened, *Señora*!'

'Tell me.'

'*Señor* Hernandez has asked me to take up duty in the kitchen. I am to be a chef.'

'Oh, that's brilliant, Pedro! I take it you're happy?'

'I am very happy, Carmencita also. Now my wages will double.'

'But you have to prove you can do the job, Pedro. It's hard work. You may not like it.'

'You forget that I have worked in kitchens before. I know what to expect. Do not worry, *Señora*. I will prove I am a good chef. This is the chance I have been hoping for.'

He went off whistling happily and Piper smiled. She continued to monitor his progress. She had recommended him: if he turned out not to be suitable, she would look bad.

She need not have worried. Each time she checked with Hernandez, he was full of praise for the new recruit: 'He is a most willing worker. He is never late. He works after hours. No job is too difficult for him. If I had some more workers like Pedro in the kitchen, I would be a very happy man.'

'But can he cook?'

'He is a magnificent cook. There is barely a dish that he can't prepare and he never has to ask for directions. And he has one other quality that is very rare in a chef. He is most even-tempered. He never gets angry. He never shouts or swears. He is a joy to work with. Believe me, I know. I have seen them all.'

***

Meanwhile, Charlie rang every day. The band's tour had kicked off in Paris to a full house, rapturous applause and rave reviews in the musical press. He was ecstatic about its reception. 'This is exactly what we needed, Piper, European exposure. It means the band will sell more CDs and their next concerts will draw bigger crowds. This tour will solidify their fan base. That's how it's done.'

'How is Sharkie fitting in?'

'The guy's a real pro. You'd think he was with the band for his entire career.'

'Well, I'm delighted for you, Charlie. You certainly worked hard for this success.'

'We all did, Piper. We mustn't forget the boys. They're the real talent.'

'Don't be so modest. You put them together and moulded them into a band.'

The tour moved on to Berlin where a similar reception awaited them. It was as if each concert sent out signals to the next date that this was a band not to be missed. By the time they got to Rome, hordes of disappointed fans were demanding tickets outside the venue. Already, music promoters were putting out feelers for another tour in a year's time.

But, happy as she was at the band's success, Piper's main focus was on the end of the tour when she would see Charlie again. The prolonged absence was proving to her just how much she loved him. She also kept in regular contact with her father. One morning while she was speaking to Henry, she dropped an idea into his head.

'You know that golf's very big on the Costa del Sol? The weather means that people can play all the year round and there are some fantastic courses.'

'I know all that.'

'I was speaking to Hernandez the other day and he told me he has a golfing party booked in.'

'You're kidding?' Henry sounded aghast. 'I know that crowd. They stay up half the night drinking and singing and keeping the other guests awake.'

'Not these ones. They're retired. In bed each night by ten o'clock and out all day on the fairways. Hernandez says they're ideal guests.'

'Well, that's a new one on me.'

'I've checked the computer. We're pretty well booked up through the autumn and winter but there are a few barren periods during the spring. I think we should promote packaged golfing holidays, but strictly for retired people. They could bring their spouses. It would be a good way to keep the rooms occupied.'

'Mmm,' Henry said. 'Let me think about it.'

'There's one other thing.'

'Yes?'

'I've checked what we're paying Hernandez. It's about half what a manager in one of our Irish hotels is getting. I suggest we give him a rise. He's well worth it. He's supremely efficient.'

'Piper, I sent you to Spain to make money for the company, not to give it away.'

She laughed. 'But this *will* make money for us. Remember what I told you before? You should see it as an investment in loyalty. People appreciate gestures like that. You don't want him being poached by some other hotel.'

'What do you suggest?'

'Raise what he's getting by fifty per cent.'

'My God, Piper, if you go on like that you'll bankrupt the company. But if you think he's worth it, go ahead.'

Her mother and Jo Ferguson were the other main contacts who kept her up to date with developments back home. One morning, as she was finishing breakfast on the terrace, she got an excited call from Rose to say that Jack and Corinne had returned from their honeymoon.

'They arrived unexpectedly yesterday afternoon. Jack spent a long time upstairs with your father and I was left to entertain your woman in the kitchen.'

'I'm sure you enjoyed that,' Piper said, mischievously.

'She's started to call me "Mum" now. It sets my teeth on edge, Piper. It's all I can do not to strangle her. She spent most of the time talking about the honeymoon – the wonderful food, the lovely weather, the beautiful scenery. To tell you the truth, I wish she'd stayed there.

'Then she was talking about the company. Seems she was able to get onto Jack's computer and look up the accounts.

204

According to Corinne, the company should be doubling its annual profit. She said McKenzie Leisure needs new thinking and new blood. She didn't say it outright but she hinted strongly that your father was no longer fit for the task. What she was really saying was that Jack should take over, which, of course, means her.'

'Did you tell Dad?'

'Are you kidding? He'd have a fit. But you've got to come home soon, Piper. We need you here to keep an eye on her. I can't be expected to do it all on my own.'

'Well, there's a slight difficulty with that. Dad's suggested I stay here for a while longer to keep out of Jack's way. He said he doesn't want us fighting. How is his general health?'

'Not good. He's very pale and tired.'

'Have you talked any more about the holiday I suggested?'

'I've tried to, but every time I mention it he changes the subject.'

'We've got to get him to go, Mum, whether he wants to or not. I'll come home with Charlie when the holiday's over. There's a very good manager in place at Hotel Azul so there's no urgent need for me to be here. I can hold the fort while you and Dad take a break. I'll be well able for it.'

'That'd be great, Piper.'

'But don't say anything to him. We'll present him with a *fait accompli*. We'll simply tell him to pack his bags and go.'

'You're a gem, Piper. What would we do without you?'

Piper laughed. 'You'd manage.'

***

205

The next few days went past in a blur of trips to the beach, picnics, lazy afternoons in the sun and constant demands from Sofía to know when her daddy was coming. Then, one evening, Piper received the phone call she had long been waiting for.

'It's me, Charlie. I'm ringing from Dublin. We had our homecoming concert last night. Sell-out. I can still hear the applause ringing in my ears. It was magic, Piper. The whole tour was a huge success.'

'Brilliant!'

'And I'm booked on the morning flight to Málaga. Expect me around midday.'

CHAPTER TWENTY-FIVE

Charlie emerged into the vast arrivals hall at exactly twelve thirty by the clock above the entrance. For a man who had just endured seven hectic nights of travelling and partying with a rock band, he looked remarkably well. There was a bright light in his eyes as he gathered his little girl up in his arms and kissed her while she squealed with delight.

'How have you been behaving while I was away? Have you been a good girl?'

'Yes, Daddy.'

'I've brought you a present, all the way from Paris.'

He put her down again and hunted in his luggage till he extracted a doll. Sofía grabbed it with glee. 'What do you say?'

'Thank you, Daddy.'

'You can start a collection,' Piper said. 'Now you've got a Spanish dolly and a French one plus the Irish ones you had already.'

Charlie turned to Margie and kissed her politely on the cheek. Then he swept Piper into his embrace and buried his face in her hair. 'It's so good to see you again. It was thinking about you that kept me going. Every night before I went to sleep, your face was the last thing in my mind.'

'Pull the other one,' Piper said, secretly pleased. 'I'll bet you were dancing till dawn.'

'I was always in bed by midnight. We had early starts, packing all the gear away and getting on the road each morning by eight. It was no picnic, I can assure you. I'm getting too old for this caper.'

'Well, it's wonderful to have you back with us. Now you can relax in the sun. And just wait till you see Hotel Azul! You'll love it.'

The new driver, José, was waiting patiently with a trolley for the luggage. Charlie helped him lift it on board and they set off for the exit and the car. José was older than Pedro and much less talkative, and within minutes they were speeding along the motorway in the direction of Marbella.

'You're here to relax,' Piper said. 'You do realise that? I'm thinking of confiscating your phone.'

'You can't do that,' Charlie said. 'You might as well chop my arm off. How would I operate?'

'I want you to spend your time with us, Charlie, so please discourage business calls. I take it the band all know you're on a break?'

'They've been told. But you don't have to worry about them. They'll be too busy chilling out and recuperating.'

'How's Pete Donohue?'

'He's been discharged from hospital.'

'So he's going to be all right?'

'Looks like it.'

'I'll bet he's sorry to have missed the tour.'

'You can say that again, particularly since it was such a huge success.'

'Well, do us all a favour, Charlie. Take a real break. Just work on your tan, have a few beers. You're on holiday now.'

'Yes, ma'am.'

Piper was thrilled to have Charlie beside her. Every so often, as the car sped towards its destination, she stole a peep at him. He was wearing a light casual suit with an open-necked shirt, and he was as handsome as ever.

Eventually they descended into Marbella and came to a halt in the forecourt of Hotel Azul. A couple of porters came scurrying out to help with the luggage while Charlie fumbled in his pockets for some change to tip them and the driver. Piper led the way to their flat at the rear of the building.

Charlie looked around the comfortable double bedroom, then opened the sliding doors and strode out onto the terrace, with its scarlet geraniums blazing in the sun, and gazed down at the sea, sparkling below. He took a deep breath and let out a contented sigh. 'This is perfect. No wonder you didn't want to come home.'

'I've arranged for Sofía to share Margie's room next door so we have this one all to ourselves.' She put her arms around his neck and gave him a passionate kiss. 'We have some romantic catching up to do, you and I. I've been lonely without you.'

'I've missed you too, Piper. Touring is a young man's game.'

'Are you hungry? Want some lunch?'

'Let me get unpacked first.' They went back inside where he opened his cases and began to take out his shirts.

'After lunch we can spend the afternoon by the pool, unless you want to go to the beach?'

At that moment, Sofía ran in to them. 'Let's go to the beach, Mummy!' she chirped. 'I want to show Daddy how I can build sandcastles.'

'The beach it is,' Charlie said. 'Now where does one get a shower around here?'

After he had changed into shorts and a golf shirt they went to the bar for lunch. While Margie and Piper contented themselves with sandwiches, Charlie ordered a large T-bone steak with onions and roast potatoes.

'Didn't they feed you on that tour?' Piper said, surprised.

'It was more like grazing,' Charlie replied. 'The main meal was breakfast, and after that it was snacks and sandwiches and whatever you could grab. You could say this is the first proper meal since before the thing started.'

Afterwards they headed for the beach, where they managed to rent loungers and umbrellas in a less crowded corner near the road. Sofía got busy with her bucket and spade and the adults applied sunscreen to themselves and the little girl.

Piper wanted to tell Charlie about the problems at home but this was not the time. He had been on the road for seven bruising nights and now he needed to rest. She could afford to wait a few days before she had a serious talk with him. Now she was determined they would enjoy some quality time together.

They spent the remainder of the afternoon reading and taking an occasional swim when they got too hot. At six o'clock they packed up their belongings and returned to the hotel.

'What about dinner?' Charlie asked enthusiastically. 'If

my memory serves, there's plenty of fine dining to be had around here.'

But nobody seemed particularly hungry so in the end they settled for a little Spanish restaurant not far from the hotel where Charlie had roast chicken and the others had a selection of tapas.

'You've certainly taken my advice,' Piper observed, as she poured some wine.

'How do you mean?'

'Your phone hasn't rung once since you got here.'

He smiled. 'That's because I've switched it to silent. Now you've reminded me to check it.'

A pile of texts and messages was waiting for him, some media requests for information about the band's future engagements, and concert promoters wanting to stage further events. 'Just give me a moment,' he said apologetically.

Piper frowned as he used the phone to ask someone to draw up a press release and send it to him for approval before it was released to the media. 'Who was that?' she asked, when he had finished.

'Your friend Alice McDowell. She's turned out to be a real treasure. She has the music hacks eating out of her hand.'

'Did you bring her on the tour with you too?'

'Of course. She was invaluable dealing with the foreign press. I wouldn't have survived without her. She speaks fluent French and Italian.'

'Bully for her,' Piper said, a little peeved that she hadn't been told earlier.

***

211

Sofía's eyes were drooping when they left the restaurant to make their way back to the hotel. Because of Charlie's arrival she had skipped her daily nap and now she was barely able to stay awake. Margie helped Piper put her to bed, and then the three adults sat on the terrace drinking wine for another hour. It was almost midnight when Charlie and Piper were finally alone in the bedroom.

He took her in his arms and covered her neck and mouth with hot kisses. Then she felt his hands on her thighs and pulling her loose dress up to her waist. With a deft movement he removed it, then her underwear.

She felt herself melt in his embrace and at once she was returning his caresses while their mouths remained glued together. Their lovemaking was fierce and passionate. When it was over, they lay side by side, bathed in sweat, as Charlie stroked her hair. 'I missed you so much,' he whispered. 'Next time we go on tour you'll have to come with me.'

'I don't think I'd like it,' Piper replied.

'You will. There's an adrenalin buzz on a tour that can't be got anywhere else, and then there are the parties – celebs and photographers, champagne flowing like water. You'll love every minute of it, Piper. It'll be just like the old days when we first met.'

'But I've got older and my tastes have changed. I've a child now and I may soon have to take on greater responsibilities with the company. Dad's working too hard and I'm worried about him. So is Mum. When I get back to Dublin we're going to persuade him to take a few weeks off at the villa in Nice.'

'I'm going to be busy too,' Charlie said. 'I have a plan

brewing but you must keep it quiet. Not a word to any of your friends in case it leaks to the media.'

'What?' she asked, raising herself on her elbow.

'Sharkie Bolger's a superb drummer. Now that the tour is over, I can't just let him go.'

By now Piper was intrigued. 'I don't understand. Pete Donohue's recovering, isn't he? You can't have two drummers in the same band.'

'No, but I can put together a new band built around Sharkie. That's my next project. When I'm back in Dublin, I'm going to start working on it.'

Piper's heart sank. 'Charlie, you can't do that. Hell's Kitchen takes up all your time as it is.'

'But what else do you expect me to do? If I let him go, someone else will snap him up. Where's the sense in that? I discovered him. It would be crazy to let some other manager reap all the rewards.'

'But then I'd never see you. I thought we'd agreed that you'd spend more time with me and Sofía.'

'Don't you see I've no option? I've got to do it.'

Piper felt a knot of tension tighten in her stomach. Charlie had just ruined their beautiful evening. She turned away from him and stared at the beams of moonlight seeping under the curtains. 'I wish you hadn't told me, Charlie.'

'I'm sorry, love. I thought you liked to know what I was up to at work.'

She decided not to mention it again for the remainder of the holiday. She would put it aside and enjoy the days that were left. But now she knew that trouble lay ahead.

***

The following morning as she was passing the manager's desk, *Señor* Hernandez stopped her. 'Can you spare a moment to talk with me, *Señora*?'

'Of course.'

They went into his office behind the desk.

'I have some news for you,' he said.

'Go on.'

'The chef has resigned.'

'The one who's been off sick?'

'Exactly. He called me this morning and said he had found another job working in a sandwich bar. Of course, the wages will be much smaller but there will be no pressure. We can offer his job to Pedro and make him permanent. But first I wanted to ask your permission.'

'Go right ahead and appoint him. You have my blessing.'

Later that afternoon, she ran into Pedro, who was grinning from ear to ear.

'I have been appointed full-time chef,' he said. '*Señor* Hernandez told me this morning. You have no idea what this means. Carmencita is delighted. Now her brute of a father can have no objection to our marriage.'

'Congratulations, Pedro. I hope you'll be happy in your job. But you must work hard and prove you're reliable. You mustn't let *Señor* Hernandez down.'

'You need not worry, *Señora*. This is my second chance. I will not allow this opportunity to fall through my fingers.'

The days slipped quickly away and the time approached for Charlie to return to work and the holiday to end. It was a blissful time: lovely bright mornings, warm sunny afternoons at the beach or the pool, balmy evenings spent eating and dancing beneath the stars. One morning, Piper sat down at her computer with a heavy heart and booked their flight to Dublin. She knew she would remember this holiday for as long as she lived.

When she had finished, she leaned back in her chair and gazed out of the window to the terrace where Charlie was drinking tea in the morning sun and Margie and Sofía were reading together.

Just then, her mobile phone rang. When she answered it she heard her mother's voice. She sounded distraught.

'Piper, thank God. I have terrible news. Your father's had a stroke.'

Chapter Twenty-Six

She felt a chill run through her bones. Her fingers gripped the phone as she forced herself to stay calm. But her heart was beating like a drum. 'Where is he?'

'At the hospital. That's where I'm calling you from.'

'What's the prognosis?'

'Nobody will tell me. They've taken him to the operating theatre. I'm waiting to hear.'

'Who's with you?'

'Jack and Corinne.'

From the window, she saw Charlie get up and stare at her.

'Tell me what happened.'

By now, her mother was weeping. 'You know how hard he's been working recently, twelve-, fourteen-hour days. But he just won't slow down, Piper, and he won't take advice. This morning when he got up, he went into the bathroom to use the shower. Then I heard a thud. When I went to see what had happened, I found him lying on the bathroom floor. His face was blue. At first I thought he was dead but then I saw he was still breathing and I rang the emergency services. They had an ambulance at the house in fifteen minutes and took him straight to the hospital.'

'Listen to me, Mum. He's in good hands. I'm on my way. Keep your phone switched on. I'll ring again as soon as I've got a flight today.'

Charlie had come into the room. He put an arm around her. 'Bad news?'

Her eyes brimmed with tears and she laid her head on his shoulder. 'Dad's just had a stroke.'

***

Charlie got on the Internet while Piper told Margie and Sofía that they had to go home immediately.

'Why, Mummy?'

'Granddad is sick. He's been taken to the hospital.' She looked at Margie and mouthed, 'Stroke.'

'Is he going to die, Mummy?'

Piper swallowed hard. This was very difficult. 'No, honey. The doctors are going to make him better. But we have to go home because Grandma needs us with her.'

Margie was already emptying drawers and wardrobes to pack the cases. It took Charlie half an hour to cancel the flight Piper had booked and make new reservations for that afternoon at two o'clock. It was now a quarter to eleven. Piper rang *Señor* Hernandez, explained that they had to return home suddenly and asked for a driver to take them to the airport.

'At once, *Señora*.'

Fifteen minutes later, they were piling into the car and Sofía was waving from the window. 'When are we coming back, Mummy?'

'As soon as we can.' She rang her mother again. 'We should be in Dublin at half past three, your time. With a bit of luck, I'll get to the hospital by four. Any more news?'

'No. The nurse says the doctor will talk to me as soon as there are any developments.'

'You have to be positive,' Piper said. 'They got him to hospital pretty fast. That's important. We'll be with you soon.'

***

The flight left on time. But it was only when Piper was strapped into her seat and saw the coast of Spain slip away that reality closed in. Her father had suffered a stroke. He might die or be left permanently disabled. One thing was certain: if he survived, he would never again be able to work as before.

She closed her eyes. Henry McKenzie was the kindest man she had ever known. He could be tough when it came to business but love, decency and fairness shone out from everything he did. Now his body had failed him and he was at death's door.

She knew the stroke had been coming for some time. He had been working too hard, concerned about the company, worrying about the family and the rift between herself and Jack. She remembered how pale and unhealthy he had looked the last time she saw him.

She should have disregarded his instructions to stay in Marbella, out of her brother's way. She should have been with her father, shouldering her share of the burden. She should have put her foot down and insisted that he take a holiday in Nice. She should have been helping him, instead of indulging herself in Spain. Now it was too late. He was lying in a hospital bed fighting for his life.

She felt Charlie's protective arm surround her and draw her close. 'I let him down,' she said.

'Don't blame yourself.'

'I should have been with him.'

'That wouldn't have changed anything. Your father is the way he is. He drives himself too hard and always has. That was how he was able to build up McKenzie Leisure from nothing.'

She laid her head on her husband's chest and let him comfort her. Thank God she had his support at this terrible time.

***

It was twenty past three when the plane landed in Dublin, slightly ahead of schedule. By the time they were outside in the fresh air, it was ten to four. Thankfully, there were taxis waiting. Margie suggested that she should take Sofía home and Piper readily agreed. They left in the first taxi, then Charlie and Piper climbed into a second.

'How do you feel now?'

'Frightened.'

'I heard you earlier telling your mother to be positive. Now it's time to apply the same advice to yourself. Somebody has to take charge of the situation. And that somebody should be you.'

He was right. Her mother was too shaken by what had happened, while Jack and Corinne would be useless. She had to appear strong and in control or they would all go to pieces.

Twenty minutes later, they were at the hospital. Charlie grasped her hand and together they walked into the crowded reception area. Piper strode quickly to the desk and introduced herself. 'I'm here to see my father, Henry McKenzie. He was brought to the hospital this morning suffering from a stroke.'

The receptionist tapped the information into her computer. 'Mr McKenzie has been taken to the Intensive Care Unit.'

'My mother is there already. Is it all right for us to join her?'

'Of course.' She gave Piper directions and they set off along the busy hospital corridors till they arrived at the ICU.

They found Jack, Corinne and Rose huddled together in the waiting room. Jack glanced up as Piper and Charlie came in. His eyes met his sister's briefly and then he looked away. Her mother stood up and Piper hugged her. 'Any more news?' she whispered.

'No.'

'Have any of the medical staff spoken to you?'

'Not yet. We're waiting to speak to the consultant.'

'Okay,' Piper said. 'Why don't you take a break? Go to the canteen. You look like you could use a strong cup of tea. Charlie and I will hold the fort.'

They left, and she lowered herself wearily into one of the chairs. Charlie sat down beside her. 'Remember what I said. You've got to be positive. He's alive and he's in one of the best hospitals in the country. He's got a top specialist working on him. I'd rate all that as pretty good.'

Eventually the others returned to resume their vigil. Piper sat beside her mother. It was now five o'clock and Rose had been waiting there for seven hours.

Time passed very slowly but at last they heard footsteps approach along the corridor outside and the door opened. A tall, thin man in a white coat came in. There was a badge at his breast pocket, which read: Dr Michael Bradford. Piper thought he looked quite young. She had been expecting someone older.

'Mrs McKenzie?' he asked.

Rose began to get up. 'Please remain seated,' the doctor said, and sat down beside her. He nodded briefly to the others and began to speak in a comforting tone. 'Your husband has suffered what is known as an ischaemic stroke. It's caused by a blood clot that has lodged in his brain. I have to be honest with you. He may not survive. We're working to save his life but it will be some time before we know if we've been successful.'

Rose began to sob.

'We're doing everything we can. You're welcome to stay here if you wish but I suggest the best thing is to go home and call the hospital in the morning. We have your contact details if there's any change in your husband's condition.' He stood up, shook hands with each of them and then he was gone.

Piper glanced at her mother. Silent tears were streaming down her cheeks. 'C'mon,' she said. 'Let's go.'

Jack had left his car in the parking area. On the way out, Charlie offered to come with them but Piper shook her head. 'There's no point. You go home to Sofía. I'll stay with Mum tonight and keep her company.'

'Are you sure?'

'I'll be all right. I'll keep in touch.'

Charlie hugged her, then left to find a cab. Piper sat in the back seat of Jack's car with her mother and they set off for Howth.

No one spoke. Everyone was tired, apprehensive and wrapped up in their own thoughts. Even Corinne had nothing to say and sat quietly, staring out of the window. When at last they reached Elsinore, Piper led her mother into the sitting room and asked if she would like something to eat.

'I'm not hungry,' she said wearily. 'I'll just watch television for a while.'

'Then I'll make some tea.' She went into the kitchen and filled the kettle. She was plugging it in when she heard the door open. She turned to see Jack enter the room. There was a grim look on his face.

'I want to talk to you,' he said.

'What about?'

'The company, of course. Someone has to run the show now Dad's ill. You heard what the doctor said. He may not survive.'

Piper had been expecting this conversation but not quite so soon. 'You don't have to worry about it. I'll take responsibility.'

'No, you won't!'

She stopped and faced her brother. 'Let's not argue about it now, Jack. Can't it wait?'

'I'm afraid not. Someone has to make the decisions.'

He took out a piece of paper and offered it to her. 'Those are Dad's instructions, written in his own hand. He has given me authority to take control of McKenzie Leisure.'

CHAPTER TWENTY-SEVEN

She snatched the note from her brother. It was typed on company letterheading. With each word she read, her heart sank.

> *I, Henry McKenzie, hereby authorise my son, Jack McKenzie, to assume the position of managing director of McKenzie Leisure in the event of my illness or incapacity. He will have complete control including the day-to-day running of the company and all decision-making.*
> *Signed*
> *Henry McKenzie*

It was dated a few days after she had left for Spain.

'You said the instructions were written in his own hand. This is typed.'

'Yes, but that's his signature. You can check it, if you want.'

'I don't even know if it's legal. There are no witnesses.'

Jack waved her objections aside. 'You're quibbling. This letter makes it plain that he wanted me to take control in the event of anything happening to him. And now it has.'

'Why did he sign it?'

'Why do you think? I'm his son and heir. He was worried about his health. He hadn't been feeling well. He was complaining of tiredness. You were holidaying in Spain at the time.'

He paused to let the remark sink in.

'Shortly after you left, he brought me into his study and said he wanted to make sure the company would be in safe hands if he was taken ill. Maybe he had a premonition. But there it is, plain as a pikestaff. He's put me in charge of running the company. It's what he wanted, Piper.'

She didn't know how to respond. It looked as if he was right. But why had her father done this? He had always been fair with her, and she had assumed she would inherit control of McKenzie Leisure with her brother whenever her father stepped down. Now it appeared she had been presumptuous.

'Okay, Jack, if that's what he wants. I'll discuss it with you in the morning.'

But her brother was shaking his head. He looked triumphant. 'There's nothing to discuss, Piper. This letter gives me the authority to take decisions. I'm starting now. I have decided that you will play no further role in McKenzie Leisure.'

***

That night she couldn't sleep. It was one of the worst nights she had ever endured. Her principal concern was her father's health but now there was the added bombshell of the letter Jack had given her. All night she tossed and turned, consumed with worry.

What had happened to change her father's mind? She thought of the numerous conversations she'd had with him, his encouragement, the confidence he had expressed so often in her abilities. It was as if there was an unwritten agreement between them. He knew Jack's limitations and was aware of Corinne's ambition and the corrosive influence she exerted over him. Why had he signed that letter?

And the doctor had told them her father might die. Even if he survived, he might be incapacitated and unable to care for himself. She shuddered as she thought of him lying unconscious, hooked up to monitors and drips, as the doctors fought to save his life.

And then there was her mother. She had been there when it happened. What terrible agonies of grief and doubt must she now be suffering? Another thought struck her. What would happen if the media got hold of the story? The last thing she wanted was to have this family tragedy splashed all over the newspapers. She made a mental note to ring Charlie in the morning and ask his advice. Around five she fell into an exhausted sleep. When she woke, it was seven o'clock and she could hear someone moving about the house.

She got up and found her mother in the kitchen in her dressing-gown. She was nursing a cup of tea, and looked old, haggard and drawn. Piper poured a cup for herself and sat down beside her. 'Did you get any sleep?' she asked.

'No. I spent the whole night praying. If he survives this, I'm taking him on a pilgrimage to Lourdes.'

'That can't do any harm.'

'What about you?'

'I dozed for a couple of hours, that's all.'

'Do you think it's too early to ring the hospital?'

'I'll do it. Why don't you make us some breakfast? It'll help take your mind off things.'

She went back to her bedroom and rang the number they had been given. She got the ward sister, who was coming off duty. She informed Piper that there had been no change in her father's condition and suggested she ring again in a couple of hours, after the doctors had examined him. When she returned to the kitchen, her mother had set out two plates of ham and eggs. Piper was pleased to see she had begun on hers.

'Well?'

'There's no change.'

Rose sighed. Piper sat beside her. 'Try to see it as progress, Mum. Every hour that he stays alive is a gain. Every breath he takes is progress.'

Her mother raised her head till she was looking straight into Piper's eyes. 'Tell me honestly what you think.'

'That he'll pull through. He's strong and he's a fighter. He won't give in easily.'

'But yesterday the consultant said—'

Piper interrupted her: 'Doctors are always cautious. It's their nature. They're afraid to say too much in case things go wrong and they get into trouble. We're different. We have no choice but to be hopeful.'

'You think so?'

'Yes, I do. You just keep on praying and looking on the bright side.' Piper picked up her knife and fork, and got on with her breakfast. She had not only convinced her mother, she had also convinced herself. She could feel it in the deepest recesses of her heart. Her father was going to survive and he was going to come back to them with his health restored.

She returned to her bedroom and got under the shower. The hot water seemed to revive her spirits further. She washed her hair, dried and brushed it, then chose a dress for the day. She added a touch of makeup – always good for morale. She was just finishing when the phone rang. It was Charlie.

'Any news about your dad?'

'No change.'

'How about your mother?'

'I'm trying to convince her to keep her spirits up.'

'Good. Just to put your mind at ease, Sofía slept well last night but she keeps asking when you're coming home.'

'I'll call and see her later today when I've been to the hospital.'

'Perfect. There is something you should bear in mind, Piper. This could be a long ordeal. A stroke is serious. You do know that?'

'Of course, but I have to keep looking on the bright side. Otherwise I'll go insane. There are a couple of other things I need to talk about.'

'Go on.'

'I'm worried about the media getting hold of the story. Can you imagine how they'd turn it into a circus?'

'You're right,' he replied. 'The bastards would have a field day. I'll ring Alice and ask her to talk to you and prepare a statement in case we get any enquiries.'

'There's something else.'

'Yes?'

She swallowed hard. 'I've been fired from the company.'

Charlie gasped. 'Fired? Are you serious?'

'Perfectly serious.'

'How did that happen?'

She explained about the letter her father had written, giving Jack power to run McKenzie Leisure and make decisions.

'I don't believe it,' Charlie said.

'It's true. I have the letter. It has my father's signature.'

'I can't believe your brother would do something like that, not at a time like this.'

'You don't know him as well as I do.'

'This doesn't sound right. There's something fishy about it. Was your father in a proper frame of mind when he signed this document?'

'I have no idea. All I know is what Jack told me. He said Dad told him he was worried about the company in case anything happened to him. It was shortly after I left for Spain.'

'Was the letter witnessed by a solicitor or some legal representative?'

'No.'

'I don't like the sound of it, Piper. You can't be fired just like that, not without good reason. What are you going to do about it?'

'I don't know if there's anything I *can* do.'

'Fax the letter across to me and I'll get my lawyers to look at it. You don't need this on top of everything else. Put it out of your mind and concentrate on your father. And ring me whenever you hear any news.'

She felt better now that she'd spoken to Charlie. She returned to the kitchen and helped her mother to clear up, then waited till ten o'clock and rang the hospital again. She was put through to the ward and was told that her father's condition had stabilised.

'Does that mean he's out of danger?'

'I can't comment on that,' the nurse replied.

'But it means he's not going to die?'

'You really need to speak to Dr Bradford,' the nurse said. 'He's the only person who can give you that information.'

'Is he there now? Can I talk to him?'

'He's in surgery.'

'Can we come out to the hospital?'

'Certainly. But there may be no further news.'

'It doesn't matter. We'd like to come.'

Piper turned to her mother, who had been sitting patiently at the kitchen table, listening to the conversation. 'We're going to the hospital,' she said.

She rang Charlie again and agreed to meet him there. Then she got into her mother's car and they set off.

'What did they tell you?' her mother asked.

'His condition has stabilised.'

'That just means it's the same.'

'No, it doesn't. It means it's not getting any worse. Remember what I told you, Mum. Every day he survives is a victory.'

She had decided not to tell her mother about the incident with Jack. She knew it would only upset her more. The most important thing now was her father and his survival. The fight over McKenzie Leisure could be put off till later.

Charlie was waiting for them and they walked together to the Intensive Care Unit. The waiting room was empty. A few minutes later the door opened and a nurse came in. 'Mrs McKenzie?'

'Yes,' Rose replied.

'If you follow me, Dr Bradford will have a word with you.'

The consultant had an office further along the corridor. When they entered, they found him seated behind a desk stacked with charts and cardboard folders.

'Good morning,' he said, standing up and shaking hands with them all. His next words brought a tremble to Rose's lips. 'I have some news for you, Mrs McKenzie.'

'Yes?'

The doctor ran his fingers through his fair hair and glanced at his watch as if to confirm the time. 'Exactly forty-seven minutes ago, your husband opened his eyes.'

Rose took out a handkerchief and dabbed away a tear, but for Piper, the words were a burst of hope. This was the first piece of good news she had heard in the past twenty-four hours. Beside her, Charlie squeezed her hand.

Dr Bradford was smiling. 'I appreciate that this has been a very difficult time for you all so I'm pleased to give you what is basically a very positive development.'

'Is he going to survive?' Rose asked.

'Let's say the indications are good. However, I must caution against raising your expectations too far. He's not out of the woods yet. There's still a long road ahead of him.'

'But he's not going to die?'

'Mrs McKenzie, only the Good Lord can decide that. But your husband is a tough man with a strong will to live.'

There was something else Piper needed to ask. 'Has he suffered any impairment?'

The doctor turned to her. 'That's difficult to say. We have to carry out further tests.'

'Can we see him?' Rose asked.

Dr Bradford lifted a phone on his desk and spoke to someone. A few minutes later the door opened again and a nurse entered. 'Would you mind taking the family to Mr McKenzie's room, Nurse? They have my permission to sit with him.'

Rose grasped the doctor's hand. 'Thank you,' she said, 'for everything you've done. You've no idea what it means to us.'

'I think I have, Mrs McKenzie.'

Chapter Twenty-Eight

The moment she entered the room, Piper recoiled in shock. She barely recognised her father. The strong, fit man she had known all her life had been reduced to a shadow. His face was gaunt and his cheeks were sunken. The skin on his hands and face was the colour of putty. Drips were attached to his arms and nose. Only the gentle rise and fall of the sheets covering his chest indicated that he was still alive.

But, despite the shock, she felt good. Dr Bradford had said her father was tough. He was going to survive. And not merely survive but recover and get better, walk and talk like the Henry McKenzie she knew and loved. She looked at Charlie and he punched the air with his fist. He put his arm around her shoulders and kissed her cheek. 'Your father's a fighter,' he whispered. 'It'd take more than a stroke to knock him out. I'll lay odds he'll be sailing his yacht around Lambay Island in a couple of weeks' time.'

Piper and her mother exchanged a glance. 'You're wrong about that, Charlie,' Rose said.

'No, I'm not.'

'He won't be sailing any yachts. As soon as he gets out of this hospital, I'm taking him to Nice for a long recuperation.'

***

Eventually Charlie left to return to work. Piper and her mother stayed at the hospital for several hours until Dr Bradford arrived to carry out some further tests. On the way home, the atmosphere in the car was in marked contrast to what it had been earlier in the day. Now the mood was much lighter. Rose was recovering some of her spirit and could barely conceal her delight at the news they had heard.

'I wonder if we should ring Jack and Corinne and tell them,' she said. 'They weren't at the hospital. They mightn't know.'

'Let them find out for themselves. How do you feel?'

'Over the moon.'

'When we get back to Elsinore, I'm going to give you a sedative and put you to bed. You need a good sleep. After that, I'm going home. I haven't seen Sofía since last night. She knows her granddad's ill and I don't want her getting upset.'

The house was empty when they arrived, with no sign of Jack or Corinne. Piper began to wonder where they might be. But she had no time to think more about it. She led her mother to her bedroom, helped her get undressed and watched while she swallowed a sleeping tablet with a glass of water. 'You'll feel much better when you wake. I'll ring you later.' She bent and kissed her mother's brow. 'Everything's going to be fine, Mum. Your prayers have been answered.'

She had barely returned to Sandymount when her phone started to ring. It was Charlie. 'How's your mum?'

'Sleeping, I hope. I put her to bed with a sedative.'

'Good idea. Does she know about this development with Jack?'

'No. I decided she had enough on her plate.'

'Any calls from the media?'

'No.'

'So far, so good. If anyone calls about your dad, you must refer them directly to Alice McDowell. She's prepared a press statement, which says he's in hospital undergoing some tests. On no account speak to them yourself.'

'What if they ring the hospital?'

'The hospital will tell them nothing. Patients' medical information is strictly confidential.'

'Okay.'

'Now, about this letter your brother gave you. I've shown it to my legal people and they tell me you have good grounds to challenge it.'

'How do I do that?'

'First, there are no independent witnesses. Second, there's the question of your father's state of mind. We know he had a stroke coming on. He might not have had complete control of his faculties when he signed that document. Then there is the matter of duress.'

'Duress? How do you mean?'

'How do we know he wasn't bullied or coerced into signing?'

Piper thought of her father. He wasn't the sort of man to be bullied into anything he didn't want to do. But if he was already sick when he signed the letter? What if Jack had taken advantage of him?

'There's more,' Charlie continued. 'I'm told that Jack can't simply dismiss you without adequate grounds. At the very least, you would be entitled to compensation. I'm told the law allows you to challenge that too. And you would have very good prospects of success.'

'Good! I'm really grateful to you, Charlie, for finding all this out.'

'I thought it might cheer you up. Now, I'm planning to get away early from work this evening to be with you. Maybe we could have a family meal together. We could send out for pizza or something. Sofía would like that. You've no plans to visit the hospital again this evening?'

'I'll call later and take Mum tomorrow.'

'Okay. Expect me around six. Love you.'

'Me too.' She ended the call. It was at times like this that Charlie was a rock of common sense and dependability. She wondered how she would have coped with this situation if he hadn't been around, and shuddered.

She felt someone tugging at her dress and looked down to see Sofía's little face peering up at her. 'Is Granddad better, Mummy?'

'Almost, honey.'

'Tell him I love him.'

***

It soon became clear that Henry was over the critical stage of the stroke, but progress was slow. Piper drove her mother to the hospital each day and they sat beside the bed while Henry's dull eyes stared at them without recognition. Then, one afternoon, a few weeks later, Dr Bradford drew them aside and delivered some more good news. 'We've concluded all our tests on your father and I'm pleased to confirm there will be no lasting damage.'

'Does that mean what I hope it does?' Rose asked excitedly.

'Yes, Mrs McKenzie. Your husband will be able to function like any normal person.'

'And his brain?'

'His brain will be fine.'

Rose turned to Piper and they threw their arms around each other.

'When?' Piper asked.

The doctor shrugged. 'We've just got to be patient. But he's definitely on the road to recovery.'

Suddenly his progress seemed to move up a notch. Every time they visited, he seemed better. His complexion returned to normal. He no longer looked like the pale ghost that had greeted them the first time they had seen him.

Then came the morning when the drips and tubes were removed and Henry was well enough to be offered solid food. Rose and Piper sat beside the bed and Rose held his hand. She began talking to him in a soft, scolding voice. 'You've got to pull yourself together, Henry McKenzie, do you hear me? You've given us all a terrible shock. This is no way to be carrying on, a man of your age, scaring the daylights out of us. We want you home with us, where you belong. So, you just listen to me. You'd better buck up and get well pretty damned quick.'

She continued to talk. Her husband stared at them with glassy eyes. Then Rose gave a sudden cry of triumph. 'Did you see that?' she asked Piper.

'What?'

'He squeezed my fingers. He knows who we are. He responded. It's only a matter of time till he starts talking.'

***

Meanwhile, Piper was concerned about Jack and Corinne. They had not been in touch since the day of her father's stroke. At first, she had believed her brother was too busy exerting his new-found authority as managing director of McKenzie Leisure. But that had been several weeks ago. Since then, he hadn't rung the house or talked to her mother. Whenever Piper visited the hospital, neither he nor Corinne was there. She grew suspicious.

One day as they were leaving, she stopped to speak to the ward sister. 'Has my brother been to see my father recently?'

'I'd need to check that with my colleagues.'

'Have *you* seen him?'

She looked embarrassed. 'No,' she said.

'Thank you,' Piper replied. She found it hard to believe that Jack could be so callous. She knew that relations between her father and brother had not been good, but to ignore Henry while he lay in hospital seriously ill was unbelievable, particularly since Henry had signed over the company to him. However, she had little time to think about it. The next time she visited the hospital with her mother, they found her father's room empty.

She asked the nurse and was told that he was with the physiotherapist. 'You mean he can walk?'

'Not yet,' the nurse replied. 'He has to undergo a course of exercises to strengthen his muscles. But I would expect it any day now.'

Piper and Rose waited till he returned from the physiotherapy session. He was helped into the room by two nurses and put to bed. He gave a sigh and sank back on the pillows. His eyes shifted from his wife to his daughter and back again. They saw his chest expand. He took a deep breath. His mouth opened and he struggled to speak.

'Hello,' he said.

***

Within a fortnight, he was walking again, moving his legs slowly and stumbling a little but definitely walking. Before long, he had recovered his speech and was able to talk properly to them. Each day seemed to bring another leap in his recovery. He could feed and shave himself. He got out of bed and sat in a chair. He began to grow restless and demanded to go home. But that took a while longer.

One day, Dr Bradford took Piper and her mother aside. 'Your husband has made a wonderful recovery,' he said to Rose. 'He's an amazing man. I don't mind telling you that I didn't rate his chances very highly at the beginning but I'm delighted to be proved wrong.'

'It's down to you and the hospital staff,' Rose said. 'We can't thank you enough.'

'Our job is to do our best, Mrs McKenzie.' He paused. 'This

239

is a good time to raise another issue. You must understand that he will never be able to work again as hard as he did. He may be strong-willed but his body is ageing. The stroke was a warning. He must slow down. He must learn to let go and relax.'

***

At last the day arrived that everyone had been waiting for. Two months after he had been admitted, Dr Bradford announced that Henry was now fit enough to be discharged from hospital. 'Remember everything I've told you. You're to take things easy and not get excited. I have to be perfectly blunt with you. You can't continue working the way you were or it will only be a matter of time before you're back in here. And next time you might not be so lucky. Do you understand?'

Henry nodded.

'The only time I want to see you in this hospital is for check-ups.'

Henry was given medication to control his blood pressure and cholesterol and a stern warning to establish an exercise regime and eat healthier food. Dr Bradford also said he wanted to review his progress at regular intervals, but for now he was free to go.

Charlie came with his car and drove them back to Howth. It was October and the leaves in the garden were turning brown. They sat on the patio and looked out over Dublin Bay. Henry smiled and sipped the tea Piper had made while he watched Sofía run around the lawn. 'Isn't life wonderful?' he said. 'To think I nearly lost all this.'

'But now you can enjoy it again,' Piper said. 'You've been given a second chance.'

'And I intend to seize it with both hands.' He looked at each of them in turn. 'I've been blessed to have you. No man could wish for a better wife and daughter.'

Rose's eyes filled with tears. 'I'm going to make a donation to the hospital,' he continued. 'I'm giving them a million euros. They can use it to buy new equipment. They saved my life. I owe it to them.'

Piper looked at the sun sparkling off the sea. She felt her heart overflow with joy. But she knew that while one battle had ended, another was about to begin. This one would be for control of McKenzie Leisure.

CHAPTER TWENTY-NINE

Piper knew that she couldn't ignore the fall-out from Jack's action for ever. At some stage she would have to bring it to her father's attention. But she decided to wait till Henry was stronger. However, time was not on her side and events were about to catch up with her.

One day, shortly after Henry had come home from hospital, she answered the landline in the kitchen. It was Ed Brannigan, the manager of the Majestic Hotel.

'Hello, Piper,' he began. 'How's your dad?'

'He's very well, Ed. He's doing everything the doctor tells him.'

'I knew he'd pull through. He's one of the old school, tough as old boots.'

'Do you want to speak to him?'

'I won't disturb him, Piper. It's your brother I'm looking for.'

'Jack doesn't live here, Ed. I can give you his number.'

'I've tried it already but he's not answering. I need to talk to him urgently.'

'What's the problem?'

'I have several suppliers demanding payment for goods and I need Jack to countersign the cheques.'

'Why don't you get a courier to bring them out here? I'll ask my father to do it.'

'That would be brilliant. When's he coming back to work?'

'It could be some time, Ed. He has to take things easy.'

'The sooner the better, if you ask me. We miss him, Piper. Tell him I was asking for him.'

She hung up with a feeling of unease. Ed Brannigan had been tactful but there was no escaping the note of disapproval in his voice about Jack's performance. The cheques arrived, and Piper brought them to her father where he was reading in his study and got him to sign them.

A few days later there was another development and this was more serious. She was in the kitchen with her mother when her father appeared in the doorway. He looked angry. 'I don't suppose you know where your brother is?' he demanded.

'Now, you're not supposed to get upset,' Rose said. 'What's the matter?'

'I've just had Campbell on the phone. That damned fool Jack was supposed to have a meeting with him and young O'Brien this morning to go over the books and he didn't show up. He never even sent any apology or explanation. This is not good enough.'

Piper knew her father placed great faith in his company's accountants. She had once heard him say that he would trust Campbell with his life.

He turned on Piper. 'What are you doing standing here? Why aren't you helping to run the company? Why aren't you keeping an eye on that fool brother of yours?'

This was the moment of truth. 'I don't work for the company any more.'

'What are you talking about?'

'Jack dismissed me.'

Henry stared at her with incomprehension. 'Jack did what?'

'He gave me a letter you signed placing him in charge of the company in the event of your illness or incapacity and giving him authority to make decisions. The first decision he took was to dismiss me.'

'How dare he?' Rose was furious.

'I never signed any such document,' her father said.

'I have it, Dad. It has your signature.'

'Why would I do such a thing? It doesn't make sense.'

He furrowed his brow and tried to concentrate. 'There was one day before I had the stroke when he came to my study with a pile of papers to sign. I was very tired and you were in Marbella. He said they were urgent invoices that required my signature.'

'You think he might have slipped the document in among the other papers?'

'I can't think of any other explanation. I would never have given him control of the company. I would never have allowed him to dismiss you. Why didn't you tell me about this sooner?'

'Because you were ill and I didn't want to upset you.'

'We have to get it sorted out immediately before he does any more damage. Where is he?'

'I've no idea. I haven't seen him or Corinne for weeks.'

'Get on the phone immediately and try to find him. Tell him I want to see him at once. He'd better have some damned good explanations.'

He left the room, his face red with fury, and they heard him returning upstairs to his study. This was what the doctor had warned them about and what Piper had tried to avoid – getting her father excited. But now there was no avoiding it.

Piper took out her phone and rang Jack's number but got no response. Next she tried the solicitor's office where Corinne worked but the young woman who answered said that Mrs McKenzie was away on leave. Had she left a number at which she could be contacted in case of an emergency?

'I'm afraid not.'

It looked like she had run into a brick wall. A dark thought began to form in Piper's mind. She went up to her father's study. 'I can't get hold of him or Corinne.'

'The idiot!' Henry seethed. 'How is he supposed to run a company if nobody can get in touch with him?'

'There's only one thing to do,' she said.

'What?'

'I'm going over to their apartment.'

'I'll come with you,' her father replied.

They got into Piper's car and set off along the coast road for Portmarnock. The ground-floor apartment Jack and Corinne had bought was in a magnificent development, overlooking the beach, but when they arrived, no one was at home. After ringing the bell several times, they gave up. Piper peered through the windows. The place looked deserted.

She went round to the back and found one tiny window open but it was too small to squeeze through. She broke a branch from a tree, climbed onto the sill and, using the branch, managed to dislodge the clasp from the main window. She pushed it open and climbed into the room.

It appeared to be an office. There was a desk, an executive chair and a large filing cabinet. In the corner of the room there was a shredding machine, its bin overflowing with strips of paper. By now, Piper's fears were growing. She opened the front door and let her father in. Together they searched the remaining rooms.

All the furniture remained, but the wardrobes were practically empty of clothes. Piper knocked on the doors of the neighbouring apartments and eventually a young woman emerged to tell them she hadn't seen Jack or Corinne for weeks.

'Did they say they were going away?' Piper asked.

'No,' the woman replied, 'and I was pretty friendly with them, particularly her. I think if they were going away she would have told me.'

Piper thanked her and returned to the car. 'Something's not right,' she said. She rang several of the hotel managers but no one had seen or heard from Jack. When she told her father, his face turned pale. He insisted on returning immediately to Elsinore. On the way he rang Peter Campbell. 'I've got a serious problem on my hands. Can you meet me at my home in half an hour?'

They spoke for several minutes. When he had finished the call, Henry's face was dark. He didn't speak for the remainder of the journey back to Howth, and when they arrived, he went straight to his study, Piper at his heels. He sat down at his computer and began trawling through various company accounts.

'What are you looking for?' she asked.

His face was grim. 'Something I hope I don't find.'

Eventually the accountant arrived and was shown up to Henry's study. Piper went back downstairs and joined her mother in the kitchen.

'Will somebody tell me what the hell is going on?' Rose asked.

'Jack and Corinne's apartment in Portmarnock has been empty for weeks and no one knows where they are.'

Rose's mouth fell open. 'You're not suggesting ...?'

Piper nodded. 'It looks like they've done a runner.'

It was several hours before Henry and the accountant finally came downstairs. Henry looked defeated and was on the verge of tears. Rose immediately went to him and put her arm around him.

'I've got bad news,' he said. 'There are almost two million euros missing from the company accounts.'

Piper was shocked. 'Where has it gone?'

'God knows.'

'What are you going to do? Should we contact the police?'

'No.' Henry brought his fist down hard on the table. 'This matter stays right here in this room. I couldn't live with the scandal if word got out. The very thought that my own son would do something like this is impossible for me to contemplate. We must tell no one.'

Piper sat down beside him and stroked his hand. Anger surged through her. For her brother to do this at all was scandalous, but to do it now, when her father was recovering from a serious illness, was beyond words. 'I blame Corinne,' she said. 'I've never trusted her. She's a schemer. She's completely dominated him.'

He turned his sad face to her. 'That may be true, but it was Jack who stole the money. Nobody held a gun to his head. He must take full responsibility.' He clasped her hand and she felt him shake with emotion.

'I'll put the money back from my personal account,' he said. 'That way everything will balance and, hopefully, this wrongdoing will never be discovered. Meanwhile, someone has to run the company. I had always hoped you would have time to work your way in and learn the business, but there's no one else.' He looked straight into her face. 'Are you ready to assume control of McKenzie Leisure?'

She drew him close. She could feel the blood rushing to her head at the dizzying prospect. 'Of course,' she said.

CHAPTER THIRTY

At the age of twenty-nine, Piper became one of the youngest managing directors in the country. It made the news, but mainly on the business pages where it belonged. The gossip columns didn't consider it sexy enough when compared to celebrities going into rehab or breaking up with their partners.

That suited her perfectly. She wanted to stay out of the limelight while she concentrated on getting to grips with the company. She recalled her father's words about keeping her private life separate from the company. It was good advice and she was determined to put it into practice.

When she rang Charlie to tell him the news, he was a little dubious. 'I always knew this day would come, Piper, and naturally I'm delighted for you. But it'll cause problems. Both of us are going to be working at full throttle. How will that affect Sofía?'

Piper had thought about this. Sofía would soon be five and ready to start school. She also had Margie, who was like a second mother to her. 'Don't worry, Charlie. I'm sure I'll find some free time. We'll work something out.'

While she was a little nervous of the task she had been asked to take on, she was grateful for one thing: that the company would remain in the family's hands. It had cost McKenzie Leisure two million euros to be rid of Corinne, but now Piper could run the firm without having constant fights with her brother and permanent worry about Corinne's interference.

She decided to take over her father's office and work from Elsinore. It had several advantages. All the company's records were stored there and she would have Henry on hand for advice and guidance. Piper was under no illusion that she would be relying heavily on him while she settled into her new job.

She was starting with some things in her favour. She had a degree in hotel management and she had spent time getting to know each of the managers in the thirteen hotels that comprised the group. She had the practical experience she had gained from negotiating for the purchase of Hotel Azul. She wasn't a complete novice. And she had her father behind her.

She threw herself wholeheartedly into her new role. The company had been allowed to slide while her father was in hospital and two million euros had been stolen from the accounts. Her first job was to sort out the problems that had accumulated and restore the company's fortunes. That meant spending long days at her desk.

From the beginning, she set herself a demanding schedule. She rose every morning at six thirty, had a half-hour sprint along Sandymount Strand, then showered, dressed, had breakfast with Charlie and drove across to Elsinore to be at her desk for eight o'clock, just as the sun was breaking through the clouds over Howth Head.

She began by dealing with the post and any text messages or emails that had come in overnight. Then she rang each manager for a consultation about bookings and to talk through any difficulties they might be encountering. She regarded it as vital that, as managing director, she should be constantly available to staff. Gradually, she devised a system with Henry's secretary, Sally Burrows, to filter out the less-important phone calls that she could deal with later.

The remainder of the day she spent struggling to get to grips with her job, which involved constant phone calls, meetings with the accountants, visits to the hotels, which were always unannounced so that she could see for herself how they were being run. Jack's job as manager of the Excelsior had been given to the under-manager, Ted O'Donnell, who had been delighted with his sudden promotion and had immediately set about achieving Henry's target of doubling the bed nights.

Once a week, she made a point of ringing *Señor* Hernandez and checking on Hotel Azul. The hotel was continuing to prosper. Pedro had turned out to be a brilliant chef, always good-natured and happy in his work. *Señor* Hernandez had taken on board her suggestion for promoting golfing holidays for seniors, and it was already showing promising results. Hotel Azul was in good hands.

In the weeks that followed, Piper got to know as many of the employees as possible. She familiarised herself with the firm's major clients and suppliers, travelling to meet them

251

whenever possible. She took the advice of department heads about methods of streamlining the firm and sought out new opportunities to grow the company.

Once she was settled in, she called a meeting of all the managers and asked each of them to prepare a report on the current situation and how they saw their hotels developing new business in the months ahead. Sally Burrows came with her to take notes. It was a day-long event, and when it was over, her head was spinning with all the information she had been forced to absorb. But it was a fruitful exercise and she came away with a much better idea of where the company stood. When the half-year results came in, McKenzie Leisure was back in profit.

But it had been a hectic time as she battled with the issues she had inherited and learned the finer details of the company. She loved every aspect of her work but she had set herself an exhausting schedule. And in the forefront of her mind was the knowledge that she could not allow the job to interfere with her family life and particularly her daughter.

***

Meanwhile, her father had set himself the task of unravelling the full extent of Jack's fraud and how it had been perpetrated. He enlisted the help of Peter Campbell and swore him to secrecy about what they might find. The work went on for weeks, until one day Henry arrived in Piper's office with Campbell in tow. He sat down and laid a heavy bundle of invoices on the desk. 'We think we've cracked it. I have to say it's ingenious. It's a pity your brother didn't put the same amount of energy into the job he was paid to do.'

'How did it work?'

'Bogus invoices. Jack sent himself bills for all sorts of goods that had never been ordered or delivered. He duly paid them from the company's money into a London bank account. What gave him away was that he used the same bank account all the time. The money rested there for one day and was then transferred to a secret account in the Cayman Islands, which we're certain he used for his own benefit. All the paperwork was in order so it would have been very difficult to uncover the fraud, even if we had been suspicious, which, of course, we weren't.'

'Can we get the money back?'

Henry shook his head. 'Highly unlikely, unless we instigate court proceedings against the bank, which I don't want to do. It would attract too much adverse publicity. And even if we did sue, there's no guarantee we'd win. Remember, your brother is a fugitive. He may have changed his name, got new identities for himself and Corinne. We don't know where to start looking for him. Besides, I'd be surprised if the money wasn't moved out of the Cayman accounts long ago. It would be like looking for a needle in a haystack.'

He sighed. 'The bottom line, Piper, is that we're never going to see the money again.'

'How long had it been going on?'

'Not very long. Jack's ultimate plan, as we both know, was to take over the company. With you out of the way in Marbella, he hatched his plot to get me to sign a blank piece of paper. When I had my stroke, he saw his chance. In the early days, I wasn't expected to live. Jack typed out the letter giving him control of the company and fired you. Now he had free rein to embezzle money from McKenzie Leisure.

'When I began to improve and it looked like I was going to survive, he panicked. That was when he decided to flee with Corinne.'

Henry took out his handkerchief and wiped his eyes. 'It's just too shameful. My own son, to think he would do such a thing.'

She looked at her father. He had devoted most of his adult life to building up the company and had worked so hard to maintain it. But now, when he should have been able to enjoy his retirement, this mess had landed in his lap.

She bent and kissed his cheek. 'Let's draw a line under it and move on, Dad. Thank God, we still have you.'

Of course, the scandal over Jack didn't simply fade away. People wondered where he had gone and what had happened. The only person outside the family who knew the truth was Peter Campbell and he loyally kept his mouth shut. Over time, people assumed there had been some sort of falling-out in the family. Piper had been appointed to the top job and Jack had taken it badly so had gone elsewhere. After a while, his name was rarely mentioned

But it was difficult, balancing the demands of McKenzie Leisure with her home life. She tried to get away from work every evening at five o'clock to spend time with her daughter before she went to bed. The same applied at weekends when they went to the beach, and to the American Diner for pizzas and hamburgers. But even when she was with her child she couldn't escape unexpected phone calls or problems. She began to get an inside picture of the impossible work rate her father had endured.

To mark her first anniversary, her father insisted that they have a celebratory dinner, just Charlie and Piper, himself and her mother. It was held in a private room at one of the better restaurants in town. As the evening came to an end, Henry got to his feet to make a little speech. He had lost a great deal of weight since his stroke but now he looked tanned and fit after the holiday in Nice.

'They say it's an ill wind that blows no good, and maybe there's some truth in that. The company has been through some very trying times, some things I'm ashamed of and won't dwell on. I blame myself for much of what has happened.

'It was always my intention that McKenzie Leisure should be the inheritance of Piper and her brother. I wanted to be fair. I wanted to avoid rancour and dissension. But I was wrong. I should have recognised from the start what was staring me in the face – that there was only one person who was fit to manage the company and that person was Piper.

'But that's all water under the bridge now and I won't refer to it again. Despite our troubles, we've emerged with a first-rate managing director we can be proud of. Piper has displayed talent and energy, attention to detail, an inventive mind and a personality for management that gets things done. With her at the helm, I can relax, safe in the knowledge that the company can only go from strength to strength.'

There was a lively round of applause and Piper felt her eyes well up with tears. She felt as happy as she had ever been. But already a new plan was forming in her mind. For

255

some while, she had been concerned about the amount of time the company devoured. She wanted to be able to spend more time with Charlie and Sofía, take more breaks, get back to Marbella and the peaceful surroundings of Hotel Azul. However, before she could do anything she had a lengthy meeting with her father to seek his advice. They debated the proposal back and forth, and in the end, Henry gave his consent.

Then she rang her best friend, Jo Ferguson.

Chapter Thirty-One

Because of her heavy workload, Piper hadn't seen her friend for several months, but they had continued to maintain regular telephone contact. Jo was still holding down her busy job as a senior manager with a multinational company. She was continuing to see her boyfriend, Carl, and still resisting his proposals of marriage.

Piper rang her on her personal line and got her at once. 'Hi there,' she said. 'How many deals have you pulled off this morning?'

'Are you kidding?' Jo laughed. 'I've been in meetings.'

'So what are they paying you that fantastic salary for? I thought your job was to make buckets of money for the company.'

'I'm only a cog in a wheel, Piper. You know how business works.'

'And how is the handsome Carl?'

'You sound like you fancy him.'

'I could, if it wasn't for Charlie. I don't think he'd take too kindly to anything of that nature. Besides, I haven't got time for romance. Does he still want to marry you?'

'Of course. But, like I told you, I'm not ready yet.'

'You'd need to watch out. Some predatory female might not be so slow.'

'That would be his loss.'

Piper laughed. 'Even when we were schoolgirls, you were always very sure of yourself.'

'You've got to be, Piper, only way to succeed. You know that.'

'Okay,' Piper said. 'Enough of the banter. I want to have a serious talk with you. When would suit?'

'I'm pretty tied up today but I could probably squeeze in fifteen minutes for a quick cup of coffee.'

'This will take longer than fifteen minutes. Tell you what. What time do you finish?'

'Six thirty.'

'Anything planned for this evening?'

'Now you've really got my full attention. You're not pregnant again, are you?'

'I don't think so.'

'Do you want to meet this evening?'

'Yes. How about the Café Noir at seven? You know where it is? Nassau Street?'

'Sure.'

'I'll see you there.'

'What's this about, Piper?'

'Just be patient. All will be revealed.'

Piper immediately called Charlie. 'Anything major planned for this evening?'

'I'm going to a gig, checking out the opposition.'

'Couldn't you see a different band another time? I need to have the evening off. And I don't think it's fair expecting Margie to take care of Sofía all night as well as all day.'

'Sure, no problem. What's so urgent that you need the evening off?'

'I'll tell you later.'

Next she rang the restaurant and booked a quiet table for two where she and her guest could talk in confidence. The head waiter, clearly suspecting this was a romantic rendezvous, assured her he had the very thing she required.

She spent the remainder of the day at her usual chores, had a sandwich and soup with her mother in the kitchen at one o'clock, and by six fifteen had showered, changed, and was on her way into town. She parked in an underground garage and walked the short distance to the restaurant, arriving at ten minutes to seven.

The restaurant was one of the best in town, with a high reputation for fine cuisine, and the head waiter had been as good as his word. The table he had reserved for her was at the back, set in a little alcove where she and Jo couldn't be seen and certainly wouldn't be overheard.

At five to seven, Jo arrived, was relieved of her coat and shown at once to Piper's table.

'Are you driving?' Piper asked.

Jo shook her head.

'So, would you like some wine?'

'What about you?'

'I must remain strictly sober unless I want to appear before the district court in the morning. The tabloids would love it.'

Jo asked for a glass of Beaune, studied the menu and the two women gave their order.

'How is Sofía enjoying school?'

'She's loving it! She's made lots of new friends and she's a bright child, Jo. She has a quick mind.'

'Takes after her mother.'

'School takes some of the pressure off me, but it's not the entire solution. That's why I want to talk to you.'

'Sounds intriguing.'

'I want to offer you a job,' Piper said.

For a moment there was silence. 'A *job*?' Jo said, incredulous.

'Exactly. But before we go any further let me explain a few things. I've just concluded my first year as managing director of McKenzie Leisure. It was the job I was always working towards because I wanted the company to stay in the family's hands. My dad built it from nothing and it would have broken my heart to see it taken over by some multinational conglomerate or fall into the hands of an outsider.'

Jo was nodding in agreement. 'I would have felt exactly the same.'

'It's been a very tough year, Jo, much harder than I expected, but we've got the company into good shape and it's making fine profits. But I feel a little guilty. I'm not seeing enough of my family. I need a deputy.'

Jo looked shocked. 'You're offering me a job as your deputy?'

'Yes.'

'Why?'

'I've just explained. But it's more than guilt. It's also selfishness. Sofía is growing up fast. I don't want to wake up one morning and discover she's a teenager and I hardly know her. I want to spend more time with her and Charlie.'

'But why me?'

'Because you'd be perfect. You have a business degree from Trinity College. You're bright and intelligent. You've got initiative. You're working as a manager for a large company so you've got the experience. But, most of all, I trust you. This is a family business, Jo. It's not some giant corporation. Personal relationships matter. You and I have known each other since we were at school. There's no one outside my immediate family I would trust more. I know we would work well together. And, what's more, I know you'd be good.'

'What would I have to do?'

'You'd stand in for me so I can take some time off. You'd undertake various projects. You'd be running the company alongside me. You're the one person I'd feel safe to have in charge when I'm not there.'

Jo took a deep breath, quickly followed by a large gulp of wine. 'I'm very flattered, Piper, but this is a complete surprise.'

'You'll be well paid. We can draw up a good package. What are you earning now?'

Jo told her. 'I'll double it. You'll get all the usual benefits: company car, expenses, health insurance, holidays, bonuses.'

'What if I make a mess of it?'

'That's not going to happen. You're a fast learner. And I don't expect you to take over from me on the first day. Obviously, there would have to be a lead-in period so you could learn the ropes. But I know you'd be right for it. However, if you're uneasy we could include a probationary period in the contract. If you feel the job isn't right for you, you can walk away and there'll be no hard feelings.'

'Aren't there other people in the firm who'll feel passed over? Won't it cause resentment?'

'No. As I said, McKenzie Leisure is a family firm. My father ran it until he was ill. It's always been expected that when he retired the top job would go to someone in the family so you needn't worry on that count. There'll be no one waiting to cut your throat.'

'Can I have a couple of days to consider it before I let you have my answer?'

'Take what time you need but just promise me one thing.'

'Yes?'

'That you'll treat this discussion as confidential.'

'You have my word.'

***

Later that evening, Piper told Charlie of her plans. 'I made a major decision today,' she said. 'I've offered Jo Ferguson a job as my deputy. It's all been done with my father's agreement.'

He seemed surprised. 'I thought you were well on top of things.'

'I am. But I want to spend more time with you and Sofía. We're a family, Charlie, and we should be together more.'

'She's an inspired choice. She'd be good. She's a smart cookie.'

'She's also a hard worker. But, most of all, she's loyal. I know I can rely on her.'

'I suppose she jumped at the offer?'

'No, she didn't. She's gone away to think about it. She'll give me her answer in a couple of days.'

'She'll take it,' Charlie said. 'She'd be crazy not to.'

While she waited to hear from Jo, Piper ploughed on with her work. By now, she was absolutely convinced of the need to have someone in a supportive role, not just to relieve the pressure but also to give her space to plan ahead and develop new ways of growing the company. With her present unrelenting workload she barely had time to think.

Piper knew she had made an attractive offer and that Jo would be tempted. The only reason she might turn it down would be fear of getting out of her depth. She had to wait several more days before she got her response. One evening as she was about to finish work, the phone rang. When she answered, her friend was on the line.

'Can we meet for a drink?'

'Sure. Marine Hotel suit you?'

'Perfect.'

'I'll see you there in half an hour.'

When Piper arrived, she found Jo, dressed in a grey business suit, waiting at a table in a quiet corner of the bar, a cup of coffee before her.

'I've given this matter a lot of thought,' she began. 'I've weighed up all the pros and cons.'

'And?'

'I've decided to accept your offer.'

Piper hugged her. 'I'm absolutely thrilled, Jo. I promise you won't regret it.'

'I have to admit I'm very nervous,' Jo continued. 'I hope I won't let you down.'

'Nonsense. You'll be fine. I wouldn't have approached you otherwise. You know, sometimes we're not aware of our talents till we put them to the test. I'm so happy.'

'I hope you're right, Piper.'

'I am. This calls for celebration. Apart from everything else, you're the first person I've actually hired. What would you like to drink? Does champagne sound okay?'

'Why the hell not?' Jo said, grinning and placing her briefcase on the seat beside her.

Piper called to the barman for two snipes of champagne. When they arrived, she filled their glasses and they drank a toast.

'I'd never thought I'd end up working for McKenzie Leisure,' Jo said, 'but now that I've made my mind up, I can't wait to start.'

'But first you have to give your present employers notice. Have you spoken to them yet?'

'I'll talk to them on Monday.'

'What does your contract say?'

'A month's notice on either side, but they might be prepared to waive that. After all, an employee who's on their way out isn't likely to be entirely focused on the job, is she?'

'I'm sure that would never apply to you.' Piper smiled.

'You're the conscientious type. That's another reason I want you.'

While they sipped their champagne, they discussed the finer details of the job.

'You'll have your own office and complete authority, but when it comes to important decisions, I want you to consult me before you take any action.'

'Of course.'

'I'll give you an induction course, introduce you to everyone and show you how the company's run. You'll pick everything up pretty quickly once you're actually doing the job. Don't be afraid to ask questions if there's anything you're unsure about.'

'Okay.'

'So, on Monday give in your notice and let me know when you can start. In the meantime, I'll get busy drawing up a contract of employment to include terms, conditions, remuneration and annual leave, all that stuff.'

'Great.'

Piper tipped her glass against Jo's. 'Here's to us. We're going to make a brilliant team, you and I, the best in the business.'

She finished her champagne and stood up to go. 'I have one more question,' Jo said.

'Yes?'

'What colour car can I have?'

'As Henry Ford said, "Any colour so long as it's black."'

CHAPTER THIRTY-TWO

Jo's hunch proved correct. When she told her employers she wished to leave to take up a new job offer, they said she could go within two weeks. She spent the time clearing up unfinished business and attending a round of farewell parties in various divisions of the company. She was popular and had made lots of friends.

Piper, meanwhile, was faced with a problem: where to put her. As her deputy, Jo would need to be close – indeed, the closer the better. Piper had inherited her father's vast study, which, apart from Sally's office, took up the entire top floor of the house. After giving the matter some consideration, she decided the best solution was to split the existing office in two and have a door connecting the rooms. Sally could remain where she was.

She contacted a reliable builder and made an appointment for him to come and give his opinion. It didn't take him long to make up his mind. He measured the office, asked what equipment would be required, then sat down with a pencil and paper and made some sketches.

'You have a large window here with spectacular views over the sea. I assume you want to keep that?'

'Yes.'

'In that case, the easiest thing is to divide the existing office with a thick partition, put in a connecting door and provide the additional office with a new window. The new office will require natural light unless the occupant wants to be looking at four blank walls all day long.'

'That sounds sensible. Would it require planning permission?'

'No. You're not adding to the size of the house.'

'Then go ahead and do it. How long will it take?'

'Couple of weeks.'

'I need you to stick strictly to schedule. No overruns. That's vitally important.'

'You have my word.'

'And the cost?'

'I'll have to work that out but you shouldn't need to take out a new mortgage.'

Piper smiled. 'When can you start?'

'Tomorrow morning.'

***

The builder kept his word. He arrived the following day with his van and a helper and began immediately. There was a lot of hammering, drilling and dust, but that couldn't be helped. To allow him to work, Piper had vacated her office and moved all her equipment and files into Sally's. That proved unviable and, in the end, the women had to move downstairs to a vacant bedroom, which meant engaging telephone engineers to transfer the phone and Internet lines. It was a very tight squeeze, with the two women practically sitting on top of each other. Even there, they didn't escape the noise and disruption emanating from upstairs. In fact, it was almost impossible to get any work done, and Piper got quite used to her phone correspondents asking if Howth was under attack from international terrorists. Even her mother complained about the racket.

Somehow Piper and Sally managed to keep McKenzie Leisure ticking over for the two weeks it took to complete the changes. The builder stuck rigidly to his deadline and finished in the time they had agreed. When the last nail had been hammered in, he engaged an industrial cleaner to come with a huge vacuum cleaner and remove all dust and debris so that the entire top floor shone. Now Piper was looking at two brand-new offices.

She got the builder to move her desk and equipment back to her office and the engineers were called out again to replace the telecommunications equipment and install new lines in Jo's. Next, she put down new carpets, added to Jo's room a desk and an executive chair, a filing cabinet, a couch and a coffee table with two more chairs. Finally she ordered a computer, printer and photocopier.

When the builder finally departed, her mother uttered a silent prayer of thanks, made a large pot of tea and took a chocolate cake out of the fridge. 'That was like living through World War Three. I hope you have no more fancy plans for turning the place upside down,' she said, as she cut two large slices.

Piper laughed. 'No, Mum. That should be the end of it.'

'Thank God for small mercies.'

***

When Jo reported for work the following Monday morning, Piper showed her into a spanking new office. 'Wow!' she said. 'I've never had a whole room to myself before. This is fantastic.'

'It's not finished yet,' Piper said. 'You'll notice I've left the walls clear. That's so you can choose some nice artwork to put up. You're with McKenzie Leisure now, Jo. We don't cut corners around here.'

Jo sat in the executive chair and let out a whoop as she propelled herself around the room on the casters while Piper stood with folded arms and smiled. 'Whenever you've finished enjoying yourself, we'll have a cup of coffee and I'll give you your induction course.'

'Right away, boss,' Jo replied.

***

All Piper's beliefs about Jo turned out to be true. She was a fast learner and immediately set about mastering the intricate workings of the company. When she had grasped the initial details, Piper took her on a tour of the hotels in the group and introduced her to the managers.

'They're the key people you'll be dealing with. They're all extremely efficient and on top of their job. In due course, you'll get to know other members of staff and the people who supply us with food and drink, furniture, laundry services and so on. But you don't have to learn everything at once, Jo. It took me about six months before I knew who was who. In fact, I'm still learning.'

'It's a bigger operation than I thought,' Jo said.

'And you haven't seen it all.'

'No?'

'There's still Hotel Azul, our jewel in Marbella where I conducted my first business deal for my father. It's the most beautiful little place you've ever seen, with magnificent gardens and a lovely beach practically outside the back door.'

Right from the beginning, Jo treated everyone courteously. If there was something she didn't know, she asked. She listened to what people had to tell her. Before long, she was exhibiting a talent for people management. Hotel staff liked, trusted and respected her.

And she had an appetite for work that was truly amazing. No task was too big for her, no load too heavy, all managed with a smile and never a complaint. That was married to good business sense and excellent judgement. Many times in the months ahead Piper had cause to thank her lucky stars for the inspiration that had brought Jo on board.

Gradually, the addition of Jo to the management staff had the desired effect. Piper was able to take time off from work to pick Sofía up from school, attend parent-teacher meetings, take her daughter on outings and spend quality time with her, reading and playing. She cooked meals and went for walks. She still spent long hours at the helm of the company but now she could be flexible because she had Jo to rely on.

The results were also evident where they counted most – in the success of the company. Piper could devote more time to planning, development and researching new opportunities. Under her guidance, the group went from strength to strength. She negotiated the purchase of several more hotels and the profit graph showed a steadily rising upward trend. McKenzie Leisure was regularly quoted in the financial press as one of the top five most successful Irish businesses.

One day her father took her aside to have a chat. Since her accession to the post of managing director, he had moved back from the company and allowed her free rein to operate as she saw fit. He had also taken the advice of Dr Bradford and now led a much less frantic life. He spent a lot of time at the villa in Nice, particularly in the spring and early summer before it got too hot and the tourists started to arrive, and he had taken to visiting the yacht club again, although he restricted his sailing to when conditions were calm. He now looked much healthier.

It was at the yacht club that he met her for afternoon tea one day. As they sat in the dining room looking out at the waves falling on the shore at Ireland's Eye, he laid his hand on hers. 'I want to congratulate you on your success. You've achieved results far beyond my wildest dreams and I'm very proud of you, Piper.'

'Thank you, Dad.'

'It was a stroke of genius, bringing that young woman aboard. I wish I'd done something similar. But I didn't have anyone I could trust, until you came of age, of course, and by then that rivalry had developed between you and your brother. By the way, I've located him at last. I've had private detectives looking for him and they've found him in Brazil.'

This was startling news. 'How is he?'

Henry's eyes watered. 'Not good, I'm afraid. He's split up with Corinne, who seems to have disappeared. He's living with a young Brazilian woman and spends all his time in nightclubs and bars. I'm told he's developed a serious cocaine habit. I'm worried about him, Piper. I had high hopes for Jack when he was younger. And, despite all that's happened, he's still my son.'

'Are you going to take action against him?'

'No. I've already said that I couldn't live with the publicity the exposure would bring. It would break my heart. But I'm having him monitored. At the pace he's living, it's only a matter of time before he has a breakdown and may have to be admitted to hospital. When that happens I'll be there for him. I'll try to persuade him to come home and go into rehab. Perhaps we might still be able to save him. But that's not the reason I wanted to talk to you.'

He paused while he took a sip of tea. 'I wanted to give you some advice. Business can become like an aphrodisiac. You get this uncontrollable urge to become more and more successful until one day you wake up and realise it's taken over your life. I spent too much of my time building up the company. Perhaps I should have been content with something smaller, but I was always striving for bigger and better things. In the end, it almost killed me.

'But I was lucky. I still have you, your mother and my beautiful little granddaughter. And my health is restored. I have all the material things I want. What I'm trying to say is that you should never be afraid to walk away. If the business takes up too much of your time, if it begins to interfere with your marriage or your peace of mind, you should always be prepared to give it up. I've learned that there's much more to life than making money.'

Her father was gazing intently into her eyes.

'Don't make the mistakes I did,' he went on. 'It was a wise move to bring Jo on board. Already I can see that she's going to be a success. And she can share the burden so you have more time for yourself. Stick with business while you're enjoying it. When it becomes a burden, be prepared to let go.'

***

Once a month, Piper and Jo had lunch at a nearby hotel where they kicked around business problems and indulged in some light-hearted chat.

'How is Carl adapting to the changed regime?' Piper asked one day.

'He doesn't mind. He's quite busy himself. It hasn't made a big difference to our relationship.'

'Are you going to marry him?'

Jo thought for a minute before she replied. 'I don't know.'

'Do you love him?'

'I ask myself that question all the time and I'm not one hundred per cent sure.'

Piper didn't respond but she thought about her own situation with Charlie. He had swept her off her feet and she had known within weeks that she was in love and he was the

273

man she wanted to marry. But she had learned that not every relationship was the same.

'How would you feel if he wasn't there?'

'I'd miss him, of course.'

'But would you be heartbroken?'

'For a while, perhaps, but I'd probably get over it.'

'He's a very attractive man, Jo. Most women would find Carl appealing.'

'But it's not all about looks, is it?'

'No. But looks are what usually kick it off. I think there has to be something else that comes over time, though, something deeper. Sometimes it's even there right from the beginning. It's a kind of feeling that this is the person who was meant for you. This is your soul mate, the one person you want to spend your life with. Mind you, it doesn't always happen.'

'Is that how you feel about Charlie?'

'Yes. If I lost Charlie, I'd be bereft.'

Chapter Thirty-Three

Piper's relationship with Charlie was the other thing that changed with the new circumstances at McKenzie Leisure. Now she was able to reclaim some of her social life. They could spend more time together, go out for meals, attend concerts and drop in to Aunt Polly's Boudoir.

But there she came up against a new realisation. She discovered that she didn't enjoy Aunt Polly's as much as she had when she was single. She had matured and grown out of that phase of her life when she had loved the buzz, and being photographed by the paparazzi.

Charlie, however, behaved as if he hadn't changed at all. He was quite happy to spend all night in clubs, huddled in corners, drinking champagne with musicians and listening to gossip, if Piper wasn't with him to drag him home to bed. Whenever she lectured him about it, he made the excuse that it was work. 'I can't switch off at six o'clock, like you can, Piper. My job never stops. I've got to be on top of everything. I have to know where the next hot ticket is coming from, what kind of music the punters want to hear, who the coming band is going to be. I can't learn that stuff by staying at home and reading the newspapers. I've got to be out and about, mixing with the movers and shakers.'

'I really wish you'd slow down, Charlie.'

'Why?'

'I want you to spend more time with me and Sofía. Besides, nightclubs bore me. It's just the same people doing the same stupid things, making the same silly remarks. It's as if they're all stuck in a time warp. You know what I enjoy most of all?'

'What?'

'Quiet nights at home when we can have a family meal around the dinner table and then a few glasses of wine, just us, by the fire. In fact, as soon as the weather improves, I'm thinking of paying a visit to Hotel Azul. We could stretch it to a week, you and me, Margie and Sofía. Jo can look after the company while I'm away. It would be a lovely break and we'd all be together.'

Charlie didn't seem terribly interested in the idea. 'I'll have to consult my diary. Talk to me about it closer to the time.'

At least he cut down on his travelling. He made an occasional foray to London to negotiate contracts or royalty deals with the music companies but much of his time was now taken up with promoting Hell's Kitchen and grooming them for international stardom.

His next big venture was another European tour, this time taking in ten cities. He spent long hours on the phone negotiating with concert promoters as he worked out venues and planned the logistics of transporting the band and their equipment from one venue to the next. He was also in negotiation with some Americans about a North American tour. And he hadn't given up on his plan to build a new band around the drummer Sharkie Bolger.

He announced it to her casually one evening when they were having a nightcap before bed. 'I'd like you to come with me to a club next week. I want a second opinion of a singer I'm interested in.'

'What sort of music?'

'Blues – he's a young guy called Mick O'Neill. With a little grooming I think he'd make a perfect lead singer.'

'For what, Charlie?'

'My new band.'

She put down her drink and stared at him. 'Please tell me you're not serious. You're really thinking of starting a new band?'

'Why are you acting surprised? I told you this in Spain after the Hell's Kitchen tour.'

'I thought that was just a passing fancy. I didn't think you actually meant it.'

'Of course I meant it. I explained it all to you. Sharkie was a sensation on the Kitchen tour. If he was a singer it might be different but he's a drummer, for God's sake, and the only thing you can do with a drummer is put him in a band. Besides, as I said before, I don't want some other manager to snap him up. I have him under contract and I intend to build another band around him. They could be even bigger than Hell's Kitchen.'

Piper gave a loud sigh. 'Charlie, Hell's Kitchen takes up all your time as it is. Even when we're alone your damned phone never stops ringing. How's it going to be if you're managing two bands? I'll never see you at all.'

He smiled and patted her knee. 'Relax. We'll work something out.'

His announcement had ruined the intimate mood. She finished her drink and went to bed, but it was a long time before she finally drifted off to sleep. She lay staring at the ceiling while she felt the resentment build within her. She had employed Jo Ferguson so she would have more time to spend with her family, and now Charlie proposed to take on even more work. It was as if the two of them were pulling in opposite directions.

The following morning, when they got up, it was as if nothing had been said. Charlie was all laughter and fun. As he was preparing to leave, he said, 'Pencil next Tuesday night in your diary. We'll go and listen to Mick O'Neill and afterwards we'll have supper somewhere romantic. If it doesn't work out, so be it. But at least let's give it a try.'

***

The venue turned out to be a dingy cellar beneath a pub in Pearse Street. It was packed when they arrived but Charlie and Piper managed to squeeze into a couple of seats near the stage. They had to endure a series of mediocre acts before Mick O'Neill was announced, and then a thin, dark-haired young man, with a bored look on his face, walked on stage. He stood before the microphone and strummed his guitar. The moment he started to sing, a hush descended.

He launched straight into a frantic rendition of 'Memphis Blues', and when he finished his set twenty minutes later, with a souped-up version of 'Baby Please Don't Go', the audience was on its feet, roaring its approval. Charlie turned to Piper with a huge grin. 'Well, what did you think?'

She was forced to concede that the young Mr O'Neill had talent. Charlie waited till he had left the stage, then nipped out of his seat and followed him to what passed for the dressing room behind the stage.

'Hi, I'm Charlie White.'

'Do I know you?'

'I manage Hell's Kitchen.'

His attitude immediately changed. 'Oh, right. I didn't recognise you.'

'I was in the audience, really enjoyed your set. I'd like to have a chat with you. I've got a proposal I want you to hear.'

'Sure, no problem.'

'I'll meet you outside in ten minutes.'

Charlie collected Piper, picked up Mick O'Neill and fifteen minutes later they were having drinks in the lounge of a nearby hotel.

'How old are you, Mick?' Charlie began.

'Nineteen.'

'Have you got a manager?'

'No, I haven't really gone professional. At least, not yet.'

'That might be about to change. What I'm about to tell you doesn't leave this room, okay?'

'Okay.'

'I'm putting together another band. I've already got a really good drummer.'

'Anyone I know?'

'I can't tell you that but he's red hot. I'm looking for a singer and two more musicians. I was very impressed with you tonight. Are you interested?'

'I sure am.'

'Give me your phone number.'

Mick O'Neill wrote it out and handed it to Charlie. 'If you're looking for musicians, I know two guys who might suit. One is a trombone player and the other is a guitarist. And one of them sings too.'

'What are their names?'

'They call themselves the Desperadoes.'

'Where can I hear them?'

'They play the Arcadia Club in Harcourt Street every Saturday night.'

'Okay, Mick. You'll be hearing from me.'

Later, as they were having supper in a restaurant in Temple Bar, Charlie said, 'Thanks for being so patient, Piper. I appreciate it.'

She shrugged. 'Looks like I don't have much choice.'

'I promise you, if this thing works out, it'll be my last venture. I take your point. We should spend more time together. But I'm a businessman, Piper, and I can't pass up a glorious opportunity when it's staring me in the face.'

***

Saturday night found Charlie and Mick in a dark, musty-smelling cavern off St Stephen's Green, sitting at the back where they wouldn't be recognised. For added protection,

Charlie was wearing his shades. The place was packed with people clutching pints of overpriced beer. But the attention given to the artists could not have been faulted. Each time an act came on stage, the audience fell silent. They were obviously aficionados.

There was a stage, a sound system and a couple of microphones, but for such a small venue, the acoustics were remarkably good. The acts seemed to fall into two categories: outright beginners who were trying to make a name and build a career, and veterans of the music business whose glory days were behind them and who were content to pick up a fee wherever they could find it.

For the first hour Charlie and Mick sat through a series of mediocre performances. Then there was a fifteen-minute break for the audience to replenish their drinks. After the interval, the Desperadoes took the stage and Charlie sat forward expectantly.

Two men in their early thirties sat down and started to play. Their music was faultless. They were professional to their fingertips. And, what was more, the guitarist sang in a mature, gravelly voice that belied his age, and projected the raw emotion of the blues he was singing. Charlie was amazed that he had never heard of them before.

As soon as they were finished, he tapped Mick on the shoulder and they made their way out of the room, then round to the back. Charlie collared the Desperadoes as they came down from the stage. 'I just heard you play,' he said. 'I'm Charlie White.'

The smaller man took a closer look at Charlie's face. 'Are you the bloke who manages Hell's Kitchen?'

'That's right. I've got an idea I'd like to discuss with you.'

'What's that?'

'Could we sit down somewhere and talk?'

They went round the corner to a quiet bar. Charlie ordered drinks and the two men introduced themselves. The guitar player was Joey Dunne and the man who played the trombone was Harry Baker.

'Mick here put me on to you,' Charlie said. 'I'm looking for a couple of really good musicians. You guys might fit the bill.'

'What for?'

'I'm forming another band.'

This announcement attracted their full attention.

'I've already got a drummer and Mick will be the lead singer. Are you interested?'

The two men looked at each other. Then they smiled.

'Tell us more,' Joey Dunne said.

Half an hour later they agreed to meet again on Saturday afternoon for a rehearsal at a warehouse Charlie used at the docks. He drove Mick home. On the way, the boy asked, 'What do you think?'

'It's looking good. But we still have a long way to go and a lot of hard work to put in. I'll know better on Saturday.'

'I think it'll work,' Mick said. 'I've got a good feeling about it.'

CHAPTER THIRY-FOUR

The musicians gathered for the rehearsal feeling nervous but excited at the prospect of making a breakthrough into the glamorous world of showbiz. Charlie was a respected manager with a reputation for success. He had taken Hell's Kitchen from small concert venues where they had played to tiny audiences and launched them on the European stage. In the process, he had helped them to make a lot of money. What was to stop him doing it again?

But there was one major difference. Hell's Kitchen had been an established band when Charlie had taken them under his wing. They had been school friends drawn together by their shared interest in music and they knew each other intimately. This time, he was attempting to take a group of disparate individuals and weld them into a band. Only two of them had ever played together. It was a risky venture. Would it work?

The first outing did not augur well. It took a long time for the four to settle down. Harry Baker's trombone tended to drown Mick O'Neill's vocals. Sharkie Bolger's drums overwhelmed Joey Dunne's guitar. The instruments clashed and the result was a mess. There was also friction over the material. After listening to them for three hours, Charlie finally brought the rehearsal to a halt. 'Guys, you need to go away and do some serious thinking. I suggest you choose six numbers, work out the arrangements and run over them till everybody knows exactly what he's doing. Then we'll meet again and take it from there.'

They looked downcast as they trooped out of the warehouse. But when they met three weeks later for their second rehearsal, there was a marked improvement. They had obviously paid attention to Charlie's advice. Now they played more fluently and sounded much more confident. But Charlie wanted more.

'Go away and do it again,' he said. 'Add some new material. Joey, why don't you try a few songs? Mick is the lead singer but he can do with some support.'

This time they were a bit more cheerful as they left.

At the third meeting, Charlie could sense they were beginning to gel into a proper band. They were no longer merely a bunch of individual talents but becoming a cohesive musical unit. For the first time since he had brought them together, he caught a glimpse of the successful band they might become. But there was still a lot of hard work to be done and Charlie wasn't about to take his foot off the pedal.

He drove them mercilessly, sending them back time and again to rehearse. He kept suggesting new material till they had built up a repertoire of twenty songs, shared between Mick and Joey. And while Sharkie, with his drumming brilliance, remained the greatest talent, a leader was beginning to emerge in the shape of Harry, the trombone player. This was exactly what the band needed and Charlie welcomed it.

But confusion remained about the band's image and style of music. Charlie was keenly aware that they had to carve out their own identity to distinguish them from Hell's Kitchen. After a lot of discussion, it was agreed they would concentrate on a blend of blues and rock'n'roll, which would appeal to an audience of young adults.

About two months after he had first brought them together, he presided over a marathon rehearsal, which lasted for five hours, and saw the band run through their entire repertoire. This time, there were few hiccups, and when the weary musicians reached the end of the session, Charlie was smiling broadly.

'Now you sound like a band I'm happy to be associated with,' he said.

'That's a relief,' Joey Dunne muttered, beneath his breath.

'I heard that,' Charlie quipped. 'And if you think you're going to go away and put your feet up, forget it. I want you to go off and concentrate on your twelve best songs. And I want you to choreograph the whole thing from start to finish – who stands where, who says what, who introduces the songs, even down to who tells what jokes. When you come back here again in six weeks' time, I want to hear a class act that's capable of going on stage and playing for forty-five minutes in front of a live audience.'

'What are you trying to do, Charlie?' Harry Baker groaned. 'Finish us off with exhaustion?'

'No,' Charlie replied. 'I'm giving you the break you wanted. I'm putting you on your first gig.'

***

While all this activity was going on, Piper was forced to sit on the sidelines as Charlie poured all his energy into developing his new band and planning Hell's Kitchen's next European tour. But she had extracted from him a promise that he would slow down once he had got the new band launched, and she was determined to ensure he kept his word.

However, it wasn't easy for her. At home, Charlie's phone was never silent. They might be sitting down to a family meal when it would ring and Charlie left the table to speak for half an hour to some promoter in Berlin about Hell's Kitchen.

Even when they were alone together, in their most intimate moments, she sensed that his mind was elsewhere. Matters came to a head one Saturday afternoon when Margie had taken Sofía to the park and they were in the bedroom about to make love. Piper was in a romantic mood as they got undressed and lay down, but just as she was becoming aroused, Charlie pulled away. 'Excuse me a moment,' he said.

She watched in utter amazement as he got up and went to his desk beside the window, took out a pen and wrote something on a piece of paper before rejoining her in bed. 'What was that all about?'

'It's just a note to remind me to phone Mick O'Neill in the morning.'

She got out of bed and began to get dressed.

'What's the matter?' Charlie asked, apparently amazed.

'You're the matter!' she shouted. 'You and that damned band. We were making love, Charlie, and you were miles away, thinking about Mick O'Neill.'

'I'm sorry, Piper. It's just I've got so much going on in my head that if I don't write it down I'll forget it.'

'That's it in a nutshell. You've got so much going on in your head that there's no room left for me. How would you react if I was to interrupt our love-making while I wrote myself notes about McKenzie Leisure? I'll bet you'd just love it.'

'I'm sorry,' he said. 'I'm under a lot of pressure right now.'

'It's pressure you brought on yourself. I'm under pressure too but I leave it in the office. I don't bring it home with me.'

'Come back to bed,' Charlie said softly. 'It won't happen again.'

***

Gradually Charlie's plans began to take shape. Hell's Kitchen's second tour of European cities was fast approaching. The entire project would take five weeks and would culminate in a massive homecoming concert in Dublin. That was when he hoped to launch the new band as a warm-up act to the main bill.

So far he had managed to keep his project under wraps and not a word had leaked out to the music press. But at some stage a carefully planned publicity campaign would have to be rolled out. It was going to be a high-wire act. The band had to be ready for their first public exposure, which meant they had to have twelve songs and a routine fully rehearsed. But now a new difficulty arose. They couldn't agree on what to call themselves.

Various suggestions had been tossed around but none seemed right. There was general agreement that the name was important. It defined their image and sent out a message about what sort of music the audience could expect. As time passed, this task began to assume critical importance. Charlie was constantly on the phone, urging them to come to an agreement so that he could start on the pre-publicity. The Moody Four, the Boys in Black, Apocalypse and the Young Hooligans were all considered and rejected. By now, Charlie was getting desperate.

Finally he took matters into his own hands. He rang Sharkie and gave him an ultimatum. 'You've wasted enough time on this. Come up with a name by tomorrow or I'll give you one myself.' He could hear an argument going on in the background. 'Twenty-four hours. Do you understand?'

'Yes.' Sharkie groaned.

But the twenty-four hours passed without agreement.

'Okay,' Charlie said. 'You've had your chance. Now I'm imposing my decision.'

'What?' Harry asked.

'The name you started out with. From now on you're the Desperadoes. I'm giving the order to put it on the publicity material tonight.'

A week later, they filed into the warehouse for their final rehearsal. They had worked hard and practised till they could have played their set in their sleep. Charlie sat at the back of the room with a grim face that gave no sign of what he was thinking. He had invested a lot of time and money in putting the band together. But he was determined not to risk his reputation by lending his name to a second-rate act.

At a signal from him, they launched into their first number – a raunchy version of the Rolling Stones' 'Satisfaction'. Charlie sat impassively as they played and Mick O'Neill sang. When this song was finished, they moved quickly on to 'My Generation', and Charlie found himself tapping his shoe on the floor. Then Joey stepped up to the microphone and the riffs from his guitar introduced the old Ray Charles classic 'Take These Chains From My Heart', with Harry's trombone lending poignant back-up.

By now, any initial nervousness had disappeared. They settled down and played the remainder of the set like veterans of many successful stage performances. At last, the forty-five minute routine came to a screaming end with Mick singing 'Whole Lot Of Shaking Going On', and Sharkie's drums bringing the performance to a crashing finale. When they had finished, they lowered their instruments and turned to Charlie for his verdict.

There was a deathly silence. Then Charlie slowly raised his hand and gave them a thumbs-up. 'You're on board,' he said. 'Now let's go and have a drink.'

***

The next move was to launch the publicity campaign. Over the years, Charlie had learned all the dark arts of media manipulation. He began by planting stories with a handful of trusted music journalists. When they appeared in the press, they had the desired effect of stimulating competition among other reporters.

289

Meanwhile, Alice McDowell had been busy organising a press conference for the eve of Hell's Kitchen's European tour. It was held in Aunt Polly's Boudoir, which was guaranteed to have the hacks fighting for invitations. But, just to be sure, Alice spent several days diligently ringing the newspaper offices and letting them know that an important story was about to break. All this ensured that Aunt Polly's was packed when the conference eventually kicked off.

A stage had been set up in a corner of the room, complete with microphones and Pete Donohue's drum kit. The reporters had already been circulated with a press release giving details of the Hell's Kitchen tour. Charlie and Pete Donohue took to the stage and began answering questions about the itinerary and how the band was fast building up a European fan base. Then Charlie smiled and said he had a very important announcement to make. At a signal from Alice, the members of the new band came out with their instruments.

'Ladies and gentlemen, I give you my new band – the Desperadoes.'

Straight away, the band launched into 'Satisfaction' and the room went wild. Cameras flashed, and as soon as the song was finished, they continued with their version of 'My Generation'. Then the questions came thick and fast.

Whose idea was it to form the band?

Where had Charlie found the musicians?

How had they chosen the name?

Charlie had plenty of experience of press conferences and used the occasion to press the Desperadoes' talent and potential while constantly stressing that the band's first outing would be at Hell's Kitchen's homecoming concert in five weeks' time. After forty-five minutes he drew the conference to a close.

'Thank you all for coming today. Anybody who wants one-on-one interviews, contact Alice and she'll try to fit you in. Now I don't know about you lot but I'm thirsty. The bar's open and the tab is on me.'

***

The next morning, the papers were filled with pictures of Charlie and members of the bands drinking champagne and celebrating the launch.

'MUSIC MAESTRO DOES IT AGAIN,' the headlines screamed, above stories that claimed Charlie was about to replicate the success of Hell's Kitchen with his new band, the Desperadoes. This led to an immediate demand for tickets for Hell's Kitchen's homecoming concert.

Two days later, Charlie left for Paris and the first night of the European tour, well satisfied with his achievement in preparing the ground for the Desperadoes' successful entry into the music super league.

Chapter Thirty-Five

Piper watched him go with mixed feelings. During the last five months, she had been forced to take a back seat while Charlie gave most of his attention to his bands and their careers. As a wife, she was proud of his achievement. He had demonstrated that he was the unchallenged king of the Irish music business. No one could come near him. He had taken four unknown musicians and moulded them into a band that was headed for stardom. And he had just put together a tour that was destined to earn him thousands of pounds in profits. It was no mean feat.

But it wasn't easy living with someone who was rushing around all day long like a pitbull terrier on steroids. He had less and less time for her and Sofía. Even when they were alone together she didn't have his full attention. She felt she was being forced to share Charlie with an army of music fans, promoters and music industry bosses, who constantly phoned and texted him.

There was a time when she would have loved all this attention and the excitement it brought, when she would have relished the champagne and the gossip and another photograph on the front page of the tabloids. But she had been younger, a single woman bent on enjoyment. Now she was a wife and mother, the holder of an important position in a major company. She had grown up and moved on, and her priorities had changed.

Gradually, a new reality began to dawn on her. Charlie had always led a busy life and she had known that when she married him. In fact, it was part of what had attracted her to him. But most of his business had been conducted in Ireland, which had meant they were rarely apart for long. Now, with his European tours, he had moved into the big time. She could see clearly what was going to happen.

Charlie would return in triumph from his present tour. He would rest for a while and then he would start planning the next. It was inevitable. She could extract all the promises she liked from him but they would mean nothing. She was caught on a merry-go-round.

Sooner or later, the itch to engineer another coup would overtake him and he would be off again, planning and plotting his next venture. And instead of one band, he now had two. She could see a life filled with long absences. And there was no solution. Short of her husband resigning from the music business altogether, she would have to accept that she would never have a normal home life like other women.

***

While he was away, Charlie kept in daily contact with her. On the morning after the opening concert in Paris, she was having breakfast with Margie and Sofía when the phone rang and he was on the line, telling her about the fantastic reception the band had had at their sell-out concert.

'You should have seen it, Piper – it was unbelievable. We filled this football stadium and even then we had to turn hundreds of fans away. The audience loved them, wouldn't let them off the stage. They ran over their scheduled time by half an hour.'

'That's brilliant, Charlie. I'm really pleased for you.'

'And the press loved them too. I've got all the papers here in front of me, rave reviews in every one. I'll ask Alice to upload them to your email address.'

'What's next?'

'I'm going to grab a few hours' sleep. We've got four more nights of this before we move on to Berlin.'

'You mean you haven't been to bed yet?' she said, astonished.

'It didn't seem worthwhile. The party was so good we decided to stay up and catch the early editions of the papers. How's Sofía? Is she there? Put her on to me so I can say hello.'

Piper handed the phone to her daughter and watched her giggle excitedly at the sound of her father's voice. At last, she handed it back to her mother. 'Daddy wants to talk to you again.'

'Piper, there's only one thing missing from a perfect scenario.'

'What?'

'You.'

***

As the weeks went past, Piper grew used to having dinner with Sofía and Margie, then going to Elsinore for Sunday lunch with her parents. At night she became accustomed to falling asleep alone. It was the longest period she had been parted from Charlie since their marriage, and as the days went slowly by, she found herself looking forward desperately to the end of the tour when she would have her husband back.

At work, she was kept busy, but even the demands of McKenzie Leisure failed to relieve her gnawing loneliness. One afternoon she went for lunch at the Marine Hotel with Jo Ferguson.

'Tell me to shut up if I'm intruding but you seem to be down in the dumps,' Jo said.

'Does it show?'

Jo nodded.

'I *am* down in the dumps. I'm missing Charlie.'

'Why didn't you go on the tour with him? I could have covered for you.'

'Are you kidding? Apart from leaving Sofía for five weeks, I would have hated it, Jo. There are women who would give their eye teeth to be married to Charlie White. But I know the music business. It appears exciting to outsiders but it's all tinsel and veneer. There's nothing there. It's just sycophants and liggers and hangers-on drinking free champagne. I would have been bored stupid.'

'How's the tour going?'

'It's been a major triumph. Charlie's sent me the reviews. It doesn't surprise me. He doesn't do failure. Anything he puts his mind to is bound to be a success.'

Jo stretched out her hand and stroked Piper's wrist. 'I don't know what to say, hon.'

'There's nothing to be said. This is what I signed up for when I married him. I suppose I'll just have to put up with it till the tour's over and I see him again.'

She was already planning what she would do when the tour ended and Charlie returned to Dublin. She was going to whisk them all away to Marbella and Hotel Azul for a couple of weeks. In the peace and tranquillity of the Spanish sunshine she would have a serious heart-to-heart talk with Charlie about where their marriage was going.

The days ticked slowly away, and the closer Charlie's homecoming came, the more desperate she was to see him. The tour was going to finish with the first public outing for the Desperadoes at a major concert in the O2 arena where they would share the bill with Hell's Kitchen. Much as she had come to dislike the razzmatazz of rock'n'roll parties, Piper decided she had to be there.

The day she had been waiting for finally arrived. She got a phone call from Charlie one morning to say the tour was about to wind up and he expected to arrive into Dublin airport the following afternoon at one o'clock. Piper arranged with Jo to take the day off and made plans to meet him at the airport with Sofía.

When they arrived, they found a small group of fans had got there before them, mainly young teenagers with banners saying, 'WELCOME HOME HELL'S KITCHEN'. Piper scanned the arrivals board to find that the flight was due in on time. Her excitement mounted as she watched the first passengers begin to filter on to the concourse.

Then she caught a glimpse of him, the first in five weeks. He was strolling along confidently, dressed in chinos, sports shirt and jacket as he pushed a trolley laden with luggage. Behind him came the band, looking tired and somewhat the worse for wear. The moment she saw him, Sofía gave a cry of delight while the fans started screaming at the sight of their idols.

Charlie spotted his family and began to wave and then he was past the barrier, scooping Sofía into his arms and tickling her cheeks. 'How's my little jewel? Did you miss me?'

'Yes, Daddy.'

'I missed you too. But I've brought you presents. They're in my bag. You can have them as soon as we get home.'

He put her down, turned to Piper and took her in his arms. She felt her heart flutter with joy as their lips met. 'At last,' he said. 'It's so good to be home.'

He waved to his musicians, and they set off in their different directions.

Charlie and Sofía piled into Piper's car and headed into the city. Sofía bombarded Charlie with questions till Sandymount came into view and they were pulling into the parking area outside their apartment. Once they were inside, Charlie poured himself a drink, went into the lounge and gazed out across the bay to where the green slopes of Howth Head were shining in the sun. 'Look at that. I've been in every major city in Europe and I've seen nothing that remotely compares with what we have right here on our doorstep.' He gave a loud sigh and flung himself down on a sofa. 'I'm whacked,' he declared. 'I've been running on raw adrenalin for the past five weeks. Now I could sleep for a month.'

'No, you don't.' Piper laughed, delighted to have him back. 'You've got a concert tonight, remember?'

'You don't have to remind me. This is the Desperadoes' big chance. I just hope they do what's expected of them.'

'Are you hungry?'

'No. What I'd really like is a long hot shower and a nap. Then I'll have to get ready for the gig.'

He opened one of his cases and took out several bags containing toys he had picked up on his travels. He gave them to Sofía, who sat on the floor and pulled them out with shrieks of delight. Charlie looked at Piper and a smile passed between them. He pulled himself up from the sofa, kissed her once more and headed for the bedroom. 'Do me a favour. Don't let me sleep past five.'

***

Half an hour before the event was due to begin, the 02 was packed to capacity for Hell's Kitchen's homecoming gig. Piper sat in the front row facing the stage while she waited

298

for her husband to join her. He was still backstage with the Desperadoes, giving them a pep talk before they made their debut. A few minutes before eight o'clock, he slipped into the seat beside her and gave her hand a squeeze. Then the spotlights shone on the four Desperadoes as they walked slowly onto the stage. A hush fell over the hall.

Sharkie gave a drum roll, Mick stepped up to the microphone and the band launched into a jazzed-up version of 'Dirty Old Town' that had the audience singing and clapping along. They followed up with 'Baby Please Don't Go', and after that they had the crowd in the palms of their hands. They could do no wrong as they confidently played their set and gave three encores before finally leaving the stage to cheers.

Charlie turned to Piper and gave her a cheeky smile. 'I think that went down okay,' he said.

***

Aunt Polly's Boudoir was jammed to capacity for the after-show party. The place was thronged with people guzzling the champagne Charlie had paid for while the bands signed autographs. Piper smiled as she walked serenely through the crowd, acknowledging the nods and greetings of familiar faces. She noticed Serge Dupont reunited with the pouting Alessandro at the bar. She was about to go and say hello when a voice said, 'This way, please, Mrs White.' When she turned, someone poked a camera into her face.

Everybody wanted to talk to Charlie and shake his hand. He was the man of the moment and they wanted a little piece of him. She finally found him on a couch with Sharkie and sat down to join them.

'Hi, Piper. I hope you enjoyed the concert tonight,' said Sharkie. 'It seemed to go down all right.'

Charlie put his arm around Sharkie's shoulders and a couple of photographers appeared from the crowd to snap them. 'It couldn't have gone better, Sharkie. You were fantastic. You heard the audience. They loved you.'

'Well, I was only one member of the band but I hope I didn't let you down.'

'You certainly didn't. You were great.'

'I don't mind admitting I was nervous as hell.'

'You've got nothing to be nervous about,' Piper put in. 'You stole the show tonight. You played like a true professional.'

Sharkie gave a boyish smile. 'I just did my best. But I'm very grateful to Charlie for giving me the break. I've always wanted to play in a band. It's been my ambition since I was a little boy.'

'Well, you've achieved it,' Charlie said. 'And you were brilliant. As soon as the dust settles I'm getting on the blower to start organising the Desperadoes' very own tour.'

***

Hours later, as they lay wrapped in each other's arms after a delicious bout of hungry lovemaking, Piper let her fingers run along Charlie's lips. 'Enjoy that?'

'Of course. I told you from the beginning there was no one better than you when it comes to rumpy-pumpy.'

'Thank you, Charlie. I heard what you said to Sharkie tonight.'

'What was that?'

'You said you were going to start organising a tour for the Desperadoes as soon as the dust had settled.'

He laughed. 'But of course. What do you expect me to do? I've just launched a successful band. Now I expect to make some money from them.'

'That's one of the things we've got to talk about,' she said, and drifted off to sleep.

Chapter Thirty-Six

Hotel Azul was shining in the afternoon sun when the driver, José, parked outside the entrance shortly after two o'clock. They had left their apartment in Dublin five hours earlier and now they were here for two weeks. Piper had wanted three but Charlie pleaded pressure of business and said one was the most he could spare. In the end, they had compromised.

Piper had thought long and hard about this break. It was an increasingly rare opportunity to spend some time alone with her husband and she intended to use it to good advantage. She wanted to unwind, catch up on her reading, eat food she hadn't cooked and relax with the people who mattered most in her life. But she also planned to use it to have the long-awaited showdown with her husband about his frantic lifestyle.

She anticipated a stormy response so she had shrewdly decided to wait till the end of the holiday before confronting him. There was no point in having a row during their first few days: it would poison the atmosphere for the rest of their holiday. But she was adamant that when they returned to Dublin some hard decisions would have been made.

Señor Hernandez hurried out to meet them. 'Welcome, welcome. We are all so happy to have you back. You are staying in the flat again. Everything is prepared. I have overseen all the arrangements. And the weather, it will be magnificent. I have checked the forecast. There is only sunshine for the next two weeks.'

That cheered Piper.

'Thank you, *Señor* Hernandez. We're delighted to be back. And I see from the accounts that the hotel is prospering under your stewardship. Well done.'

He blushed. 'We all strive to do our best, *Señora*.'

'Well, we're very pleased with the way you're running the hotel.'

The porters had collected the luggage and Piper, Charlie, Margie and Sofía followed Hernandez to the flat. As soon as the porters had been tipped and departed, the manager glanced quickly around the living room. 'Everything is to your satisfaction, *Señora*?'

'Everything is perfect.'

'I took the liberty of leaving some cava to welcome you.' He pointed to the bottle of sparkling wine in an ice bucket on a table in a corner. 'If there is anything else you require, please ring Room Service.'

'Thank you, *Señor*,' Piper said.

He made a little bow and departed with a wide smile on his face.

As soon as he was gone, Piper walked to the window, pulled back the curtains and looked out at the terrace. The lawn was newly trimmed, the gardens were in full flower and the sea sparkled like crystal.

Charlie came and put his face to hers, his arm draped round her shoulders. 'Happy?'

'Delirious,' she said, as his lips brushed hers. 'I've been looking forward to this trip for months. Now, is anybody hungry?'

'I am,' Charlie said.

'Then let's all head off to the bar and grab a bit of lunch. Then I'm going to sit by the pool for the remainder of the afternoon. We'll decide about dinner later.'

After they had eaten, they changed into their swimming gear and walked the short distance to the hotel pool. A couple of guests were already stretched out on loungers. Piper got out her sunscreen, put some on Sofía and herself, then perched her Ray-Bans on her nose and lay back.

Meanwhile, she was glad to see Charlie take out the paperback he had bought at the airport and start to skim through the pages. She felt a delicious contentment steal over her as the warm sun caressed her face and she listened to the lazy buzzing of the bees in the rosebushes.

They spent the afternoon reading and taking dips in the pool, and had an occasional sip of wine, which Piper had brought in a cooler.

A shadow fell across her face and she sat up to see Pedro, the former driver, now chef, standing over her. 'I hope I am not disturbing you, *Señora*,' he began. 'I heard you had arrived and I wanted to welcome you. You are looking very well. So is your lovely family.' He smiled at Charlie, Margie and Sofía.

'How are you, Pedro? Are you still enjoying your new job?'

'Yes, indeed, very much. I have been promoted. I am now the assistant chief chef.'

'Congratulations. I'm very pleased for you. You must have worked very hard.'

'But I enjoy it so much, *Señora*. It is what I was meant to do. And there is something else. Carmencita's father has agreed that we can be married. He is very proud of me. He tells all his friends that his daughter is to be married to the assistant chief chef in Hotel Azul. When I meet him now, he is courteous to me. He invites me to have a drink with him. Before, he would hardly speak to me. So, you see the big difference it has made to my life!'

'I'm very happy for you, Pedro. When are you getting married?'

'It will be next year. First we have to save the money to buy a house.'

'The time will go by quickly, you'll see.'

'Thank you, *Señora*. Now I must go to the kitchen and start work. But we will talk again. *Adios*.'

That evening, they dressed in casual clothes and started off towards the seafront in search of somewhere to eat. The evening was warm and crowds were thronging the promenade. No one was particularly hungry so they ended up eating pizza at a pavement café where they could watch the strollers drifting along the Paseo Maritimo. By the time they returned to Hotel Azul, it was after ten o'clock. Piper decided to turn in and make an early start in the morning.

As Charlie's strong arms encircled her and drew her close, a thought crossed her mind. His phone hadn't rung all day.

She smiled to herself. Their holiday was starting off on the right note.

***

The day was already bright as she set off through the gardens the following morning at seven o'clock. This was the time she liked best, before it got too hot and her energy began to flag. She slipped into the refreshing water of the pool, then swam for twenty minutes and got out. She towelled herself, then put on her dressing-gown. When she got back to the flat, she found Charlie sitting on the terrace with his laptop.

'Margie's up but Sofía is still sleeping. There's coffee brewing in the kitchen.'

'What are you doing, Charlie?'

'Just checking my emails.'

She frowned. 'I hope you're not going to spend the holiday working. We're here to relax, remember?'

'Of course, but I can't isolate myself from the world, Piper. Neither can you. Your mother rang while you were having your swim. I told her you'd call her back.'

Piper poured a cup of coffee, sat down beside Charlie and picked up her phone.

'Everything okay?' Rose wanted to know.

'So far, so good, flight left on time, weather's perfect. We're just taking it easy. How's Dad?'

'He's fine, sends his love. How's Sofía?'

'In her element. I promised to take her to the beach today. She likes that.'

'And Charlie?'

She glanced at her husband. 'He's on his computer but he kept his phone on silent all day yesterday. I think he's getting the message.'

She heard her mother laughing. 'Okay, I was just catching up. Keep in touch.'

'Will do.'

Next she rang Jo and checked that everything was under control at McKenzie Leisure. Then she set off for the bar to buy some croissants for breakfast. By ten o'clock they had packed their beach bags and were making their way down to the sea.

Sofía built sandcastles and paddled with Margie. Piper listened to her radio, and Charlie continued to turn the pages of his airport thriller, while around them holidaymakers stretched out in the sun. At one o'clock they trooped up to the beach bar and ate fried calamari rings with salad. Charlie drank a glass of wine and gave a sigh of contentment. 'I'm beginning to feel the benefit of this break already,' he said.

'That's the whole point!' Piper told him. 'You work too hard. You've got to learn to relax.'

He kissed her cheek. 'I was thinking we might go out to a decent restaurant tonight.'

'We could eat here at the hotel. The food's excellent. I can vouch for it.'

'Let's go somewhere different.'

'Okay, I'll ask *Señor* Hernandez to recommend somewhere special.'

'Brilliant,' Charlie said. Now I'll go back to my lounger and have a snooze.'

Piper smiled. That was exactly the sort of thing she wanted to hear. She was beginning to hope that she had finally convinced her husband of the wisdom of her advice.

That evening they dined at an upmarket restaurant in the centre of Marbella called El Molino, The Windmill. When they got home, they put Sofía to bed and sat on the terrace sipping wine in the moonlight. By midnight, they were tucked up in bed and Charlie was stroking her thigh. Piper closed her eyes. It had been a perfect day. She couldn't have felt happier.

The week continued in a similar fashion, with only slight variations. Piper was up each morning at seven and started the day with a brisk swim. Then it was breakfast and a trip to the beach or the pool. In the cool of the evening, they would stroll along the promenade, past the clowns and mime artists to have dinner.

A couple of times, they ate at the hotel where the food was superb. On two occasions, they got José to drive them along the coast and spent the afternoon walking around Puerto Banús or San Pedro. It was idyllic.

But it didn't last. One morning in the middle of the second week, Piper returned from her morning swim to find Charlie pacing up and down the terrace, his phone clamped to his ear, engaged in a heated conversation. At last he snapped it shut and sat down, scowling.

Piper stared at him. 'What's the problem?'

'That was Harry Stokes,' he growled.

'Should I know him?'

'He's a record producer. I did a deal with him for the Desperadoes' first release before I came away. Now he's trying to renege on his commitment. He wants to reduce the terms.'

'Why don't you tell him you're on holiday and you'll deal with it when you get back?'

He looked at her scornfully. 'By then it'll be too late. I have to deal with it now, Piper. There's a lot of money involved. These things can't wait.'

She had hoped to put off their talk till the end of the holiday but now she realised she had no choice. 'Put your phone away for a few minutes, Charlie. I want to talk to you.'

'What about?'

'Us.'

She sat down beside him. 'I was hoping to postpone this conversation but I think we'd better have it now.'

'I haven't got time, Piper. Can't it wait till later?'

'No, it can't. Now, please switch off your phone and put it away.'

Reluctantly he did as she requested. 'Well?' he said, his face still angry.

'You have to slow down. You have to spend more time with me and Sofía. I can't live like this. It's making me depressed.'

'But this is my business, Piper. It's different from yours. You've got Jo to look after things when you're away. I'm on my own.'

'Precisely. So why don't you follow my example? Why don't you hire someone to help you so you've got more free time?'

He laughed. 'Are you kidding? I wouldn't leave my business with anyone else. How do I know they wouldn't run off with some of my clients?'

'You choose someone you can trust.'

'You don't know the music business like I do, Piper. It's full of sharks. The minute my back was turned, my so-called partner would be robbing me blind.'

'I'm sure you could find someone if you tried. There must be some young person out there who's anxious to get a toehold in the scene.'

'Piper, you're not listening to me. It isn't possible. This is my business. I'm not sharing it with anyone.'

'Then cut back on your commitments. You told me when you were putting the Desperadoes together that it would be your last venture. Now you're working harder than ever.'

'Things have changed.'

'But your bands don't have to be touring all the time.'

He snorted. 'There are times when I think you're living in a fantasy world. The bands want to make money. So do I. And if I won't find them work, they'll go to someone who will.'

'I work in business too, a much bigger business than yours. I know how tough it can be. But I've managed to combine the two. Please, Charlie, can't you see what this is doing to our marriage?'

He sighed. 'Piper, I love you and Sofía. I want us all to be happy. But what you're asking is impossible.'

Her heart sank. She'd been hoping she might be able to convince him. Now she could see it was a waste of time. 'Are you saying you won't change?'

Charlie shook his head. 'It's not that I won't change. It's simply that I can't.'

CHAPTER THIRTY-SEVEN

The rest of the holiday limped along to its conclusion. Piper kept her feelings to herself because she didn't want to upset Sofía and Margie but inwardly she was fuming. When they got back to Dublin, Charlie flung himself into his work with all the zest he had displayed before he came away. He would leave in the mornings and wouldn't return till after midnight. He made several trips to London, and sometimes stayed for two and three days. If he wasn't on his phone talking to someone, he was busy firing off text messages.

A gulf began to open between them. Slowly, Piper began to see something that should have been obvious from the beginning. Charlie White was one of those men who couldn't stand still. He didn't play golf and had no interest in soccer, rugby or any other sport. He had no real friends, just a gang of hangers-on and sycophants. His only interest was his work in the music business. He had spoken the truth when he said he couldn't change. But worse was to come.

One morning, a few weeks later, Jo came into Piper's office looking uneasy and embarrassed. She made sure that the door was firmly closed before she sat down. She took a letter out of a file and placed it in front of her. 'I thought you should see this. I apologise for opening it by mistake. I couldn't read the typing on the envelope. But it's intended for you.'

Piper took the envelope and studied it. She could sympathise with Jo's difficulty. The name had been practically obliterated by the rain so that only the address was visible. 'What is it?'

'You'd better read it.'

Piper carefully opened the envelope and withdrew a page torn from a large notebook. Words cut from newspapers had been stuck on it.

YOU THINK YOU'RE THE QUEEN BEE DON'T YOU? WELL THINK AGAIN. YOUR HUSBAND CHARLIE WHITE IS TWO-TIMING YOU ALL OVER TOWN. I'VE SEEN IT WITH MY OWN EYES. UNLESS YOU PAY ME I WILL GO TO THE PAPERS. HOW WILL YOU LIKE THAT? I WILL CONTACT YOU AGAIN SOON.

As Piper read it, she was trembling. Finally, she put it down and stared at Jo. 'Where did it come from?'

'It arrived with the morning post.'

'Has anyone else seen it?'

'Only me.'

'This is awful,' she said. She buried her head in her hands. 'What am I going to do?'

Jo got up and came to stand beside her, stroking Piper's hair. 'I'm sure it's a shock, but if I was you, I'd ignore it.'

'But what if it's true? What if the person who sent this carries out their threat?'

'You don't think it's true, do you?'

'Not that Charlie's been unfaithful, of course not. But what if this person goes to the papers with some story? It doesn't have to be true to cause trouble. Think of the harm it would do. Think of the hurt to Sofía and my parents.'

'Destroy it, Piper. If the person who sent it is serious, they'll contact you again. They said so in the letter.'

Piper took a deep breath and tried to pull herself together. 'Thanks for bringing it to me, Jo. I need to think about this a bit more and then I'll decide what to do.'

'I'm really sorry,' her friend said. 'I don't know what more to say. There are a lot of sick people out there. Try not to let it upset you.'

***

Piper stayed in the office, but her mind wasn't on her work. It was dominated by the letter and the threat it posed. Only gradually did the allegations begin to filter into her brain. What if there was some substance to them? What if Charlie really had been unfaithful? She kept pushing the doubts out of her mind but they insisted on returning.

Never in all the years she had known him had he given her any reason to doubt his fidelity. But Charlie was a man. And he had plenty of opportunities. He spent a lot of his time at parties and nightclubs without her. And she knew that plenty of women would regard it as a triumph to get Charlie White into bed. What if he had succumbed?

In the end she decided to go home. She said goodbye to Jo and set out for Sandymount. She still hadn't made up her mind what to do with the letter. Should she take Jo's advice and ignore it or should she confront Charlie? But she had no evidence against him, only the claims in the letter, and Jo had already suggested it was the outpouring of a sick mind. If she raised the matter with her husband it would be certain to drive a further wedge between them. How would he react if she confronted him solely on the word of an anonymous blackmailer?

She had to get advice about the letter from someone who would know or it would worry her to distraction. There was only one group of people who had experience with this sort of thing: the police. She pulled over to the side of the road, took out her phone and rang the nearest station. Within minutes, she was put through to a young woman police officer, who gave her name as Grace Devine. She listened while Piper outlined her problem. 'Where are you now?'

Piper told her.

'Have you got the letter with you?'

'Yes.'

'Why don't you call in and talk to me?'

Grace Devine was in her mid-twenties, with short dark hair. She led Piper into an interview room and offered tea. When Piper accepted, she left the room and returned shortly with two mugs.

'Let me see the letter.'

Piper took the envelope from her bag and placed it on the table. Grace put on a pair of latex gloves, lifted it and examined it front and back. She took out the letter and started to read. When she had finished, she glanced up at Piper. 'Pretty nasty stuff. When did it arrive?'

'This morning.'

'Who else knows about it?'

'Just my deputy and the person who sent it, of course.'

'Do you mind if I hold on to it?'

'Go ahead.'

'We'll try to determine where it was posted and when, but it'll be like looking for a needle in a haystack.'

Piper nodded. She had already come to the same conclusion.

'However, there is something that strikes me as odd. Usually in cases like this, the blackmailer doesn't beat about the bush. They give detailed instructions about how much they want and how payment is to be made. This writer simply says they'll contact you again.' She paused. 'It makes me wonder if he or she is really serious. In many cases like this, the perpetrator is someone with a grudge who just wants to inflict pain in the most cowardly way possible. You are quite well known, Mrs White. You're successful in your own right and you're married to a prominent man. Unfortunately, people like you attract envy. My instinct tells me this letter was written by someone who is jealous of you.'

'But what if it's serious?'

'The writer will contact you again with instructions about payment. If they do, you must get in touch with us immediately and we'll take action to apprehend them. On no account should you attempt to deal with them on your own.

If you do, they'll just keep coming back for more till they've bled you dry.'

'Thank you,' Piper said.

'There's something else. If the person who wrote this letter really has evidence about your husband, why didn't they blackmail him? That would be the most obvious thing. Why target you?'

'Why do you think?'

'Because you're the one they want to hurt. They want to fill your mind with doubt. They want to torment you. I don't think this is about money. I think it's about making you suffer. And if I was you, I wouldn't allow them to succeed.'

* * *

Piper left the station feeling much better. She had done the right thing by taking the letter to the police. But she didn't relax entirely. From now on, she insisted that she opened all personal mail at McKenzie Leisure, but the second letter from the blackmailer never came. Grace Devine had been correct in her assessment. The person who had sent the threat had simply wanted to make her suffer by destroying her peace of mind.

One day she received a call from the young policewoman. 'I haven't heard from you,' she said. 'Am I right to assume that the demand letter never arrived?'

'Yes,' Piper said.

'That's what I hoped. I don't have much to report at our end. We haven't been able to trace the sender. I told you I didn't think it was very likely that we would.'

'You did. But you were very helpful and I want to thank you most sincerely.'

'That's just my job,' Grace Devine said. 'I'm glad it all turned out well. Do you mind if I hold on to the letter, just in case?'

'Not at all,' Piper said. 'I never want to see it again.'

Even though the threat had receded, Piper kept wondering who had sent the letter, in particular if it was someone she knew. Who hated her so much that they wanted to inflict such pain? If Corinne was still around, she might have suspected her. But her sister-in-law had disappeared to some distant land beyond the reach of the law. Whoever had sent the blackmail threat, it wasn't her. She finally concluded that it was as Jo Ferguson had said, some sick person jealous of her success, someone she probably didn't even know who just wanted to make her suffer.

Piper and Charlie continued to be busy at work. Indeed, he was working harder than ever, constantly on the go with new schemes and ideas. Increasingly, they were living almost separate lives. Piper wondered how long it could last.

One afternoon she was collecting together some clothes for the dry-cleaner and took one of Charlie's suits out of his wardrobe. As usual, she checked the pockets and felt something small and hard in one. Curious, she put her hand inside and withdrew a silver earring.

She examined it. It looked expensive. But what was it doing in Charlie's pocket? She put the earring into an envelope in her bureau drawer, sent the suit to the cleaner and said nothing to Charlie.

But the doubt was now in full flood. She could find no innocent explanation for the presence of an earring in Charlie's pocket. She thought about it for a week and then she took action.

The office was above a block of shops in Abbey Street, central Dublin, with 'PARSONS PRIVATE INVESTIGATIONS' in large letters on the frosted-glass window. Inside, a man in a smart grey suit was sitting behind a desk. He looked up as she came in.

'Mrs White? Please sit down.' He pointed to a chair. 'Did you bring the information we discussed earlier on the phone?'

Piper opened her bag and took out a recent photograph of Charlie, his business address, mobile phone number, car make, colour and registration. The man took it and put it in a drawer. 'Leave it with me, Mrs White. I'll contact you as soon as my inquiry is complete.'

He stood up and shook hands. Piper walked down the stairs and out to the street. Her heart was thumping. She had just crossed a line. Something told her that things would never be the same again.

*****

At home, she tried to pretend that everything was normal but it was difficult. It was hard to look Charlie in the eye, eat at the same table and sleep in the same bed and not think about the private detective gathering evidence of his infidelity. Even worse was the thought of what he might find.

He rang one morning while she was at work and asked if he could see her. Half an hour later she was once more climbing the stairs to his office. He was sitting behind the same desk wearing the same suit. In front of him was a folder. She knew in her heart it was not good news.

He waited till she was seated. 'Mrs White, do you know a woman called Alice McDowell?'

CHAPTER THIRTY-EIGHT

Piper sat still. In a flash, she saw what lay ahead: the end of her marriage and all she had once held dear. Her first thought was for Sofía. She loved her daddy. 'Yes,' she replied.

'Your husband is conducting an affair with her.'

'Are you sure?' she whispered, but as she uttered the words she knew how foolish they sounded.

'I'm certain, Mrs White.' He tapped the folder in front of him. 'We have all the information here, dates, times, locations. We have photographs, video and audio evidence. There is absolutely no doubt.'

He opened the folder and passed a set of photographs across the desk. She looked at the first. It showed Charlie and Alice McDowell in a bar with their heads together, smiling into each other's faces. The next one showed them kissing. Piper couldn't look at the rest. She pushed them away. 'Those photos don't prove they're having an affair.'

'I agree. But this does.'

He delved into the folder again and brought out a small audio cassette. 'Would you like me to play it for you?'

She nodded. He slipped it into a machine and turned up the volume. She heard Charlie's voice, then Alice's. There was laughter and the unmistakable sound of a couple making love. She felt her stomach tighten. She reached out quickly and turned it off. 'How did you get that?'

'We have our methods,' the man said.

'You bugged his office?'

'Somewhere else.'

'A hotel room?'

'Yes.'

'God damn it,' she said. She felt dirty and cheap. She had commissioned this sleazy material. She had paid this man to spy on her husband. She felt sick.

'Mrs White, the less you know about how this information was obtained, the better. All that matters is we have the evidence you asked for. Did you recognise your husband's voice?'

'Yes.'

'And Ms McDowell's?'

'Yes.'

He passed the photographs across again. 'Is that your husband and Ms McDowell?'

'Yes.'

'We also have video evidence of them together. Do you want to see it?'

'No,' Piper said.

They sat looking at each other in silence.

'I appreciate this is very difficult for you,' he said. 'It's always shocking to discover we've been betrayed by someone we trust, even when we've suspected it.'

'How often did they meet?'

He flicked open the file again and studied a printed sheet. 'Eight times in the past three weeks, mainly in the evening but not always. There were two meetings in the Phoenix Park at lunchtime. They sat in your husband's car. All the dates, times and locations are logged here. What do you plan to do with this material?'

'Confront him with it, of course.'

'I would suggest you seek legal advice if you intend to take the matter further. We can hold the material for you if you prefer.'

'Please do that.'

'In that case, if you're satisfied with our work, I'd like to present you with an invoice for our fees. All outlay and expenditure are clearly explained. There is also a charge for VAT at twenty-one per cent.'

He slid the bill across the desk.

***

Piper stumbled down the stairs and into the street. In the twenty minutes she had sat in the investigator's office, her life had fallen apart. In that short time she had lost her marriage to the man she had once loved and admired. How had it happened? What had she done wrong?

Her head was reeling. She needed to sit somewhere quiet, away from the honking traffic and the milling crowds, some little oasis where she could gather her thoughts and decide how to proceed. She thought of Trinity College. It would take ten minutes to walk there and she knew she would find the tranquillity she was seeking. She rang Jo, told her that something had come up and she was taking the rest of the day off. Then she set out for Trinity.

The college was gleaming in the autumn sun. As she walked along the cobbled paths towards the Buttery Café, she thought bitterly of Alice and the last time she had seen her. She was just an ordinary young woman. By no stretch of the imagination could she be regarded as beautiful. What had Charlie seen in her? Rage surged from somewhere deep inside her. She had introduced Alice to Charlie one night in Aunt Polly's and this was her reward. For her husband, the smooth-tongued adulterer, she felt nothing but contempt. He didn't know it yet but he had thrown away a pearl beyond price.

She found a bench and sat down. Gradually, the fury subsided and a cold clarity took its place. She would not make a scene. She would not allow Charlie to see how hurt she was. It would be hard but she would conduct herself with dignity. She would confront him with the knowledge she had gained from the private detective. She would take Sofía and go to live with her parents. Once she had sought legal advice she would file for divorce.

At last, she got up from the bench and began walking again. Her pride was shattered. The media would have a field day when they found out. It would be splashed all over the tabloids. They had helped to build her up when she was a young woman-about-town and now they wouldn't hesitate to drag her down.

She drove home and told Margie she had a personal matter to discuss with Charlie and that she could take a few days off. She fed Sofía and bathed her. Then she read her a story and put her to bed. She packed her bags and put them in the car. Then she settled down to wait for Charlie's return while in her head she rehearsed what she would say. Outside the window, she watched the sun sink over the bay.

As she sat in the quiet apartment, Piper was strangely calm. She knew that her marriage had been dying for some time. Charlie had struck the *coup de grâce*. But the marriage could have been saved if he had been prepared to meet her halfway. Now, with the evidence of his adultery, there was no turning back.

At nine o'clock, she heard his car drive through the gates. and a few minutes later, his key in the lock. The door opened and he bounded in. He was smiling, the same old Charlie in his fine suit and expensive shoes, the debonair playboy who had stolen her heart with his charming ways and now had broken it with his deceit. He stopped when he saw her sitting alone by the window.

'Where's Sofía?' he asked.

'I've put her to bed. I don't want her to hear what I have to say.'

'Oh,' Charlie said. His manner changed and he became cautious. Perhaps he sensed trouble.

'Please sit down.'

He lowered himself into a chair beside her. 'What's wrong, Piper? Something's upset you.'

She steeled herself. Whatever happened she must remain calm and not get angry. 'I know about you and Alice McDowell.'

His face changed colour. For a moment, he looked confused but he quickly pulled himself together. 'Alice McDowell? What about her?'

323

'You're having an affair with her.'

He laughed but it sounded hollow. 'An affair? Are you mad? What put that idea into your head?'

'You've been seen with her.'

'Of course. She does a lot of PR work for me.'

'You took her with you on the Hell's Kitchen European tour.'

'Sure I did. I needed her to handle the publicity.'

'So your relationship is purely professional?'

'Exactly.'

'Then why have you been meeting her in your car in the Phoenix Park? Why have you been taking her to hotel rooms? I know all the dates and times and locations. I've even heard you having sex with her, you bastard.'

He stared at her for a minute. 'You've been following me?'

'Not me, someone else.'

'A private detective?'

'Yes.'

His head dropped into his hands and he sighed. 'Why did you do that, Piper?'

'Because I suspected you were up to something and I was right. You left her earring in your suit pocket.'

His face went pale.

'I have all the evidence I need, Charlie. I trusted you and you betrayed me. Now I'm leaving and I'm taking Sofía. Don't try to stop me. I'm filing for a divorce. Any further communications between us will be conducted through my solicitor. She'll write to you shortly.'

She got up but Charlie made one more desperate effort to

hold her. 'Wait,' he said. 'Let me try to explain. I have been seeing Alice, that's true. But it's not what you think. It means nothing to me. It was sex, that's all. There is no emotional involvement. I don't love her, Piper. You're the one I love. You're the only one I have ever loved.'

She looked at him. He was pleading with her. 'How long has it been going on?'

'About six months.'

'Who started it?'

'I don't know. We were working closely together. Who knows how these things happen?'

'You never thought of me waiting for you here in this apartment when you were taking her to hotels for sex?'

He hung his head. 'I've done wrong. I admit it. But we can start again with a clean slate. Please don't throw everything away.'

'You're the one who threw it away,' she said bitterly.

'Please, I'm asking you to give me one more chance. I beg you, Piper.'

She felt pity come from somewhere in her breast. This was the man she had known and loved for a long time, the father of her child. He was pleading with her for one more chance. Was it too much to grant?

For an instant, she hesitated. But she had vowed to be cool and rational. He was sorry now but how long would it last? How could she ever trust him again after what he had done?

'Charlie, our marriage has been in trouble for a long time. I brought you down to Hotel Azul and begged you to cut down on your workload so we could spend more time together as a family. I asked you to hire an assistant to help you, and you refused point-blank. Do you remember what I said that time you disappeared to London and wouldn't return my calls?'

'What?'

'I told you never to take me for granted.'

'I remember that.'

'And do you remember what I said would happen if you ever did?'

'Tell me.'

'I said I'd be gone and there would be no second chance.'

Charlie looked stunned.

'There's one thing you should have learned about me, Charlie. I keep my word.'

She woke Sofía, brought her out to the car and strapped her into the back seat. A few minutes later she was driving away.

CHAPTER THIRTY-NINE

She drove straight to Elsinore. Her parents were surprised to see her and appalled when she explained the circumstances, but they agreed immediately that she could have her old bedroom. As the days went past, Sofía adapted to her new surroundings where she now had doting grandparents to cosset and spoil her.

But the matter didn't end there. Despite Piper's warning to communicate through her solicitor, Charlie wouldn't give up. After he had recovered from the bombshell of her departure, he besieged her with phone calls and text messages, begging for a meeting at which they could try to smooth things out.

Piper never weakened in her resolve. She had made her decision and was determined to stick with it. Slowly, Charlie seemed to realise that she was not going to change her mind and switched his attention to securing visiting rights to Sofía.

This was something on which Piper was prepared to negotiate. Charlie was the little girl's father and he had been a good parent. She agreed that he could see his daughter at weekends at Elsinore. On those occasions she took care to absent herself so that they wouldn't meet.

The first thing she had planned to do once she had settled into her parents' house and removed her belongings from the apartment was to consult the family solicitor about a divorce. Before she did this her mother asked if she could talk to her. They sat in the drawing room and Rose got straight to the point. 'Are you absolutely sure you want to go ahead with this?' she asked.

'Yes.'

'Your father and I are shocked by what has happened. We liked Charlie. We always thought you were happy together.'

'We *were* happy,' Piper replied. 'But he spent all his time at work. I begged him to slow down but it was like talking to a brick wall. Then I discovered he was carrying on an affair with another woman behind my back. You have to see this from my side, Mum. I'm the innocent party. I did nothing wrong.'

'Can't you forgive him? Let him have another chance? He's had a fright. Your father never strayed, thank God, but I know plenty of men who did. They think they're supermen, masters of the universe. All they need is one good shock and they never do it again. I'm sure Charlie will learn his lesson.'

'How can I be certain?'

Rose shrugged. 'You can't. You just have to trust him.'

'But that's the whole point, Mum. I can't trust him. I know Charlie better than you. I know exactly what he's like. He has women throwing themselves at him all the time. I couldn't live with the uncertainty, checking my watch every evening to make sure he's home on time. Charlie is Charlie. He's not going to change.'

Her mother gave a deep sigh. 'It's your business. I shouldn't interfere.'

'I know you mean well.'

'I was thinking of you and the little one. She needs a father.'

'I know that, too, Mum, but my mind is made up.'

'All right,' her mother said. 'I won't mention it again.'

***

Her mother wasn't the only person to urge Piper to reconsider. Some of her friends, including Jo Ferguson, made the same suggestion once they'd got over the shock of the news.

'Is there no other way round this?' Jo asked. 'Is there no possibility of reconciliation?'

'None.'

'You told me once that if you ever lost Charlie you'd be bereft.'

'That's true. Don't think I feel happy about it, Jo, because I don't. But I'll get over it.'

'It might have been just a fling. As they get older, some men get these crazy urges to prove they can still attract women. It's a psychological thing with them.'

'I'm not sure this was just a fling, and I'm not convinced it was only going on for six months. I think it might have been much longer.'

'Can't you cut him some slack?'

'Let me ask you something,' Piper said. 'What would you do in my shoes?'

'I'd take him back. He's a great guy. I'd let him sweat for a while till he got the message and then I'd relent. With strict conditions, of course.'

'I can't do that,' Piper said.

She was getting tired of people giving her well-intentioned advice even if she sometimes wondered if they might be right. It was true that Charlie was a great guy. He had swept her off her feet. For most of the time she had known him, he had behaved impeccably, always charming, generous, kind and considerate. In most ways, they had been a perfect match.

Despite the stiff upper lip she portrayed to the outside world, Piper's heart was breaking. She had loved Charlie with every fibre of her being. Of all the men she had known, he was the only man she had truly loved.

But she couldn't forgive the betrayal. Perhaps it was pride or maybe something deeper. In being unfaithful, Charlie had shattered some spell. He had turned out not to be the man she'd thought he was. And, with this realisation, the magic had vanished. Charlie had feet of clay, like all the other men she had known.

She instructed her solicitor to begin divorce proceedings. Then she buried herself in work in the hope that it would provide distraction. But she found it difficult to adapt to single life again. She missed Charlie's company, his charm and his warm body lying beside her in bed.

And, of course, any remaining social life she had was now completely suspended. She could hardly go out partying on her own without raising eyebrows and starting tongues wagging. So far, she had managed to keep the break-up under wraps and only a small handful of people knew about it. But that was about to change.

One morning, as she was returning to Elsinore from her regular run across Howth Head, she heard someone call her name. When she turned, a photographer began snapping like crazy. Then a reporter appeared out of the bushes. 'Mrs White, can you confirm that you have split up with your husband?'

She felt her stomach turn over. Her secret was out. 'No comment,' she said, and let herself into the grounds. She went straight up to her office and met Jo.

'What's happened?' her friend asked. 'You look like you've seen a ghost.'

Piper's hand was trembling as she sat down at her desk. 'I've just been ambushed by a photographer and a reporter. They were asking about the break-up with Charlie. The news is out, Jo. They're going to splash it all over the tabloids. This is what I dreaded most.'

'You need to talk to a professional,' Jo said, firmly, 'someone who can handle these things. I know a woman who might be able to help. Her name is Midge McCarthy. Would you like me to call her?'

'Who is she?'

'She's a public relations consultant. She'll know what to do.'

Piper nodded.

'I'll call her right away,' Jo said. 'But first I'm going to get you a strong cup of coffee.'

Twenty minutes later Midge McCarthy rang Piper. After introducing herself, she got straight to the point. 'Jo tells me you've got a problem.'

331

'Are we speaking strictly confidentially?'

'Of course.'

'My husband is Charlie White, the music promoter.'

'I know who he is.'

So Midge McCarthy's clued in, Piper thought. That's a promising start. 'Our marriage recently broke up and we're living apart. I'd been hoping to keep it private but today I was doorstepped by a photographer and a reporter outside my parents' house.'

'Did you tell them anything?'

'No.'

'Good. Don't talk to them under any circumstances. If you said it was a nice day they'd twist it into something. This is the downside of all that hype you and Charlie have been getting. Those people would devour their own children. Jo tells me you work from your parents' place?'

'That's right.'

'Stay there. Don't go out. Keep a low profile for a few days and it might blow over. If it doesn't, ring me again.'

'Okay.'

'And I'm really sorry about you and your husband.'

Piper felt slightly relieved after that conversation. Around midday when she was sure the newspapermen had gone, she sent Jo on an errand to the convenience store to check the early editions of the evening papers. She returned with a copy of the *Gazette* and a doleful look on her face. She handed it to Piper. The story was splashed across the front page.

CELEBRITY COUPLE PART

....

Dublin's dream couple, the music supremo Charlie White and his stunning wife, Piper McKenzie, boss of McKenzie Leisure, have split up after seven years of marriage, the *Gazette* has learned.

The couple who have been the toast of the Dublin social scene are now living apart. A close friend told the *Gazette* today that they had recently been experiencing matrimonial difficulties. The couple have one child. When asked about the dramatic developments, Mrs White refused to comment.

The report was accompanied by a photograph of a harassed-looking Piper in her running gear dashing into Elsinore. Inside, there was a two-page spread detailing her and Charlie's achievements. It was plastered with pictures of them drinking champagne at Aunt Polly's and other celebrity watering holes.

She steeled herself for trouble. She knew how the press worked. Now that the *Gazette* had published the story, the others would be after it too. It was only a matter of time before the storm broke.

But she couldn't have prepared herself for what happened next. Half an hour later, the landline rang. When she lifted it, a voice said, 'Mrs White?'

'Yes.'

'This is Freddie Harris of the *Tribune*. I wonder if you'd like to comment—'

Piper slammed down the phone. Immediately it was ringing again. She removed it from its cradle and left it to lie on the table. No sooner had she done that than the intercom on the security gates was buzzing. When she answered, a reporter from one of the tabloids asked if she could spare five minutes to talk to him. She switched him off.

Her father came into the room – the noise had alerted him. 'What's going on, Piper?'

'The press have got wind of Charlie and me and they're looking for interviews. They're gathering outside the house.'

He snorted. 'I'll turn the garden hose on them.'

'That won't shift them.'

He shook his head sadly. 'I wish you'd never got involved with these people, Piper. You've become public property and now they're latching on to your distress.'

She used her mobile to ring Midge McCarthy. While she waited for her to answer, she pulled back the curtains and peeped out. A jeep was parked on the road outside the house and four men were standing beside it. Two had cameras and were taking photos of Elsinore. She let the curtains fall back with a sinking heart.

'Hello?' Midge said.

'It's Piper. The story's broken. The media are gathering outside my parents' house as I speak.'

Midge sounded surprised. 'That was fast. They've obviously decided to go big on this. There's probably a similar posse right now outside your husband's place.'

'What will I do? Can I call the police to remove them?'

'Only if they're trespassing.'

'So what am I supposed to do? I'm a prisoner in my home.'

'Let me think about it and I'll get back to you.'

Piper turned off the phone and looked out of the window again. Another car had joined the jeep and two more men were getting out. In no time others would have gathered and they would have the house surrounded. This was a crisis. She had to act quickly.

Just then her phone rang again. It was Midge.

'We'll have to get you out of there,' she said. 'It's the only way. Now, listen carefully to what I say.'

She went and spoke to Margie and told her to pack a bag. Then she went into Jo's office. 'I want you to leave here right away and take Margie with you. Take your car and go home. Drive slowly as you leave so they can see it's you and not me. On no account speak to them. When you get home, stay there till I contact you again.'

'What's going on?'

'I'll explain later.'

Finally, she started packing bags for herself and Sofía. Then she went to find her father. 'I need to ask a favour, Dad. I want you to drive me and Sofía to Jo Ferguson's house.'

'Why on earth are you going there?'

'We have to get away.'

'You're letting those parasites drive you out of your home?'

'Yes. So long as I'm here, they'll be camped at the gates.'

'All right,' he said wearily.

***

335

Twenty minutes later, Henry drove his Mercedes out of the garage and down the drive to the gates. He sat with his head uncovered so that he could be clearly seen. In the back, crouched on the floor and covered with a blanket, Piper lay with Sofía in her arms. The car slowed and waited for the gates to open. As soon as it drove onto the road, the cameras were flashing.

She could hear the reporters shouting questions and then the car gathered speed as it left Elsinore behind. 'Are they following?' she asked nervously.

'I don't think so. They're still standing on the road.'

'Good.'

So far, her plan appeared to be working. The only people the reporters had seen leaving Elsinore were Jo and her father. She was hoping they would conclude that she was still barricaded inside the house. Fifteen minutes later she heard the Mercedes pull up and stop. She waited for the word from her father.

'All clear,' he said. 'You can get out.'

Piper sat up and climbed out with Sofía. Jo's Fiat was parked alongside with Jo at the wheel. Margie took Sofía and cuddled her while Piper put the bags in the boot and got in beside them.

Her father put his head through the window. 'Good luck,' he said. 'I'm sorry it's come to this.'

'Thanks for everything, Dad. I'll give you a call as soon as we arrive.'

The Fiat started up. Piper took a scarf from her bag and

wrapped it round her head, then clamped her sunglasses to her face. 'I'm grateful, Jo. I really am.'

'Oh, give over!' Jo laughed. 'I'm enjoying this. Did I ever tell you I always wanted to be a spy?'

At the airport, Jo said goodbye and they hurried inside to Departures. Piper bought the tickets and proceeded to check-in. Then, when they were through security, safely beyond the reach of prying reporters, she could relax.

After that, everything went smoothly. The plane left on time and touched down in Málaga at seven thirty. The sun was descending, a bright orange globe in the sky. When Piper walked outside to the taxi rank, the first thing she recognised was the sweet scent of the flowers.

CHAPTER FORTY

Señor Hernandez was waiting to welcome them when they arrived at Hotel Azul and had the flat ready. Piper had called him from Dublin airport to tell him she was coming and he had sent José to meet them. After the media frenzy she had left in Dublin, the little hotel was like a sanctuary of calm. In Spain, she would find peace. Hopefully, the media pack would never track her here.

The first thing she did, when she had unpacked the bags and sorted out the sleeping arrangements, was to ring home. Her mother answered.

'We've arrived safely.'

'Thank God for that,' Rose replied.

'Are the press still outside the house?'

'More of them than ever. They're parked all over the road. The neighbours are complaining and I can't say I blame them. People don't like this sort of hullabaloo.'

'It won't last long,' Piper said. 'Once they realise I've gone, they'll move somewhere else.'

'Let's hope you're right. I don't like having that mob out there. How's the little one?'

'She's fine.'

I miss her already,' her mother said. 'And you. How long do you think you'll stay down there?'

'I don't know. At least till the fuss blows over.'

'I'll call you again tomorrow. Now, I'm putting you on to your father. He wants a word.'

She spoke to Henry, told him that everything was fine, then rang Jo, who assured her that she would look after everything while she was away and Piper needn't worry. Finally she called Midge McCarthy. 'You can let those jackals know I'm no longer at home.'

'Good. Now they'll turn all their attention to your husband.'

'Where is he?'

'Holed up in his apartment. Unlike you, he has nowhere to run. It can't be easy for him.'

'What are you planning to do?'

'I've drafted a press statement in your joint names. It simply says you've agreed to separate. It doesn't mention divorce or go into any details. He's okayed it.'

'Do you think it'll work?'

'We'll see. I'll email a copy for your approval and, if you're happy, we'll release it.'

'Okay. There's one other thing, Midge. Under no circumstances tell him where I am. The fewer people who know, the better.'

The statement arrived fifteen minutes later. It was brief and stuck rigidly to the facts. Piper emailed her approval. She was beginning to feel a tinge of sympathy for Charlie. She had escaped but he was still in Dublin and would have to face the music. Her father had been right. The gloss was wearing off her celebrity lifestyle. She was learning the hard way that there was a price to pay for living in the limelight.

By now, the stars were out and the sound of music came drifting on the balmy night air from the seafront. But Piper wasn't in a relaxing mood. She had just been through a harrowing experience and now she felt exhausted. They ordered sandwiches from the bar and ate them on the terrace. By half past eleven, they were safely asleep in their beds.

***

She woke early the following morning, refreshed. While Margie and Sofía slept on, she slipped out and went for a dip in the pool, then met the others for breakfast in the dining room. Piper was still nervous about leaving the hotel. Marbella was a favourite haunt of Irish holidaymakers: someone might recognise her and word would filter back to Dublin. The media pack would think nothing of hopping on a plane and pursuing her here. In fact, they'd probably enjoy it.

But Sofía was impatient to get to the beach.

'Not today, honey.'

'Why not, Mummy? I like the beach.'

'Today we're going to stay in the garden.'

As soon as it was nine o'clock Irish time, she rang Sofía's school, spoke to the headmistress and explained that she had to take her daughter out of class for a while because an emergency situation had arisen. She promised to have her back again as soon as possible. The headmistress was sympathetic. She had probably read the newspapers.

For the next few days, they remained confined to the hotel and spent their time around the pool. Each morning, Piper talked to Jo, who brought her up to date on the affairs of McKenzie Leisure. She spoke to her parents. She monitored the media situation with Midge McCarthy. The tabloids had called off their siege of Elsinore but they were still baying for blood.

One evening she decided to walk into Marbella. She left Sofía with Margie, put on her shades and a baseball cap and set off through the winding cobbled streets till she came to the outskirts of the town. The sun was going down and a cool breeze drifted up from the sea. From bar doorways, she could hear music and laughter. She turned a corner and came across a little restaurant.

She caught her breath. It was the very one where she had met Eduardo. Some impulse drew her in. She sat down at a table in the garden and asked for a glass of wine while she took in the surroundings. It hadn't changed. The same red geraniums blazed along the wall and the yellow nasturtiums tumbled from their pots. Over there was the table where she had sat talking with him. She closed her eyes and the memories flooded back.

Eduardo had taken her to dinner later that day, and afterwards he had walked back with her to the villa. They had paused by the gates and he had kissed her. She could still remember the thrill that had swept through her and the fire that had burned in her veins.

She had wanted Eduardo, wanted him desperately, but she had sent him away and told him they must never meet again.

341

She could recall the hurt in his eyes as he turned from her to walk out of her life.

She finished her wine, left some coins on the table and departed with a heavy heart.

***

The following morning, she woke early and had a swim. While she drank her coffee on the terrace, she thought of how her life had turned out. She could see now that she had married the wrong man. Charlie White, with his dashing debonair ways, had brought her unhappiness and, in the end, he had betrayed her.

As the morning sun began to warm the air, a plan took shape in her mind. What had Eduardo told her the last time they met? That he had qualified and was now working as a doctor at a hospital in Málaga. She wondered if he was still there.

She took out her phone and rang Jo. 'Tied to your desk, I hope?'

'Piper! I wasn't expecting to hear from you so early.'

'I'm keeping you on your toes.'

'What's the weather like?'

'Nice and bright this morning and still quite warm.'

'Any sign of those creepy tabloid hacks?'

'Not so far.'

'You're safe, Piper. They won't find you there.'

'I want to pick your brains,' Piper said. 'Remember Eduardo and Cesar, the students we met in Marbella when we were young and foolish?'

'What about them?'

'Can you remember their surnames?'

Her friend laughed. 'What's this about?'

'Just an idea I've got. They told us their names. I can remember that much.'

'I can remember Eduardo's.'

Piper felt her heart skip. 'What was it?'

'Garcia.'

'How can you be sure?'

'Because I was studying the work of the Spanish poet Federico Garcia Lorca at the time and I was struck by the coincidence. It's stayed in my mind ever since.'

'You're certain?'

'Absolutely.'

'You're a treasure, Jo. I'll talk to you later.'

'Wait! You haven't told me what this is about.'

'Be patient. All will be revealed.'

Piper switched her phone off. So far, so good, but she still had a lot to do.

She went inside the flat. Sofía and Margie were still sleeping. She got dressed, then walked the short distance to the foyer where *Señor* Hernandez was at the desk, consulting a register. 'Could I have a word with you, *Señor*?'

He looked up and smiled. 'Of course, *Señora*. Please come into my office.' He brought her into the cool room and offered coffee, which she declined.

'I need your advice. I'm trying to find a doctor who works in Málaga. I have his name and not much more. But I know he works in one of the hospitals there.'

343

He knitted his brow, then pulled a telephone directory off a shelf and quickly turned the pages. 'There are six major hospitals in Málaga, *Señora*. Do you know which area of medicine he works in?'

Piper shook her head.

He thought for a moment longer. 'I'm not sure if this will work but perhaps the simplest thing is to ring each hospital and ask if this person is on the staff.' He took a pen, copied the phone numbers from the telephone directory on to a sheet of paper and passed it across the table to her. 'Good luck,' he said.

She checked the time. It was not yet ten o'clock. She went back to the flat and found Sofía and Margie having breakfast.

'Can we go to the beach today, Mummy?' Sofía asked, as soon as she saw her.

'I'll think about it, honey, but first I have a little job to do.'

She told Margie she had to go into Marbella but would be back within an hour. Then she set off towards the town. She needed to think hard before she started ringing the hospitals. She would probably be put through to a switchboard and the operators were unlikely to speak English. How would she explain herself?

Then she had a brainwave. In a side street, she came across an Internet café. Most such places were used by tourists and foreigners so there was a good possibility that someone would speak English. The place was empty, apart from a young man sitting behind a desk. He looked up as she came in.

'*Habla inglés?*' she asked.

'Yes, *Señora*.'

'I need a favour. I'm willing to pay you fifty euros if you can help me.' Piper opened her purse and took out a note. The young man sat up and his eyes brightened.

Piper explained her situation and how she needed someone to help her find a Dr Eduardo Garcia, whom she believed worked in one of the six hospitals whose numbers she had written down. She gave him the list.

'I can try,' the young man said, 'but it won't be easy. This doctor may not work in any of these hospitals or he may have moved elsewhere. There are so many difficulties.'

'Just do your best and I'll pay you anyway.'

The young man picked up the phone and dialled. Every so often he would break into rapid Spanish and she would hear Eduardo's name mentioned. Then he would shake his head and start again.

Piper watched with growing desperation. On the fifth call, there was a breakthrough. The young man grinned. He continued speaking in Spanish, paused and drummed his fingers on the desk, then talked again. At last he handed the phone to her.

'Have you got him?' she asked, her spirits lifting.

'No, but this man knows him. He speaks English.'

'Hello,' Piper began. 'I'm a friend of Dr Garcia. I'm trying to find him. Is he there?'

'No,' the voice said. 'Not today. He is on leave.'

'Can you give me his phone number so I can call him?'

'I'm afraid I'm not allowed to do that, *Señora*.'

'It's very important that I contact him. What do you suggest I do?'

'If you leave me your name and number, I will make sure he gets it. Then he can call you.'

'Okay,' Piper said. 'Have you got a pen?' She spelt out her name and phone number. 'Thank you very much,' she said.

'*De nada*,' the voice replied, and the line went dead.

***

She left the café with mixed feelings. She had got further than she'd expected but there were still obstacles in her way. The man she had spoken to might not pass on her message. Even if he did, Eduardo might not want to return her call. She could hardly blame him, after the way she had treated him. She had to face the fact that she might have wasted her time and might never see him again.

She walked back to the hotel, trying to keep in the shade. She found Margie and Sofía playing in the garden. As she approached, the nanny stood up. She looked uneasy. 'There was a call for you while you were away.'

'Who was it?' Piper asked.

'Charlie. He rang the hotel.'

CHAPTER FORTY-ONE

Piper's heart sank. She removed her sunglasses. Charlie knew she was in Marbella. 'What did he want?'

'He wants you to call him urgently.'

She thanked Margie and went into the flat, sat down at the kitchen table and took out her phone. Charlie answered at the first ring.

'How did you know I was here?'

'That was easy. When I heard you'd gone, Hotel Azul was the obvious place.'

'Who else knows?'

'No one.'

'Didn't I tell you only to communicate through my solicitor?'

'You did, and I apologise, but this is important. It's something only you and I can sort out between us.'

'What?'

'Before we start, how's Sofía?'

'She's fine, Charlie. You've got nothing to worry about on her account.'

'I wish I could see her. I miss her. I miss you both, Piper.'

'You'll be able to see her again when things quieten down and we can return to Dublin.'

'Well, that's exactly what I want to talk about. I need you to do me a favour. The media are persecuting me. They have the apartment under constant surveillance. Everywhere I go, they follow me. If I turn up at Aunt Polly's, they're waiting to ambush me. If I talk to a woman, our pictures are in the papers the next day. It's Hell on earth, Piper. I can't do my job properly. My business is suffering.'

She was tempted to tell him he had brought it on his own head and hers by his affair with Alice McDowell. 'What do you expect *me* to do about it?'

'I've been told the only way to call them off is to hold a joint press conference, you and me.'

'A what?'

'A joint press conference, let them fire their questions, clear the air. It'll lance the boil and then they'll leave us alone, so you can come home and I can get on with my work.'

'Are you out of your mind?'

'How do you mean?'

'This isn't the launch of a concert tour. They'd tear us apart. They'd ask all sorts of intimate questions. They'd grill you about Alice McDowell.'

'They don't know about her.'

'Give them time. They're probably digging for dirt right now. And you want me to take part in this circus? You want me to sit there in front of those sewer rats while they trawl through your dirty laundry and then splash it all over the papers for every little voyeur to gloat over? You must be mad if you expect me to agree to something like that.'

'I'm sorry you feel that way, Piper.'

'Well, I do. And if you had any sense, you'd follow my example and disappear for a few weeks. Then they'd have nothing to write about.'

'And who'd run my business? Who'd look after the bands? They're already suffering as it is.'

'I told you to get an assistant. If you'd listened to me you wouldn't be in this predicament.'

'So what am I supposed to do?'

'I'm sorry but I can't help you, Charlie. Nothing would persuade me to give a press conference to those lowlifes.'

There was a pause. His next remark rocked her back on her feet. 'Well, in that case, I'll just have to do it myself.'

'You do what you like, but I'm warning you, Charlie, you mention my name and I'll have my lawyers on to you in a flash.'

She switched off the phone. Her head was spinning. She'd thought she'd escaped but the poison had followed her to Spain. God damn Charlie White, she thought. If only he'd behaved himself none of this would have happened and this shit storm would never have descended on their heads. He was utterly naïve if he thought a press conference would satisfy those vultures. It would be like throwing petrol on a fire. It would simply reignite the scandal and give it new life.

She thought of Alice McDowell. How long would it be before they ran her to ground? Or, worse still, before she came forward to volunteer? The tabloids had deep pockets. It would be nothing for them to write her a cheque for €100,000 to sell her story. Faced with a tempting offer like that, how long would she remain loyal to Charlie?

These thoughts were depressing her. She went back out to the garden where Margie was playing with Sofía. She lifted the child and swung her round in her arms.

'Still want to go to the beach?'

'Oh, yes, Mummy!'

'Then let's pack the bags and go.'

***

The beach was filling up when they arrived. They hired some loungers near the shore and Margie and Sofía went paddling. So far, it had been a tumultuous morning.

'How's Charlie?' Margie asked, when they returned to Piper. 'Are the reporters still chasing after him?'

'Yes.'

'So we won't be going back soon?'

'I'm not going back till I'm sure it's safe.'

'You know I don't mind staying down here,' Margie said. 'I'm enjoying it. So is Sofía. She loves it in Spain.'

Piper looked at the cloudless sky and the sea where the yachts were scudding along the horizon. Margie was right. Marbella was the perfect haven from all the hassle that awaited her in Dublin, with its grey skies, the pressure of business and the tabloid vultures threatening to dissect the corpse of her marriage and splash every sordid detail over the front pages.

She took out her phone and rang Jo to check on McKenzie Leisure.

'Relax, why don't you? I have everything under control.'

'You're a star, Jo. Appointing you was the best thing I ever did.'

'Oh, you'd have managed perfectly well without me. Incidentally, did you find whatever it was you were looking for regarding Eduardo?'

Piper laughed. 'You didn't forget!'

'Of course not!'

'Well, I've nothing to report on that front. As soon as I have, I'll let you know.'

She lay back and let the sun warm her face. But she was still worried about Alice McDowell. She was a loose cannon and there was no way Piper could stop her if she decided to talk. She shuddered to think of the possible consequences if the tabloids got their hands on her. She could imagine the headlines. 'MY NIGHTS OF PASSION WITH PLAYBOY ROCK KING'. 'HOW HE TOLD ME HE LOVED ME'.

Piper would be a laughing stock in Dublin. She would never be able to walk its streets again without people pointing her out with hypocritical sympathy. And what about her parents? What shame and embarrassment would they suffer?

Another thought struck her. Now that Charlie knew she was in Marbella, could he be trusted to keep the information to himself? What if he let it slip and the media got to hear? She might wake up some morning to find them camped outside the hotel.

The whole dirty business was turning into a nightmare. She wished now that when she was young she had never courted the reporters. She wished she'd had the good sense to stay in the background. But she had loved the publicity too much. She had revelled in it. She had relished the sight of her picture in the papers and the flattering stories they had written about her. She had encouraged them, and now they had turned on her.

The days passed and nothing happened. She checked the Internet every morning for indications that Alice McDowell might have sold out but nothing appeared. She waited for news of the press conference that Charlie had threatened to call but there was no sign of that either. It was like waiting for a storm to blow up or a volcano to erupt. She felt utterly helpless in the face of impending disaster.

Apart from her one short sortie into Marbella and a few excursions to the beach they had remained confined to the hotel. One morning she suggested to Margie that they go for lunch at a nearby restaurant, and at one o'clock, they set off down the hill towards the town. As long as they didn't approach the Paseo Maritimo, where the tourists tended to congregate, they should be fairly safe. They came across a restaurant that seemed to offer a good selection of dishes so they went in and took a table at the back, away from the door.

They ate grilled sole, salad and fried potatoes, and drank a carafe of wine. By the time they had paid the bill and started back to the villa, Piper was feeling more relaxed. She had barely returned to the hotel when her phone rang. She recognised Midge McCarthy's number.

'I've got bad news,' she began.

So, the volcano had erupted. Alice McDowell had talked to the press.

'Tell me.'

'Serge Dupont has been murdered.'

For a moment, Piper was unable to speak. She thought of the flamboyant couturier who had been one of the regulars at Aunt Polly's. 'My God, what happened?'

'His boyfriend stabbed him. You know that creepy little guy he was living with?'

'Alessandro?'

'That's him. The cops have got him in custody. It looks like a lovers' tiff. But it's an ill wind, Piper. It's all over the front pages. Every hack in town has been put on to the story. It looks like your break-up with Charlie is old hat.'

'They're not interested in us any more?'

'I didn't say that. But your situation is no longer hot news. Now all they want is stories about poor Serge. In a contest between a celebrity marriage break-up and a celebrity murder, the murder comes out on top every time.'

Piper finished the call and immediately sat down at her laptop and checked the web editions of the Irish papers. The story was splashed in lurid detail across all the front pages with acres of coverage. Midge was right. Her split with Charlie had been pushed into the background.

She felt relief mingled with sorrow. She would miss Serge. She had many happy memories of him. But his death had done her a big favour.

She became aware that her mobile was ringing. She picked it up and clamped it to her ear, expecting to hear her mother or Jo. But the voice was male and sounded foreign. 'Who is this?' she asked.

'It's Eduardo. I received a message to say you were trying to contact me.'

CHAPTER FORTY-TWO

Two mornings later, Piper left Sofía in Margie's care and set off by taxi for Málaga. She was nervous, but exhilarated too. Her phone conversation with Eduardo had been brief and courteous. He had told her he had progressed in his career: he was now a senior doctor at the hospital and enjoyed his work. There had been little time to learn much more except that he was glad she had made contact and would be happy to meet her.

The call had lifted her spirits. But Piper didn't know what to expect as she travelled the road from Marbella to Málaga. Would the magic that had sparked between them when they last met still be there? Or would it be a meeting of two people who had once been attracted to each other but had since drifted irretrievably apart?

It was a pleasant journey along the motorway that took about thirty minutes before Piper could see the domes and spires of the city sparkling in the morning sun. Then they began to descend, and soon after, the taxi was dropping her at the bustling Alameda Principal in the centre of the city. Eduardo had said he would meet her at a place called Bar Monica and had given her directions. She quickly spotted it near the bottom of the busy thoroughfare and quickened her pace.

She recognised him at once. He was seated at a table outside the café and was wearing a light suit with an open-necked shirt. He had put on a little weight but otherwise he was exactly as she remembered him. She hurried forward, then slowed when she noticed a little boy of about twenty months sitting beside him. He was the image of Eduardo, right down to his dark brown eyes.

By now, Eduardo had seen her too. His face broke into a welcoming smile. He stood up, held out his hands and kissed her cheek. She looked into his eyes, the dark eyes that had once beguiled her.

'It is so good to see you again, Piper. How was your journey? Please sit down and I will get you something to drink. What would you like?'

The little boy was staring at her intently.

Eduardo turned to him and laughed. 'Let me introduce you. This little fellow is also called Eduardo.'

Piper forced herself to smile.

'This beautiful *señorita* is called Piper, Eduardo. She is from Ireland. She is a very good friend but we have not met for a long time.'

The child giggled, and hid his face in his sleeve.

'He's a little shy with strangers. I brought him along

especially today so you could meet him. Let me introduce my nephew, Eduardo Delgado Garcia.'

Her heart filled with joy. 'I'm very pleased to meet you, Eduardo,' she said, and shook his little hand.

It was only now that Piper realised how much she had invested in this meeting. It had been a massive gamble and she had set herself up for heartbreak if it failed, but now that the ice was broken, they chatted like the old friends they were. Eduardo ordered coffee for them both, and orange juice for his nephew. He brought her up to date with his busy career at the hospital. He told her he was living in a flat close to his workplace and was very happy. He made no mention of any girlfriend.

When he had finished, he turned to her. 'And now what has been happening to you?' he asked. 'Are you still working with your father?'

'He has retired.'

'So who is running the company?'

'I am,' Piper replied. 'I am the managing director of McKenzie Leisure.'

His eyes twinkled. 'Congratulations, Piper. I told you when we first met that one day you would be a successful businesswoman. What happened to your brother?'

The shame of Jack's behaviour was too much to admit. 'He got married and went to live abroad.'

'So now you are in complete control?'

'Yes. But I have help. You remember Jo, my friend?'

'Of course.'

'She's my deputy.'

'The perfect arrangement. And how is your daughter? Her name is Sofía, no?'

'I brought her with me. She loves Spain.'

'And your husband?'

Piper stared at the ground, then slowly raised her eyes till she was looking directly at him. 'I'm divorcing him.'

'Oh?' Eduardo's face showed concern. 'I am sorry to hear that, Piper. What happened?'

'He was unfaithful with another woman.'

For a few moments, Eduardo didn't speak. Then he reached out and gently took her hand. 'Has it caused you very much pain?'

'It has shattered me.'

'But now you are putting it behind you and beginning life afresh?'

'Yes – and what about you? Did you marry?'

'No. I never met another woman I could love.'

They talked for a while longer and then Eduardo insisted that they have lunch. They went to an open-air restaurant in a nearby park and the little boy sat quietly beside them while they ate. It was four o'clock when Piper finally said she must go.

Eduardo paid the bill and walked with her to where some taxis were waiting. He took her hand once more. 'Will we meet again?'

'I'd like that very much.'

He smiled. 'Shall we say the same time next week?'

'Yes.'

He took her in his arms and kissed her on each cheek. Then he hesitated for a moment and kissed her once more. 'You remember what that means?'

'Three kisses for a special friend.'

***

The traffic was heavier on the return journey and it was five o'clock when Piper finally arrived at Hotel Azul. All the way back, her heart had sung with joy. It had been such a memorable day. Despite the years, she had found the same Eduardo she remembered so well from the past. It was as if he had been waiting for her to return. She couldn't wait to see him again.

***

That evening, when she went to bed, Piper's thoughts turned once more to her visit to Málaga. She had been given a second chance, and this time she was determined to seize it with both hands.

The week passed quickly. Each day she was in touch with her parents and Jo. The company was ticking over smoothly. There was nothing to worry about. She also rang Midge McCarthy, who assured her that press interest in Charlie and her had died and it was safe to come home.

But Piper wasn't going back to Dublin just yet. She had her second visit to Málaga to look forward to. This time, she brought an overnight bag and found Eduardo waiting for her at the same table outside Bar Monica. He was alone. They didn't stay for coffee. He had his car parked nearby and suggested he take her to see his flat. It took ten minutes to drive there. Once they were inside the door, he took her in his arms and kissed her face, her cheeks and finally her lips. She felt a delicious thrill run through her.

Slowly he undressed her, then led her to the bedroom where they began to make love. It was exactly as she imagined it would be, gentle and generous, yet overlaid with passion till at last they lay side by side, sated. She touched his cheek with a finger. 'Do you remember that night we had dinner in Marbella? I asked if you believed in love and you said yes.'

'Of course I remember.'

'And I asked if you believed that for each person there was one other who was destined for them?'

'I still believe it. Why do you think I waited for you?'

'You knew I would come back?'

'I hoped you would. I knew you would not be happy till you did.'

She drew him closer and held him tight. 'There's something else I must tell you. The night when I sent you away...'

He laid a finger over her lips. 'Please, Piper, let's not talk about it. It's the past. Don't bring it back.'

'But I must. I'm saying it for me. It broke my heart to send you away. I wanted you desperately but I couldn't betray my husband, even though I ached for you. And that night I lay in bed and couldn't sleep because I believed I had just made a terrible mistake .'

'You did the honourable thing, Piper. That is something to be admired.'

'But it was the *wrong* thing. I thought he was the man who was destined for me. But I was mistaken. You were.'

He drew her close and kissed her. 'Let's not talk of it again. Now you have come back. We are together, just as we were always meant to be. And this time nothing shall keep us apart.'

CHAPTER FORTY-THREE

Three days later, Piper said goodbye to *Señor* Hernandez and left Hotel Azul with Margie and Sofía to return to Dublin. She had no need of headscarf or dark glasses. The bloodhounds had been called off and she didn't fear being ambushed by reporters.

In Ireland, once more, the taxi took them straight to Howth where her parents were waiting. They made a fuss of Sofía as she ran around the kitchen while they drank tea and ate home-baked scones.

'You can't get these in Spain,' Piper said, as she plastered jam onto a piece and took a satisfying bite.

'I think there's a little English bakery in Fuengirola that makes them,' her mother said.

Piper smiled. 'I'll bet they're not as good as yours.'

'Flatterer!' Rose laughed. 'How was your trip?'

'Great – once we were sure we'd shaken off the sewer rats.'

Her mother gave her a quizzical look. 'The what?'

'The tabloid reporters.'

'Oh, that's all gone away. You can relax now.'

'Not quite,' Piper said.

'Oh?'

'I'm going back to Spain, but not before I've had a serious chat with Dad.'

At this, her father looked up. 'What's up?'

'The company, Dad. What else?'

***

The following morning when Jo arrived for work, Piper was waiting for her.

'So you're back, safe and sound?' her friend said. 'It's great to see you. You look fantastic. You'll find everything's under control. Let's have a cup of coffee and I'll take you through it all.'

Piper laid a hand on her arm. 'Before you do that, there's something we have to discuss. Go into my office. I'll get the coffee.' She joined Jo a few minutes later with steaming mugs and a plate of biscuits. 'I met someone on that trip to Marbella,' she began.

Her friend laughed. 'You saw Eduardo, didn't you? I knew you were up to something. That's why you asked for his surname.'

'You're right. He's hardly changed. He's still the same beautiful man we met on our first trip to Marbella. He's a doctor now and works in a hospital in Málaga. And meeting him made me realise that I'll never be completely happy until I'm with him. You'll probably think this is daft, but I believe he's the man who was meant for me.'

363

'It's not daft, it's very romantic!'

'So I've been thinking, and now I've got an important proposition to put to you.'

'What?'

'How would you like to be managing director of the firm?'

Jo's face registered total shock. 'Are you serious?'

'Absolutely. I've discussed it with my father. The family will continue to hold the controlling interest but you'll be the boss. You'll run the show. You've proved you can do it. We trust your judgement. And we'll pay you extremely well.'

'What will you do?'

'Sofía and I are going to Spain to live with Eduardo.'

Jo's eyes were popping.

'It's what I crave, Jo – a normal family life, caring for my child, doing the things any normal mother does.'

'Charlie might have something to say about it.'

'He's in no position to look after her, with the life he lives. He'll still have visiting rights. She can come to him for holidays. It'll all be done legally, with her father's consent.'

'And I would be managing director?'

'Yes. It's the same as when I asked you to be my deputy. I can trust you and you know the company inside out. You've been running it without me for the past few weeks anyway.'

Jo sighed. 'It's a very generous offer – and a total surprise.'

'I appreciate that. Take some time to think about it. In the meantime, I'll get a contract drawn up. Is a week enough time for you to make up your mind?'

'I should think it's more than enough.'

'I'll talk to you again. Till then, your lips are sealed. Right?'

'Right,' Jo said.

***

Next, she rang Charlie and arranged to meet him in a quiet hotel in Dalkey where she hoped they wouldn't be recognised. As he was free, for once, they agreed they'd go straight there. When Piper arrived, he was already installed at the bar and had bought himself a beer. He summoned a waitress, who brought Piper a glass of sparkling water.

She cut immediately to the chase. 'I'm going to live in Spain,' she said, 'and I'm taking Sofía with me. I'm asking you not to fight me over this. You can visit whenever you like and she can spend time with you in Dublin. I'll draw up a legally binding contract, if that's what you want.'

Charlie's face collapsed. She had never seen him look so crushed. 'This will break my heart, Piper. Do you have to do it?'

'Charlie, I'm not trying to punish you. Our marriage is over and Sofía needs a stable environment. I can provide it and you can't. I wish you well. I hope you find whatever it is you're looking for.'

'Have you?' he asked.

'I've found the person I should have married instead of you.' She reached out and took his hand. 'You really hurt me, Charlie, but I've forgiven you. I have some very good memories of our time together and no bitterness. Can we remain friends?'

He nodded.

'And you'll agree to my proposal?'

'Yes,' he said.

***

Over the next few weeks, Piper was extremely busy. As she had expected, Jo accepted her offer. She received a very generous remuneration package and a profit-sharing arrangement. Piper knew she was leaving the company in good hands.

She packed boxes of clothes and books and had them shipped to Hotel Azul, where Margie and Sofía were now waiting to receive them. Margie had agreed to come with Piper to Spain and continue as Sofía's nanny. Meanwhile, Piper would buy a house in Marbella, enrol Sofía in the local international school, and Eduardo would try to find a job at the nearby hospital.

The last days were spent in a hectic round of leave-taking as she said goodbye to Jo and other friends, extending invitations to visit. Finally, the date of her departure arrived. Her father drove her to the airport and walked with her to the departure gates. Her parents had arranged to come to Spain the following week to help her settle in and to meet Eduardo.

'I'm going to miss you,' Henry said. 'There's always plenty of excitement when you're around.'

'Didn't Dr Bradford tell you you're not supposed to get excited?' She laughed.

'You kept me young, Piper. You have so much energy.'

'I won't be far away. We'll talk all the time.'

'Are you sure you're doing the right thing?'

'I haven't a single doubt in my mind.'

'Then I wish you well with this young man.'

The plane left on time. Piper gripped the seat, closed her eyes and prayed hard as it rose steadily into the air. When she opened her eyes again they were airborne. From the window, she watched the clouds part as the plane swept across Lambay Island and out over the Irish Sea. She leaned her head back and closed her eyes again. She had been given a second chance. She was starting a new life in a new country with a new partner.

She was going back to Spain to be reunited with the man of her dreams.

Epilogue

There was a lot of activity in the garden at Hotel Azul and Sofía was very excited. She kept staring at herself in the mirror in the foyer, admiring her dress. She had been living in Marbella for six months now and lots of exciting things had happened but this was the best of all. She was to be a flower girl at the wedding of Pedro and Carmencita.

She turned to her mother, who was standing beside her. 'Do I look pretty, Mummy?'

'You're as pretty as a flower, honey.'

'Are you sure? They're going to take my picture.'

'Of course I'm sure.'

Piper looked at Eduardo, who smiled. Earlier, they had attended the wedding ceremony at the local church and now they were waiting for the festivities to begin. A marquee had been erected in the garden and trays of drinks and food laid out. A space had been cleared for dancing and a group of musicians were carefully tuning their instruments. Everyone was anxious for the party to begin. But first they had to complete the wedding photographs.

Just then Pedro appeared from the garden. He looked very handsome in his well-cut suit. He swooped on Sofía and took her hand. 'There you are, *niña*. Come with me and have your photo taken. We cannot keep the bride waiting.'

Piper and Eduardo followed them out to the garden where the bridal party was lined up on the lawn, the parents, bridesmaids and groomsmen in their finery while pride of place went to Carmencita, ravishing in a dress of white silk.

The photographer went down on one knee and began snapping. Then he rearranged the group, herding them closer together, and took more photos till they began to grow restless. The sun was out, it was hot, and the trays of cold drinks were very enticing.

At last he had finished and people came forward to congratulate the happy couple. Piper and Eduardo stayed in the shade of the porch, happily watching the proceedings. Eventually Pedro led his bride to them. He introduced Eduardo, then turned his attention to Piper.

'You have already met Carmencita,' he said. 'Carmencita, you know it is because of *Señora* McKenzie that we are married today. It was she who persuaded *Señor* Hernandez to promote me to become a chef.'

Piper laughed. 'Who told you that?'

Pedro grinned. 'It is true, *Señora*. I know it.'

'It was your talent that got you the job, Pedro.'

'No, it was you, and we will always be grateful. So I wish to thank you and also to tell you how happy we are that you are able to attend our wedding.'

'*De nada,*' Piper replied.

Outside the musicians had started up and their lively music drifted up from the garden.

Eduardo took Piper's hand, and smiled into her face. 'Shall we dance?'

ACKNOWLEDGEMENTS

Writing can be a solitary trade so I would like to thank my family and friends for their constant support and encouragement. Thanks also to my readers who faithfully buy my books in increasing numbers. Finally, I want to thank all the staff at Hachette Books Ireland, particularly my editor, Ciara Considine.
Enjoy!

Reading is so much more than the act of moving from page to page. It's the exploration of new worlds; the pursuit of adventure; the forging of friendships; the breaking of hearts; and the chance to begin to live through a new story each time the first sentence is devoured.

We at Hachette Ireland are very passionate about what we read, and what we publish. And we'd love to hear what you think about our books.

If you'd like to let us know, or to find out more about us and our titles, please visit www.hachette.ie or our Facebook page www.facebook.com/hachetteireland, or follow us on Twitter @HachetteIre